THE RIVALS WE HATE

BRAYSEN U

SERIES #1

USA TODAY BESTSELLING AUTHOR

BROOKE O'BRIEN

THE RIVALS WE HATE

USA Today Bestselling author Brooke O'Brien brings all the hate-to-love feels in this rivals to lovers, small town college football romance.

Football players are treated like royalty in our small town, which makes Beckham Carver their king. And as the new quarterback of the Braysen Bulldogs, he's also my boyfriend's biggest rival.

Add that to the list of reasons I should stay far away from him.

But when my truck breaks down, Beckham makes me an offer I can't refuse: He'll repair my pickup in exchange for me tutoring him.

I have only one stipulation—no one, including my boyfriend, can find out.

The more I try to convince myself and Beckham that I hate him, the more he pushes my buttons to prove me wrong.

Worse, the lines we've drawn between us blur as we spend more time together. And when my relationship comes crashing down around me, I almost forget why I couldn't stand him all along.

If I've learned one thing about Beckham Carver, it's that he always gets what he wants...

... and now, he's set his sights on me.

BRAYSEN U SERIES
READING ORDER

Braysen U is a small-town college football romance series. Each book in the series follows a different player for the Braysen Bulldogs.

The Rivals We Hate

Beckham and Hallyn

A rivals to lovers, boyfriend's rival romance small town

The Plays We Fake

Hayes and Everly

A fake dating, opposites attract romance

Grab the rest of the Braysen U series at:
www.authorbrookeobrien.com/braysenu

DEDICATION

To my grandma, for all the times she let me crawl onto the recliner next to her while she'd read to me.

I love you, a bushel and a peck.

CHAPTER 1

BECKHAM

"I hope we don't have this conversation again, Carver. Take this as my first and only warning. Get your ass to class and your grades up, or you won't be the starting QB at Braysen U."

I press my lips into a firm line and roll my head to the side. I know better than to speak my mind to Coach right now. It's not worth the shitstorm he'd rain down on me if I did.

Coach Frye has made a name for himself in college sports as a force to be reckoned with. It's why he's one of the best of the best.

He knows what it takes to build a championship team. He's won the last three conference championships, and he went on to earn national titles with two of those.

"Now get the hell out of my office," he grunts, and I push myself to stand.

We don't bother with goodbyes. He passes me the list of tutors from my professors, a point he so kindly emphasized.

As soon as I step out of his office and round the corner, I crinkle the paper into a ball and shove it into my pocket.

In my first year of college, I busted my ass playing for Rixton University, and we never made it close to playing for a conference championship. As much as I loved it there, Rixton was all about their hockey team, which wasn't giving me the opportunity to play at a higher level.

If I wanted to make it to the NFL, difficult decisions needed to be made. So I packed up my shit and headed east to play with my brother, Hayes, at Braysen.

Braysen, South Carolina, is a small college town on the Georgia-South Carolina border, where the Savannah River meets the ocean.

Football runs this town, and being a Bulldog meant you were treated like royalty. I've heard all about the trouble Hayes and his friends got into last year, and the community welcomed me with open arms.

"What'd you do to piss Coach off?" Hayes asks when I climb into my pickup. He's waiting for me in the passenger seat, scrolling through his phone.

He barely lifts his head to acknowledge me.

"My grades. It's the same thing I expected to hear when he called me in there. I need to get my shit together."

I arch my back to reach into my pocket for the list of tutors, shoving it into my bag and tossing it behind me onto the crew cab seat.

I'll figure out a way to get my grades up. I don't need Coach's help, and I sure as hell don't need a tutor.

His brows bunch together, studying me. I shrug, shoving the key into the ignition and hit the gas, peeling out of there.

Hayes is no stranger to Coach's no-nonsense approach. We're only three weeks into the school year. Coach needed to give me a break and give it time. I'd prove he didn't have anything to worry about—on or off the field.

The drive back to our house takes no more than five minutes. You can hear the music blaring before you even turn on our road or see the crowd spilling out of our house into the front yard.

Tables set up in the grass have people playing flip cup and beer pong. Girls wear their swimsuit tops and shorts. The ones not focused on a game hold their plastic cups in the air while they sing to Garth Brooks about having friends in low places. A few guys in the mix are dancing and grinding with them too.

Eventually, people make their way out back to take a dip in the pool. It's one last bash before the season starts.

I pull my truck into the grass near the trees along the side of our driveway so it's out of the way. The last thing I want is anyone fuckin' with my truck.

The crowd cheers when Hayes and I head up the driveway. Hayes holds up his hand and joins in on the singing before he takes a beer when someone tosses one his way. I recognize a few people who call out my name and motion for me to grab a drink of my own.

I wave them off and head toward the house, my gym bag slung over my shoulder. I'm still sticky with sweat from practice and want to shower before I crack open a cold one.

Our living room is packed with people, most of whom I've never seen before in my life. They call out my name once more, but I don't hang around to chat. Instead, I make a break for it and head down the hall toward my bedroom.

It's my only solace away from all the noise, and I keep it off-limits for a reason.

So when I find the oak door cracked open, I steel my spine and grit my teeth, slamming my fist against the wood to push it the rest of the way open.

My eyes are wide as I search for any sign someone messed with my shit, but the room looks untouched.

My phone vibrates against my thigh, and I reach into my pocket to pull it out, seeing Talon's name flash on the screen.

"Well, look who the fuck it is." I laugh, kicking the door shut behind me.

I drop my bag at the foot of my bed and toe off my shoes. I hit the button to put the call on speakerphone and set it down on my dresser.

"Man, it's just not the same around here without you," Talon groans.

We've been best friends since the third grade but are more like brothers. There's nothing I wouldn't do for him, and I know it's the same for him.

"Same," I grunt. "It's like a different world being here. I miss Tennessee, but you know I'll be back as soon as the season is over."

I shed my T-shirt, tossing it toward my hamper.

"Speaking of which, what's the word on the street?" I ask, my voice dropping lower. "How's Tatum doing?"

We haven't spoken about what happened that night, and it's a promise I'll take to the grave. I hate the fact I left him there to deal with the fallout and repercussions.

When he got the call from his sister, Tatum, after she left a party one night and she described the horrors she went through, I knew Talon would turn the town upside down if he didn't make the fuckers who hurt her pay.

"I haven't heard a word since," he says. "It'll be blood on his hands, not mine, if I see him again too."

There's rustling coming from my bathroom as I hear the toilet flush. I quickly reach for my phone to turn it off speaker and press it to my ear.

"Man, I've gotta go. Someone just showed up here. Let me call you back in an hour."

We end the call just as the door opens and a blonde appears in the doorway. Her hair is pulled back in a clip, with a few strands framing her face.

She's dressed in a white Bulldogs tank top and a pair of denim shorts, frayed along the edges and rolled at her waist, showing her swimsuit underneath.

"May I fuckin' help you?" I bellow, clenching my jaw.

If I wasn't livid at the thought of her overhearing my conversation, I'd probably handle this better. Never mind the fact she's in my room, and I have no idea how the hell she got in here.

Her eyes dart around the space, taking in the Braysen football poster we got last week hung up on the wall and my jersey draped over my desk chair.

She doesn't bother to answer the question, her eyes roaming over my body before she reaches my face. My eyes widen, and I hold out my arms, emphasizing her lack of response.

"You want to answer my question? What the hell are you doin' in my room?"

She fumbles over her words, pointing her dainty finger toward the door, and mutters, "Someone told me I could use the bathroom."

"Who?" I bark.

Her eyes study my face, roaming over my shoulders and down to my arms crossed over my chest. She seems to pay special interest to my last name tattooed on my forearm before her eyes flick back over to the poster on the wall.

"Beckham Carver," she whispers low. I almost question if I heard her at all.

She steels her spine and narrows her eyes. "You'll have to forgive me. Some guy came stumbling out of here, and I asked him where the bathroom was. He pointed behind him and told me I could use the one in here. You know what, the next time it happens, I'll make sure to stop him and ask for his name, just for you."

"There won't be a next time," I deadpan. "You can leave now."

She gives me an amused smirk and rolls her eyes. For the first time since I found her in my room, I let my gaze trail down her body, running over her toned legs to her bare feet. I'm honestly surprised she had the decency to take off her shoes since most people don't at a party.

Her green eyes stand out against her tan skin, freckles peppering the apple of her cheeks.

She's as beautiful as she is sassy. Somehow, I find it even more attractive.

Most of the girls back at Rixton were quick to flutter their lashes and smooth their hands over my chest while they practically fawned over me. It's one of the perks that comes with being a QB, I guess.

I have to admit, though, after a while, it gets old, and you want to be left alone.

She mutters, "Why am I not surprised?" as she stalks past me.

"Wait." I hurry to grab her wrist to stop her.

Her eyes go wild, and she spins around toward me.

"Get your hands off me." She gasps when she nearly crashes into my chest.

Her intoxicating scent reaches me, a mixture of sea salt and coconut.

I smirk. "All right, feisty, I didn't mean to rile you up."

She keeps her face straight, staring at my chest with only a foot separating us. She slowly raises her eyes until her gaze locks on mine.

I lean in close to her and whisper, "Unless you're into that sort of thing and want me to get you all worked up." I wink.

Her nostrils flare, and a look of disgust transforms her face.

Well, there's a first time for everything.

"It'll be a cold day in hell before that ever happens."

I wait for her to storm out of my room, but for some reason she doesn't.

"Do I know you from somewhere?" I circle back to her earlier comment. "What did you mean about not being surprised?"

Her eyes go wide, and she laughs. "It's nothing. It's just ... I've heard of you before, and I guess I can say you lived up to your reputation."

I cross my arms over my chest again and lift my chin. "It's good to hear my reputation precedes me."

I nod toward the door, urging her to leave now. She might be beautiful, and I may have debated tossing her on my bed with plans of having those legs wrapped around my waist and my head, but now she's proven to be an uptight snot and not worth the headache.

"I don't think that's something I'd brag about." She chuckles. "I'm sure you know my boyfriend, though. Tanner Freeman?" Her eyes flash before she corrects herself. "I mean, ex-boyfriend. It's complicated." She shakes her head.

I ignore the hurt on her face and the pain in her voice and focus on what the hell the girlfriend of Keaton's quarterback is doing at Braysen?

She sucks in a sharp breath when I step toward her again. Lowering my voice, I say, "Well, you tell Freeman his girl looks good in her Braysen top. The longer you keep hanging out in my room, though, the more I'll think you want me to help you out of it."

I push the strand of hair in her face back and tuck it behind her ear.

She gasps. "You did say he's your ex-boyfriend, right? We can even keep it between the two of us."

"Fuck you," she huffs and storms away, jerking the door open.

I drop my hand to my side and grin.

"Name the time and place, feisty girl, and I'll be ready."

CHAPTER 2

HALLYN

We're only a few weeks into classes, and I'm already kicking my ass for not picking up a second job over the summer.

I brush my finger over my trackpad, scrolling through the messages left in response to my recent bulletin offering tutoring services. I already have a packed schedule between dance and classes, but I need to figure something out if I have any hope of getting by after paying for my books, dance uniform, and other expenses.

I've dreamed of being at this moment for what feels like forever. Braysen U was added to my vision board when I entered my sophomore year of high school.

Except it didn't work out the way I hoped it would.

It was supposed to be me and Tanner—he'd land the QB spot for the Bulldogs, and I'd join the dance team, cheering him on from the sidelines.

Our plans changed when he found out he didn't get the offer, which meant he'd be taking his second choice, sending him thirty minutes away to play at Keaton.

I'd be lying if I said it hadn't caused turmoil in our relationship, especially after I told him I turned in my acceptance and would be getting a place with my best friend, Ava.

We spent the summer apart. I went north to Virginia to stay with my grandparents, giving us both time away from each other, and in the end, it brought us back together.

It wasn't going to be easy being apart again, especially with how busy our lives are now that football season is here. We're getting by with video chats and text messages, and we've promised to make the drive as much as our schedules allow.

Although, I've been the only one to make the drive so far. I haven't mentioned the small problem of gas money, and he hasn't considered it either.

Money has never been a problem for Tanner. We grew up differently. He comes from a wealthy family—his dad is an investment banker, and his mom works as a pediatric nurse.

It's a far cry from my life with my mom, who raised me on her own and pinched pennies to pay for my dance classes my entire life.

She's helped me in more ways than I could ever repay her, which is why I'm determined to figure out a solution to make extra cash without burdening her anymore.

The coffee house on campus overflows with people. I stare at the line forming toward the door from where I sit, then down to the leftover remnants from the sandwich I bought for dinner.

My phone vibrates on the small bistro table. I swipe the screen to see the notification, reminding me of the tutor session scheduled in twenty minutes. It's the only one I have off campus. I'm still trying to figure my way around Braysen, so I'd want to leave soon to ensure I'm not late.

My eyes survey the bustling café and decide against grabbing another coffee on my way out the door. I'll desperately need a pick-me-up later, but that's a problem for future Hallyn to sort out.

Right now, I need to get my ass out the door if I have any hope of making it on time.

After stacking my books, I shove them into my backpack. I adjust my grip on the strap and scurry out the door, walking and zipping my bag at the same time before shrugging it over my shoulder.

My '79 Ford F250 is parked off on the side of the lot, away from everyone else. She's an old Tiffany Blue pickup, passed down to me from my grandpa, so it holds more sentimental value than anything.

I toss my bag across the bench seat when I climb in and crank the engine. The radio station plays Luke Combs. My worries slip away for those few minutes as I listen to the welcoming sound of his deep voice.

I almost forget where I'm going until the muffled sound of the GPS directs me to make a right turn in less than half a mile. I'm weaving around several potholes on the worn-down highway and mistake one for a puddle after the heavy thunderstorm the night before. The sound of my tire bouncing over it has me clenching my teeth, sending my phone across the truck and onto the floor.

"Dammit." My eyes flick to the floor and back to the road.

I don't see the second pothole past the bridge until it jerks my steering wheel to the right and nearly causes me to sideswipe the guardrail. I overcorrect and swerve into the other lane. Cars honk, and I narrowly miss colliding head-on with a sports car before I veer off onto the side of the road.

I cut the engine, and tears leak from my eyes. Squeezing the steering wheel, I glance at the time on my watch. I only have six minutes until my tutor session is scheduled to start.

Leaning across the bench seat, I reach for my phone. My hands shake, and my heart still beats wildly in my chest.

As if I'm not already being tested by the universe today, when I turn the key in the ignition, a clicking sound is followed by another low rumble of the engine as it attempts to turn over.

"Nooo, c'mon! Please don't let this be real." I wince, exhaling heavily.

I don't know much about cars aside from what I learned in the auto class I took in high school. I picked up a few things, like how to change a tire, give myself an oil change, and other basic tune-ups.

Judging by the smoke billowing from under the hood now, it's safe to say this one is out of my wheelhouse.

I pull up my messages with Shiloh, the girl I was meeting for the tutoring session I'm now late for. She's sweet and understanding when I explain what happened, and I apologize for canceling, promising to reschedule once I get things sorted.

I do a quick search for the nearest repair shop and hit the call button.

"Kavlik's," a deep voice answers.

Judging by the gruff sound of his voice, I'd guess he's an older man. In my mind, I picture him looking like my grandpa, and the thought makes me smile.

"Yes, um, hi. Is there any chance you offer towing services?"

"Sure thing. Where about are ya?"

His comforting Southern twang somehow manages to relax me enough to provide the details from my GPS on where I'm at.

He says to hang tight and reassures me he'll have someone out to help me in about twenty to thirty minutes.

I hold my hand against my forehead to shield against the sunshine as I wait, trying not to let myself stress about what I'll do about transportation, much less worry about how I'll make it back to my apartment.

Sure enough, twenty minutes pass by before a large truck with a flatbed pulls up behind me. I glance in the rearview mirror, noticing the mascara smeared under my eyes. I quickly wipe it away before the tall, broad-shouldered man appears at my door.

He's wearing a backward baseball cap and a black T-shirt with the sleeves cut off and jeans. He taps on the window.

Something is familiar about the curve of his lip when he smirks, watching me through the glass while I roll down the window.

"I didn't even know there were still trucks with the ole crank handles." He chuckles with an amused smile on his face.

"Up until about thirty minutes ago, she was running like a champ."

"I'll get you hooked up and tow you back to our shop. We'll take a look and see what's goin' on for you."

He glances down at the clipboard in his hands and back at me.

I nod. "That would be great. Thank you, sir."

He appears to study my face, pausing on my lips. I'm still trying to pinpoint where I've seen him before. He clenches his jaw, and my eyes flash down to the tattoo spanning his forearm.

Carver.

Without another word or a second glance, he returns to his truck, and I can breathe again for the first time in minutes.

What the hell is Beckham Carver doing towing my truck?

He climbs into his rig and moves it to park in front of me. He jumps back out and gets to work on hooking up his tow.

When I get out, I give him space to do his thing while I pace back and forth in the grass on the side of the road.

The downside to being new to Braysen and the area is I'm still meeting new people. I made a few friends, mostly girls on my dance team and our coach or students who I'm helping tutor.

I attempt to call Ava, trying to jog my memory of her schedule hanging on our fridge. I can't remember if she's working at the local dance studio, teaching little girls and boys how to dance.

I'm praying she's not and maybe could pick me up on her way home from class.

I massage my fingers into my forehead.

The only other option would be to call Tanner. He's probably just getting out of practice right now. It's a bit of a drive, but he's my boyfriend. He should want to help me, right?

By the time he gets here, though, it will probably be dark, and the last thing I want is to wait on the side of the road for him.

I glance up and catch Beckham studying me. His eyes drag over my body, and I cross my arms to cover myself from the intensity of his gaze.

He's the reason Tanner didn't land the QB spot, at least that's what I tell myself. If that wasn't reason enough to dislike him, the way we met the night of the party seals the deal.

Beckham Carver is a jackass, and I can't stand him.

That's why, even if I can't find a ride back to the tow shop, I refuse to accept a lift with him.

The fact he keeps looking at me with his infuriating smirk only solidifies it. It's like he knows he's handsome and uses it to get what he wants.

I hate to break it to him, but he can't use his good looks and charm on me.

Not in a million fuckin' years.

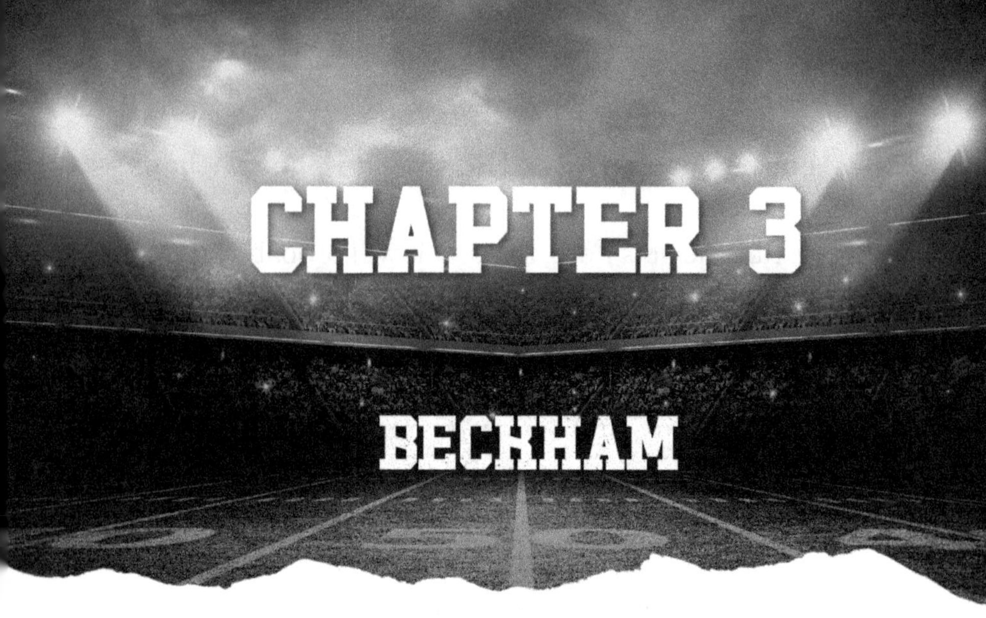

I barely make it to the shop for my shift before Hank hollers my name. After shoving the tow call papers in my hands, he pushes me back out the door.

Now I'm standing on the side of the highway with the sun beating down on me. It was hard to make out her face at first. It wasn't until I started hooking up her old beat-to-shit pickup and caught her pacing back and forth in the plot of grass off to the side that I got a good look at her... and fuck me.

She's just as beautiful as she was the night she stormed out of my bathroom, all feisty with her sassy mouth when I asked her what the hell she was doing in my room.

I study her as she tucks her wavy blonde hair behind one of her ears. Her cheeks are red, but I'm not sure if it's from the sun or if she's upset. Maybe a mix of both, as she nervously runs her fingers through her hair with her phone pressed to her ear.

She seems different from the girl I met the night of the party.

I notice how she anxiously bounces her leg and scoffs when she hangs up, evidently not able to get through to whoever she's calling.

Her tense muscles capture my attention, and all I can think about is how perfect they'd be wrapped around my head.

It's that moment she picks to glance my way, catching my eyes burning into her. She clears her throat, sending my gaze snapping up to meet hers.

Her eyes flash as if she can read my thoughts. Now it's her turn, letting her gaze trail down my body.

I'm praying to God she can't see the rod growing in my jeans.

Her eyes flutter. "Everything all right?" My voice deepens, and even I notice it.

She clutches her phone to her chest and nods. She drags her lip between her teeth, considering her next words.

I tilt my head to the side when she doesn't respond and chuckle.

Passing by her, I grab the chains from the flatbed and kneel on the ground to hook them under her truck. I climb inside and shift it into neutral before loading her truck up the ramp.

Once it's loaded and secured, I dust my hands off on the front of my worn jeans. Her throat bobs as she studies me.

"You want a ride back to the shop with me?" I nod toward the passenger side.

She holds her hand up and shakes her head. "No, thank you. That'll be all right. I'm waiting for my friend to call me back, but if she doesn't, I can just get an Uber."

"You want to wait on your friend by yourself out here on the side of this gravel road in hopes they answer? If not, you'd rather pay for someone to give you a lift?" I question, studying her face.

She nods slowly.

"What, you don't want to ride with me?"

"I barely even know who you are," she fires off.

"Somethin' tells me you wouldn't know that Uber driver either, but to each their own." I kick my boots along the ground, sending a few rocks skipping down the roadside as I head back toward my truck.

"Wait," she calls, halting my footsteps.

Her fingers are pressed to her mouth when I turn back to her as if she hadn't expected me to stop. She chews on her lower lip again.

"What makes you think I would trust you after the first night we met?"

I'm starting to wonder if she heard more of my conversation with Talon, but I don't mention it in hopes maybe I'm wrong.

"All right, fine." I cross my arms over my chest. "Let's start over then, shall we? I'm Beckham Carver. I play football and am a student at Braysen U. I work part-time at Kavlik's. You text your friend you're tryin' to get ahold of and tell her you're with me. That way, if you turn up missin', she'll know who you were with."

"If I turn up missing?" She straightens her shoulders, her gaze narrowing on me.

I curl my lip and chuckle. "Well, it's not like we're strangers anyway. Somethin' tells me she's heard of me too."

She curls her lips. "I'm sure every woman in town knows who you are." She scoffs.

I answer with an amused smile. "Why's that, feisty girl?"

She rolls her eyes. "You really are full of yourself, aren't you? I just meant I've heard about you. And it's less about your game on the field and more about your bedroom activities."

My face drops, and I narrow my eyes. I pull my gloves off, shoving them into my back pocket. She analyzes me, trailing her eyes over my arms, before making their way back to my face.

What is it about this girl that drives me crazy?

Hell, even that night, she managed to get under my skin in a way no one else has before.

I can't even remember the last time a woman rejected me. And certainly not when I offered to throw her on my bed and give her a reason to get all riled up.

"It's not often I have a woman turn down a ride from me, certainly not twice, but have it your way."

I shrug, and she bursts out in a laugh. She covers her hand over her mouth, her arm clutching her waist.

"Somethin' tells me you're used to getting what you want," she fires off. "At least until you met me."

"Oh, trust me. I always get what I want." I smirk. "Suit yourself, though." I point my thumb over my shoulder toward her piece of shit pickup. "Give us a call tomorrow, and one of us can talk to you about lookin' at your truck. Although, it might be time for you to ask Daddy for a new one."

I pass by her and start to round the front of the tow truck when she stops me.

"Excuse me, ask Daddy?"

I pat the hood of the truck and shrug.

"I'll have you know, I haven't seen or spoken to my father since I was three. That was right before he tucked me in for bed, only for him to sneak out in the middle of the night while we were sleeping. So whatever preconceived notion you have about me being some stuck-up rich girl, you can take it and shove it up your ass."

Now it's her turn to cross her arms over her chest.

What does it say about me that I love riling her up like this?

Why does it turn me on?

"Listen, as much as I love arguing with you on the side of the road, I'd like to get your truck back to the shop before we close. Do you want a ride or not?"

She stares past me at the cars zooming by on the highway, her hair blowing in the breeze behind her before she turns her frustrated gaze to me.

"I'll get a lift from you," she grumbles, stalking toward the passenger door.

I sidestep in front of her, reaching for the handle and opening it for her.

She presses her lips together in a thin line, her nostrils flaring and her jaw set. Goddamn, would I love just to reach out and touch her, just to see if I could make her melt for me like I did that night.

I don't, though, because no matter what I thought we felt, she apparently has a man now, and it just so happens to be the quarterback for Keaton University, Braysen's biggest rival.

She reaches for the bar outside the truck and steps on the footrest, climbing into the passenger seat, waving her sweet ass in my face as she does.

I slam the door shut as soon as she's in and grunt, using the size of the rig to grant me a second of privacy while I adjust myself.

She has one leg crossed over the other, her toned tan legs forcing me to take a heavy swallow. I keep my eyes trained on the road to safely get our asses back to Kavlik's.

The sooner we can get there, the faster I can gain some distance from her.

The entire drive to the shop is quiet, aside from the radio playing. She tenses and keeps her face forward when I hold her headrest while turning to back the rig in.

"I'll unload it if you want to head on inside."

She exhales heavily and nods, pushing her door open and jumping out. As soon as she slams the door shut, I let out a low grunt.

The smell of her floral perfume lingers in the air. It's different from what I remember that night, mixed with the subtle smell of coconut from hours in the sun that day.

Thank fuck it's almost closing time, so I won't have to be here for much longer.

She's sitting in the waiting room when I saunter inside ten minutes later. Her legs are once again crossed, one foot bouncing on the ground.

Something about her attitude and her impatience makes me want to dig under her skin even more.

Hank whistles at me from across the room and nods in her direction when he hears me enter. I raise my hand to wave him off, reassuring him I got it from here.

Hank's a nice guy, even if he's an old pain in the ass sometimes. He's just set in his ways, and I guess when you get to his point in life, it's the way it is.

"Hallyn," I say, calling her name.

She glances up from where she's typing away on her phone and stands to head toward me. I keep my eyes trained on the computer screen until she leans her forearm on the counter.

"It looks like we'll have time tomorrow afternoon to get your truck in and take a look at it."

"Dang, okay, I guess I'll have to make it work. Can you hold off on doing any repairs until you talk to me, though?"

I nod. "Someone will get ahold of you to let you know what they find."

"All right, thank you." She sags in defeat and nods. Stepping back from the counter, she spins to head for the door before she turns back to me. "Oh, before I forget, thanks for the lift."

She nods toward the door. The bell dings when she pushes it open and disappears outside.

I expect her to be gone by the time we close for the night, so when I walk toward my truck and find her sitting on the bench an hour later, my eyes flash in surprise.

The sun has started to go down. I'm not sure where she lives. Braysen is small, but the campus is big compared to Rixton. There's a lot of student housing, but most are on the other side of town.

"You need a ride home, too?" I ask, breaking the silence.

She sighs. I thought she would've fought me on it, tossing more attitude my way, only this time, it never comes.

"If you don't mind." She grabs her bag next to her and heads toward me. She must've retrieved it from her truck.

She looks tired and disappointed, so I don't press her on it.

"Don't worry about it," I whisper. Only a couple of feet separates us now. "We don't even have to tell anyone either. I'll keep it between you and me."

Beckham leads me around to the passenger side and opens the door. I stare at him, unsure what to make of the gesture the second time.

His face drops, and he shakes his head. "Just get in, Hallyn."

Maybe it's because I'm tired, or perhaps it's because I'm irritated about my truck. It's probably a bit of both combined.

Either way, I don't have it in me to say what's on my mind.

Beckham circles the back of the pickup, and we climb in together. It takes me a minute to get in since it's lifted an extra couple of feet off the ground.

With nothing but the dashboard illuminating the space, he glances over at me in the dim moonlight.

He hands over his phone. "Go ahead and punch in your address."

He shifts the car into drive and flicks on the radio. Chase Rice plays low, filling the silence. I hadn't realized how small the space of his pickup is until all the oxygen feels like it's been sucked out of every inch.

The lyrics of the song pull me in. I've heard it a couple of times, but it isn't until now that I've been keenly aware of each word.

He sings about feeling her body against his and wanting to make her knees weak. When the chorus starts playing about riding on her all night long, I use my fingers to cover my gasp.

I glance over at Beckham from the corner of my eye and see his grip tighten on the steering wheel, causing the cords in his forearms to flex.

I clear my throat and turn my gaze outside, watching the houses and streetlights pass by. He doesn't say anything, and neither do I.

Eventually, the song changes, and before long, he flicks his turn signal to pull onto my street and into a spot outside the apartment I share with Ava.

I reach down to pick up my purse and my backpack. I'm glad I thought to grab it. I was so ready to get home that I almost forgot about it. I would've been sorry tomorrow, though, when I woke up and had class only to realize I left my stuff behind.

"Thanks again for the ride," I say, reaching for the door handle, clearing my throat when I realize my choice of words.

Beckham chuckles. "It's my pleasure."

I shake my head and turn back to him. "I mean it, though. You didn't have to offer me a lift, and I appreciate it."

His face changes, and he nods. I climb out of his truck and head to the secure entrance, punching in my code to unlock the door.

I look back at the road and notice him still waiting. He doesn't drive off until I enter, and the door shuts behind me.

As I trek up the stairs to our apartment, I try to shove the thoughts of Beckham out of my mind. That isn't hard to do when my phone vibrates in my pocket, and I pull it out to see a picture of Tanner and me from our senior prom.

He has his arm wrapped around me, and we're both smiling. That night is one of the happiest memories I have with Tanner, which is why I saved the photo as his contact.

"Hey, you," I say, trying to muster up more energy than I have.

"What are you doing?" he asks. His direct tone cuts to the chase, and it throws me off.

"I'm just getting home. You wouldn't believe the hellish day I've had."

I shove the key into my lock and push the door open, hitting it with my hip to close it behind me.

"What happened?"

"I was on my way to one of my tutor client's house. They live in the newer housing development on the edge of Braysen. While driving on the highway toward their place, I hit a pothole and nearly got into an accident when I lost control. Thankfully, I was able to get ahold of one of the shops in town, and they had one of their guys tow my truck back to their place until I can figure out what's wrong with it."

"Damn," he says. "And Ava gave you a ride home?"

I frown, confused by his question. He didn't seem concerned about the fact that I broke down or could've been hurt.

I shake my head as if trying to rid those thoughts from my mind.

Maybe it's all the arguing lately or his incessant complaints about my truck. I guess he wouldn't be too disappointed if I told him it kicked the bucket.

He doesn't seem to care in the least why the truck holds sentimental value to me.

Growing up, all I had were my mom and my grandparents. We ended up moving away from them the summer before I went into middle school, and that's when I met Ava.

It also brought me to Tanner.

The hard part was being away from my grandparents, though. My grandfather, Henry, was more like a father to me in the sense that my dad skipped out on us. He and my mom had separated long before I arrived, but he stuck around and put on a show pretending to play the role before he cut out of town.

I think my grandparents expected it to happen. Although it took longer before my mom came around to accepting it.

I still have some faint memories of her crying on the floor in her closet when she didn't think I could see or hear her. She did everything she could to provide for me, and when it came down to taking a job offer to work for a law office in Beaufort, she packed up and moved us away from my grandparents because she knew it would provide a better life for us.

It was, in the sense that living in a small town has its perks. Living in a big city means more expenses, and those were things she didn't have to worry about.

During summer break, I'd make the trip back to our hometown in Virginia and spend a couple of months with my grandparents. It gave my mom a break, and she was always refreshed when I returned. Those few weeks we spent together each summer before I went to school were some of my favorite memories.

The old pickup I drive has been in our family for years, so when I returned to Virginia to spend those few weeks with my grandpa before his heart attack, I held tight to those memories.

Just like I held on to the pickup he gave me.

"No," I prepare to lie, realizing I hadn't answered his question. The visions of me sitting in the truck with my grandpa, singing along to Dolly Parton and Johnny Cash, flash through my mind. "I, uh, called an Uber to pick me up. Ava had to work tonight."

I don't know why I lied to him, and something about it makes my stomach turn. He wouldn't understand why I accepted a ride from Beckham, no matter how many times I tried to break it down that it wasn't what he thought.

"Oh," he answers.

He doesn't say anything else, so we sit in an uncomfortable silence. I change the subject, asking him about practice, and he seems to perk up at the mention of Keaton and football.

I try not to show any signs that it gets to me to hear him talking about going out after practice. He suggests I come down next weekend, saying he wants to introduce me to a group of guys he's become friends with. He thinks I'd get along well with their girlfriends.

We're almost a month into the school year, and he's still trying to sell me on transferring to Keaton, so I'm careful with my words.

He seems to forget about the small fact I'm now without a car too.

I hear the lock on the door to my apartment click before Ava kicks it open with her foot. She's carrying her backpack, dance bag, and half a dozen grocery sacks.

"Oh, hey sweetie..." I pause Tanner in the middle of his story about the run-in he had with their QB last year. It turns out Tanner took his spot, and there's been some tension between them. "Ava just got home and needs a hand. Plus, I kind of need to jump in the shower. I'll call you when I crawl into bed."

He responds with a clipped okay, telling me to call him whenever I have a minute.

Ava sets the bags down on the counter with a huff and turns to me.

"Why does it sound like that conversation wasn't going too well?"

I kick off the shoes I'm still wearing, letting out a low sigh. It's like taking off your bra after a long day.

Ava's unpacking her groceries on the counter, and I saunter into the kitchen behind her. I lean against the tabletop, folding my arms over my chest and stare blankly at her.

"Is it really that obvious?" I ask, and she nods.

"You just haven't been yourself the past few weeks. I get it's the beginning of the school year, and you and Tanner are still working things out, trying to sort through being in different towns while attending different schools. Are you sure you're not rushing it, though, getting back together? Maybe you both need time to figure things out without trying to force it right now."

I swallow through the ball of cotton in my throat.

"I know how it looks, Av, but I promise it's not all bad. I think the stress you heard when you got here was from my craptastic day."

"What happened?"

"Well, for starters, I'm running short on funds since I finished buying my books and ordered the uniforms for dance. I haven't had a whole lot of luck finding tutoring clients. Then on my way to one of my sessions, my truck broke down."

"Shit, what are you gonna do?" She stretches her mouth into a flat smile, gritting her teeth.

"I guess I'll have to bust out my bike." I giggle. "I mean, they have buses, right? I could throw some money your way for gas to carpool with you to dance or games until I figure out a plan to get it fixed. It could take a few weeks, maybe a month, but I'm sure I'll sort it out."

She nods. Ava understands my hesitation to burden my mom with things like this. I'll figure it out one way or another.

"Maybe ask Tanner if he could loan you the money. Certainly, he'd want to help, especially with you driving down to Keaton to see him every weekend."

I narrow my eyes, leveling her with an "Are you serious?" stare.

She holds her hands up and laughs. "I mean, it's not like it would put him out or anything. Plus, you're his girlfriend. He should want to help you if he can, right?"

I ignore that she's voicing the same thing I told myself earlier.

"What's that shit you always say? Everything happens for a reason?" I ask. She rolls her eyes, and I chuckle. "There has to be some big epic plan for why things are falling apart right now."

Ava's always been the spiritual one between the two of us. It's right on par with her to believe it's divine timing and that there's a bigger purpose to why life throws you chaos.

She'd say, "It'll all come together the way it's meant to be."

Not me, though. Call me a realist, or maybe I'm just cynical. I think the universe would say it's just my luck. What other reason explains why Beckham Carver always seems to be right there, no matter where I turn, when I've only been in Braysen for a few weeks?

"Speaking of boyfriends..." I change the subject.

Ava suddenly takes an interest in putting the rest of her groceries away, and I laugh, knowing exactly what she's doing.

"You want to tell me what's going on with you and Colter?"

She's spent some time with Colter Vaughn, one of Braysen's offensive linemen, after a whole fiasco at the beginning of the school year when our apartment wasn't ready. It left her with nowhere else to go, so she crashed at his place.

Sure, she had the option to pack up and head to Keaton, where she could've stayed with her brother until things sorted themselves out, but what's the fun in doing that?

"Not much to tell." She shrugs, but I know my best friend better than to believe it. "I mean, I stayed with him for those ten days. Things got heated between us a couple of times, and one thing led to another. We're friends, though. Why do you ask?"

"I don't know too many friends who hook up, but if you say so." I hold my hands up, turning to open the fridge and swiping the bottle of orange juice I picked up from the cafeteria this morning.

"I'm curious, what do you know about Beckham Carver?"

She's gotten to know more of the football players than I have since her "friendship" with Colter began.

Her brows deepen. "Well, he's one of Colter's roommates. Why are you asking about Beckham?" she retorts.

I shake my head, trying to downplay it. "Well, I mean, we both know he's the QB for the Bulldogs, but it turns out he works for the auto shop I called. He towed my truck there for me."

She nods slowly, waiting for me to elaborate. Her eyes stay trained on my face while I swallow what's left of my OJ.

"What? Why are you looking at me that way?"

"What way?" she jests. "I'm just curious as to why you seem more interested in talking about Beckham than the situation between you and Tanner."

"All I asked is what you knew about the guy who towed my truck."

She nods. "You say that like I don't know *you*." She takes my words and turns them back on me. "I know that look. You don't even have to tell me. You have a crush on Beckham."

I scoff. "Are you kidding? Actually, if you care to know, I think he's an asshole. I ran into him that night at the party a few weeks ago, and you could say he proved to be a royal jackass. I do *not* have a crush on Beckham."

She chuckles. "Riiiiight."

I shake my head and stalk past her, tossing the now empty bottle of juice into the trash before spinning on my heel.

"Thanks for the chat tonight, Av. I'm gonna go shower now."

"Don't worry, Halls, if you want to flick the bean tonight to thoughts of Carver, I'll put in headphones and pretend I don't hear you. Your secret is safe with me."

If I didn't know better, I'd think she and Beckham were conspiring together.

I raise my middle finger and flip her off behind me, sending her into a fit of giggles.

I hate how easily she can read me.

Let's hope it's not so easy for Beckham, or I might be in deep trouble.

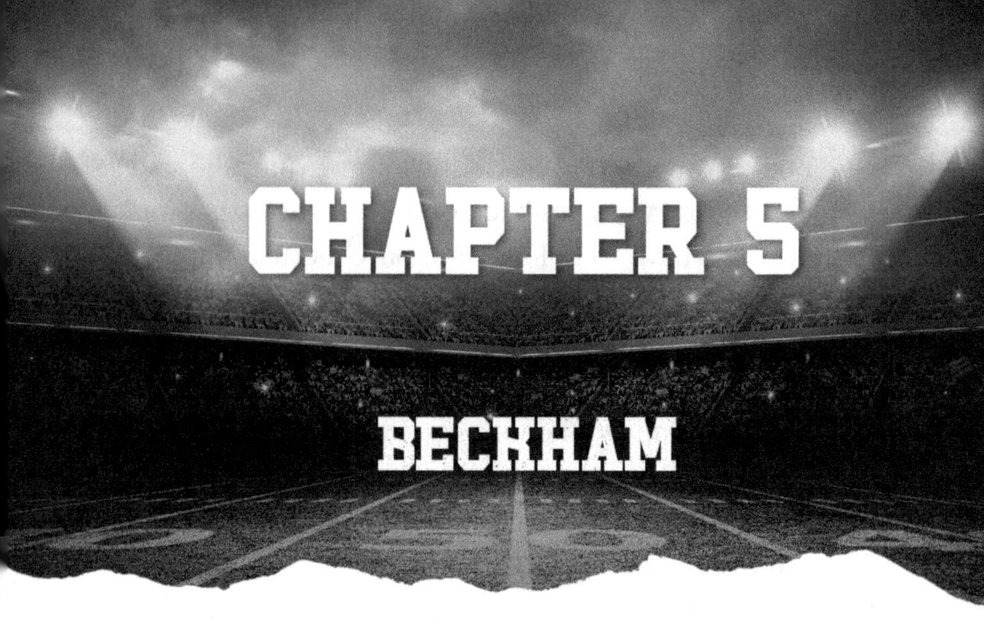

CHAPTER 5

BECKHAM

"Carver, my office." Coach Frye's voice echoes down the long hallway, stopping me mid-step as I push open the locker room door.

Reed, one of my good friends and roommates, stands behind me. His back faces Coach, so only I see the "oh shit" look on his face.

"I'll be right there," I holler back, holding my finger up to let him know it'll be a minute.

"What the hell does he wanna see you for?" Reed drops his voice low.

"I'm guessing it's about my grade in chemistry," I grumble. "I got a D on the test, so now I'm straddling the line of failing. He's been on me about getting my grades up before our first game."

He mutters, "Good luck," as I pass by him and amble down the hall toward Coach's office.

I wish I could pull one of those ole switcheroos with Hayes. He's always been smart, whereas I goofed off in class and hardly ever paid attention. That's part of my problem—I've been skipping class. I tend to mess around until the last minute and usually spend all my time figuring out a way to quickly clean up the mess I've made.

Coach sits in his chair, his eyes on a piece of paper in front of him, when I tap my knuckles against the door and push it open.

"Take a seat." He motions to the two chairs facing him, and I follow suit.

The look on his face is more serious than the last time I was in this chair. It has me sitting up a little higher, giving him my attention.

"So, what have you been doing about your grades since our last conversation?"

I clap my hands together and adjust the hem of my shorts, attempting to buy myself some time.

What have I done? Well, the truth is *nothing*.

I've spent the past few days fuckin' around and didn't bother to even study for the test I had earlier this week.

I should've known it would get me in trouble, but did I care? Not so much.

I chalked it up to it being early in the school year, and once I had more assignments, my grades would improve.

Turns out I was wrong.

"I'm working on getting one of those tutors you suggested," I lie. "I'm waiting on a couple of them to get back with me."

He nods his head, his eyes narrowing on me.

"You lying to me, son?"

I swallow hard and shake my head. "No, sir," I lie again. There's a lump in my throat, and my mouth is as dry as the Sahara Desert.

He flares his nostrils and tilts his chin, leaning back in his chair.

"Well, your teacher tells me that you have two assignments due in the next two weeks, and if you can manage to get a ninety or higher, you should be able to pull your grade up enough to get me off your back."

A ninety will require an act of God, but if I want to get the dogs off me, I guess I need to figure my shit out.

The only other option would be to go back to my earlier suggestion of convincing Hayes to take it for me. There's no way he'll do it, though, no matter how bad he wants me to play with him.

The last thing we need is for both of us to sit out of a game.

"I'll get on things with the tutor, and I'll make sure I pull my grade up before the first game."

He nods once more. "All right, then. Now, get the hell out of here."

I push my hands off the armrests, helping me to stand, and thank him before I hightail it out of his office.

I have thirty minutes to get cleaned up before my shift at Kavlik's, and judging by the quiet locker room, most of my teammates have already taken off.

Since I don't have much time, I opt to shower there and throw on my clothes I wore earlier. I pull out the paper I shoved in my bag, scanning over the list of tutors Coach gave me, before my eyes zero in on one name.

Hallyn Rivers.

Well, I'll be damned. Turns out Little Miss Feisty might be the only thing saving me now.

And I have just the idea of how to make it happen.

Kavlik's is one of the few car dealerships and auto shops in Braysen, although it's the biggest of them all.

I pull into the parking lot not long after practice and park near the shop. The dealership is located in the front and the repair and detail shop in the back.

It's relatively quiet at this point, as most of the mechanics have taken off for the day. We still take customers until closing, although things die down in the evening.

That's one good thing about livin' in the South—they're big on family time, and when dinner is served, a lot of folks expect to have everyone around the table to join them.

I hear Hayes's voice before I see him, and I'm a few steps behind catching who he's talking to. The first thing I see is her long blonde hair pulled into a high ponytail.

"You new to Braysen?" Hayes asks.

He's clearly into her. He has no problem in the women department, but he's not normally one to flirt, so it's obvious when he's attracted to someone. Judging by his tone, he's laying it on thick.

It's *Hallyn.*

I grit my teeth and clench my jaw. Something about the sight of the two of them together grinds on my nerves, even if it's like picturing her with me.

Hayes has no idea about our brief but recent history. Not that there's much to tell anyway.

"Yeah." Her voice sounds softer, sweeter than before. "I'm originally from Beaufort, North Carolina."

"Is that right?" He curves his mouth into a smile and leans against the counter in front of her.

She takes a step back, and I wonder if she thinks it's me or if she's realized it's not.

Hayes wears a Kavlik's navy blue T-shirt and a pair of denim jeans. We both have a name tag that Hank rides our ass to wear, but since Hayes is often in the shop detailing cars, he forgets to put it on.

"It's a shame I haven't seen you around more. You ever stop out at Whiskey Sinner's?" he asks, but that's when I've had enough.

I clear my throat, sending Hallyn's long hair swinging as she spins around to face me, and her mouth drops open when she notices me coming.

She glances back and forth between the two of us, and I greet her with a signature smirk.

"I see you've met my brother," I grunt, nodding toward him as I pass by to circle around the counter to where he's standing.

Hayes pushes off the counter, his brows deepening, picking up on my smart-ass tone. I tilt my head to the side as if to tell him to get the fuck outta here.

He bursts out laughing before he turns back to Hallyn.

"My apologies, sweetheart. I hadn't realized you've already been spoken for."

"Take a hike, will ya?" I grunt, interrupting Hallyn before she has a chance to clarify.

Once it's just the two of us, I turn my attention back on her.

She's dressed in a pair of leggings and a fitted tank top. She looks like she just came from a workout, and I take a moment to thank whoever invented those pants because goddamn does she make them look good.

Just like the first night I met her, she's not wearing a speck of makeup, and I can make out the dusting of freckles along her cheeks.

Her green eyes sparkle like emeralds, burning into me. Any sign she might be happy to see me is out the window, and her cold-as-stone exterior from the last time I saw her is back.

"Did he happen to tell you what's goin' on with your ole beater before the two of you started whatever it is you were talkin' about when I walked in?"

If I was trying to play it off like I didn't give a shit, I was doing a piss-poor job of it, but I didn't care.

I'm not sure if I'm more ticked about Hayes hitting on her or the sour look on her face now that she knows she's talking to me.

Honestly, it's a bit of both.

"No, that's why I'm here, so why don't you break it to me for him."

I exhale a heavy sigh and shake my head. "Well, it turns out the alternator is going out. At this point, I gotta admit, I don't think it's worth fixin' unless you want to throw more money into that ole thing. If you ask me, I don't think it's worth it."

She sags in defeat, likely hoping this wasn't going to be the answer.

"How much does something like that cost?"

"With parts and labor, you're looking at about nine hundred."

"Shit," she mutters before she presses her fingers to her mouth.

She grits her teeth and drops her chin to her chest. I almost feel bad for her, especially when she glances up at me, and I catch the slight glisten in her eyes.

She looks like she's on the verge of tears.

"I'm gonna need a few days to figure something out. I'm sorry, I just don't have that kind of money right now."

I nod. "It's no problem. We can keep your truck parked here in the lot until you decide what you'd like for us to do."

She tucks a strand of hair behind her ear, and I catch her subtly try to brush the moisture from the corner of her eye.

"How about this?" I suggest, the words flying out of my mouth. "I can tell you're upset, and I think there might be somethin' I can do to help you out."

Her face falls, and her eyes narrow. "What's that include exactly?"

The wheels turn in her head, and I can only guess where she thinks this might be going.

"Well, I've been meaning to get in touch with a tutor. I haven't been doing so well in my chemistry class, and, uhh, I noticed your name was on the bulletin of tutors available."

She nods her head slowly as if the pieces of the puzzle start to come together.

"What do you say I hire you to help me for the rest of the semester, and in return, I'll take care of getting your truck fixed."

She trails her tongue along her lips. My eyes zero in on the move, watching as she presses them together.

Silence falls over the two of us, and I can practically hear the seconds tick by as I wait for her to respond.

"I don't think that's a good idea."

"Why not?"

"Well, for starters, I have a boyfriend, and he wouldn't be too happy if he knew I was tutoring you."

Boyfriend.

I guess that means she and Freeman got back together after all.

The news lands like a punch in the gut.

"What, you don't tutor other guys too?"

She flares her nostrils, and her throat bobs when she swallows.

"Well, yeah..."

"Okay, so then what's the problem?"

"It's just, it's *you.*"

I grin. "Are you saying there's something between us that he has a reason to be jealous of?"

"See, this is exactly why it wouldn't be a good idea."

I hold my hand up, attempting to stop her when she pushes off the counter to leave.

"Whoa, all right, fine. I get it."

Her thoughts play out on her face, and it's as if a war rages through her mind. If I have any hope of her helping me out, I need to concede a little here.

"Fine, I'll cool it on the antics. Okay?"

She crosses her arms, and it takes everything in me not to let my eyes trail over her body. Somehow, I manage to keep them focused on her face.

She lifts her brow. I don't know if she's amused or surprised, but she nods.

"Can you give me a couple of days to think about it?"

I have chemistry twice a week, every Tuesday and Thursday. We got our grades handed out to us today. I can give her the rest of the week if she wants to drag this out.

In the end, though, she needs my help, and I know I need hers.

Eventually, her little boyfriend will find out, and it's a bonus to know I'll be getting under his skin too.

"Whatever you need." I wink.

She rolls her eyes and drops her arms. Without another word, she spins on her heel and storms out, and I'm left once again thanking God for those fuckin' pants.

CHAPTER 6

HALLYN

I toss my poms onto the stage in the practice gym and jump up to take a seat on the ledge.

Ava lifts the hem of her tank, using the cotton material to wipe her brow before she takes a drink while I do the same.

SJ's been busting our asses to get us ready for the football season kickoff. It's given me something to take the stress off, balancing school, dance, and finding time to pick up more tutoring jobs.

Now, the big question is if I'll accept Beckham's offer and tutor him, knowing it could be the end of my relationship with Tanner if he found out.

Things are already strained between us. When we got back together, we both promised we'd put in the effort to make it work.

"You comin' out with us tonight?" Ava asks, taking another drink from her water bottle.

"What's goin' on tonight?" I question, glancing from her to Mandy and Summer.

"I guess there's a group meeting up at Whiskey Sinner's tonight. I figured you could use a night out. It's been a while since we've gone dancing."

That's the truth. Growing up, I often hung out at the small-town bar my mom worked at back in Beaufort. Every Friday and Saturday night, they had bands playing, often cover bands.

On the nights when my mom bartended and couldn't find a babysitter, she took me out with her. Sometimes, she'd even let Ava tag along.

We were both in everything from tap, ballet, and even hip-hop but hangin' out at the tavern is where we were first exposed to line dancing. So when Ava mentions how it's been a while since we've gone dancing, the glimmer in her eye tells me exactly what she has in mind.

"I could definitely use a night out," I agree. "I haven't heard from Tanner for most of the day."

I lean across the stage and tug my backpack toward me. My phone is tucked in the side pocket, so I pull it out and check the notifications.

When I talked to Tanner earlier, I asked him about our plan for tonight. Every weekend since the school year began, I've made the drive down to Keaton to see him. So when I suggested maybe this time he could make the trip to me, he stopped responding to my messages.

Ava leans against my shoulder, snapping my attention back to her when I realize she had been talking to me while I zoned out scrolling through my messages.

"Maybe just text him, tell him you're goin' out to Whiskey Sinner's, and if he chooses to come, then we'll meet him there."

I bite the edge of my lip, debating before I nod. I'm not going to sit around and wait on him while he gives me the silent treatment.

Ava always knows how to pull me out of my funk. So, after we agreed to meet the girls at Whiskey Sinner's, we rode back to our apartment to get ready for the night.

On the entire drive home, she has the music turned all the way up. At one point, when she glanced over and caught me not singing along, she reached for my wrist, using my fist as a microphone while she belted out the lyrics to Carrie Underwood.

Later, I stand in front of the large gold ornate-framed mirror in the corner of my bedroom when Ava pokes her head in. My fingers run through my long blonde curls before I adjust my belt.

"Girl, if Tanner isn't falling over himself when he sees you, I'm telling him I'm takin' you home for myself."

She wags her brows at me in the mirror, and I smirk, shaking my head.

A crowd forms out the door of Whiskey Sinner's when we pull up shortly after. My phone vibrates in the back pocket of my denim shorts.

Tanner: We'll be there soon.

"Tanner sent me a message. He said they'll be here in twenty."

"Does that mean Alec is coming with him?" Ava's eyes widen, and I give her a straight smile.

"When do they ever go out without the other?" I retort, and we both know I'm right.

Tanner and Alec have been best friends for nearly as long as Ava and I have. That's how he and I first met and started talking.

Alec has always been overprotective of Ava, so if he finds out she's been hanging out with Colter, there's no telling how he'll react, but we both know it won't be good.

The bouncer at the door checks our IDs and lets us in. We managed to score a couple of fakes when we moved to Braysen, which is how we've been able to get inside.

"C'mon." Ava links her arm in mine. "We both need a drink now, especially after your hellish week."

A large bar is centered in the middle of the open room. Two sides are lined with barstools, and the other two serve patrons who walk up, likely looking for a drink between dancing.

There are booth seats and high-top tables up front, with the dance floor and stage near the back. Large rustic beams are spread throughout with black iron details.

"Colter's here," Ava whispers, brushing her hand over my forearm. I glance over at where she's nodding, and my eyes lock on Beckham's.

He's already spotted the two of us. When he catches me looking in his direction, he lifts his beer to his lips and nods before taking a drink.

He's leaning his arm on the table, his leg crossed over the other, looking confident and relaxed, like he knows he could have any woman in this room if he wanted her.

Except for you, Hallyn.

I hate to admit I've noticed, but he looks damn good in his maroon T-shirt and distressed black jeans. I tell myself not to glance in his direction so he doesn't catch me staring and get any ideas that I'm checking him out.

So, when I spot a girl sliding up next to him and drawing his attention away, I let my eyes do a brief once-over. Enough to satisfy my urge, taking in his square-toe boots and the black cord around his wrist.

The muscles in his forearm tense when he lifts his beer again, and Ava elbows me in the side.

"I think that's Beckham," Ava says. "It's hard to tell him and his brother apart." She thinks I only know him from the party and from him towing my truck back to the shop.

She has no idea about how he gave me a ride there and home after, or about the deal he tried to strike up when I went to talk to them about the repairs.

I can only imagine her reaction if I told her that Hayes has longer hair and Beckham has the tattoo on his forearm. Those are details I shouldn't have picked up on in the little time I've interacted with them.

I slowly turn back toward Ava as we take another step closer to the bar. We're next in line, and I'm ready for that drink she mentioned earlier.

"The guy standing behind him talking to the blonde is his twin brother, Hayes. He played for Braysen last year. I guess Beckham went to some school in Tennessee. He transferred here to play with his brother."

I nod, trying not to show I'm curious about him. I shouldn't be either.

He's an asshole, and he's proven himself to be since the first time we met a month ago.

The way I see it, if he hadn't decided to transfer to Braysen, Tanner would've gotten his spot, and all the strain we've had on our relationship wouldn't be happening.

Even though I know it's not his fault, it's easier to hate him when I tell myself it is.

"The guy talking to Colter is Reed Hendrix. The four of them are roommates. He plays for the Bulldogs too."

Colter notices Ava looking in his direction, and I elbow her and grin when we both catch the slow smile stretching across his face.

My heart warms for my best friend. I remember the early stages of my relationship with Tanner. The butterflies in my stomach, the way my skin pricked when he kissed me.

I saw him a lot whenever I hung out over at Ava's house, which was often growing up. Feelings were always there on my side, and sometimes I find myself wondering how things could change, like it was flipped over on a dime.

Strong arms wrap around my middle, and I glance down, noticing the familiar tattoo near his wrist. I spin around to Tanner, expecting him to greet me with the same warm smile Colter gave Ava, only to be met with a neutral and unreadable expression.

"Hey." I reach my arms around his neck, pulling him into me, and he buries his face into my shoulder. His body seems to relax when I whisper, "I missed you," in his ear.

He steps away, letting his eyes drag down my body before they quickly snap back to meet mine.

"You couldn't wear something a little less revealing?" he asks.

Ava's head flies around, shooting a pissed-off glare in his direction. I can see the fire in her gaze when she looks at me and mutters, "Dick," under her breath. She's not usually one to start drama, so while I want to believe she meant to keep her voice down, there's no doubt in my mind he heard her.

She turns away from the two of us, stepping up to the bar to order our drinks. I cross my arms over my chest, suddenly feeling self-conscious.

"What's wrong with what I'm wearing?" I steel my spine and narrow my eyes on him.

"Nothing," he responds defensively. "I just don't under-stand why you have to wear tops that show your stomach and those short-ass shorts. If you bent down, everyone could see your ass hanging out."

"Well, I guess it's a good thing I'm not doing any bending over, then, huh?" I fire back. "There's no difference between this and my dance uniform, so get over yourself. Is this what you came all this way for? I haven't seen you in a week, and all you want to do is fight with me."

My heart hammers in my chest. He shakes his head and turns, and for the first time, I notice Alec and a few guys I've never met standing with him.

"Here you go." Ava hands me a shot and then snickers when I realize the other one in her hand is meant for me too. "You deserve it." She winks.

We both cheers before we down one of them. When I glance back at Tanner, I notice he and his friends have claimed another nearby table. He clenches his jaw as if he's waiting for me to take the second.

I smile at him even though I know I'm being a smart-ass and take the other.

"C'mon." Ava presses her mouth against my ear. "Let's go dance."

I cast one last look over at Tanner and wave while Ava tugs on my arm. We weave through the crowd of people toward the dance floor before Ava stops when we reach the table where Colter and Beckham stand.

"Something tells me your boyfriend isn't gonna like it when he realizes who's over here." Beckham grins.

I finally recognize the blonde I saw approach him earlier. Her name is Leslie, and she's one of the seniors on the cheerleading squad.

She rubs her lips together, flicking her eyes from Beckham over to me as if trying to piece together our connection.

"Yeah, well, somethin' tells me when you take Leslie here home for the night, she'll be disappointed too."

Beckham's eyes glitter, and the subtle twitch on his face gives away he's resisting the urge to laugh.

"You wish it were you, Hallyn." Beckham tilts his head to the side, wrapping his arm around Leslie's shoulder. "Why don't you tell her how bad you wish this were you right now."

I glance at Ava, curious if she heard anything Beckham said.

"How many women in this bar have you been with since you got to Braysen, Beckham? What's there to be jealous of when you're desperate to give it up to anyone and everyone?"

My response earns a few laughs from his friends, and Beckham clenches his jaw.

"Now, if you'll excuse us, we have a dance floor to tear up." I grin, reaching for Ava's arm.

"Let's go, Av. You promised me dancing."

CHAPTER 7

BECKHAM

I'd like to smack the smug-as-fuck look off her boyfriend's face.

After Hallyn's little smart-ass comment, she and her friend disappeared onto the dance floor. I resisted the urge to watch her walk away, but when the song changed to Ed Sheeran and the crowd lined up to dance, I gave in to the temptation and stared at her.

She's dressed in a pair of shorts, frayed along the edges, and a black corset top with silver-studded fringe hanging along the bottom. When she rolls her hips and sways, the material moves with her, giving a glimpse of her tan stomach underneath.

My throat bobs when I swallow hard, watching her kick her leg out and stomp as she turns, this time her ass facing me. Her ass and legs look incredible. I clench my jaw, and my temple pulsates at the thought of her going home with Freeman tonight and him devouring every inch of her sinful body.

She's wearing black booties, and her hair falls down her back in waves. When she finally turns back to face me, she runs her hands through her hair. Her face and chest glisten in a sheen of sweat.

I've never seen someone dance the way she does. It's like she can feel the music flowing through every inch of her body. She catches me watching her when she rolls her hips, and I wonder if she imagines she's dancing for me the way I am.

The song changes, and she turns toward her friend. They bump their hips together and clap hands, sauntering between the two high-top bars lining the dance floor.

She makes a beeline across the room toward where her boyfriend stands, waiting for her.

"I need another drink," I mutter to Reed. "You want one?"

I still have half my beer in my cup. He glances down and back at me, his lip curling in a smirk.

"If you're going, I guess grab me another one too."

He overheard my conversation with her earlier, so something tells me he's onto me.

I down the rest of my beer and stalk across the bar to join the line where they're standing. His hand presses against her lower back, holding her against him.

The sight of his hands on her sets off something inside me, and I don't want to think about why. Now that I'm within earshot, I'm able to hear their conversation.

"Why did you drive to Braysen if all you want to do is fight?"

I pretend I'm not eavesdropping, keeping my eyes focused ahead. The bartender waves me over, and I shout my order to him across the bar.

Hallyn moves beside me, her body tensing when she turns in his arms to find me standing there.

"What the hell are you doing?" she barks.

"Aren't you going to introduce us?" I quirk my brow, glancing over at Tanner.

His face is as hard as stone, his gaze burning into me.

"Halls can be so rude sometimes. I'm Beckham." I smirk, holding my hand out between us.

Hallyn's mouth falls open, and she holds up her hand between us.

"What the hell are you doing?"

"That's a bit rude, don't you think?" I scold her. She exhales a heavy breath, her nostrils flaring and her jaw clenching.

"How do the two of you know each other?" Tanner interjects, and I drop my hand to my side.

"Well, we met at a party a few weeks ago. Now, that was an interesting run-in." I chuckle, shaking my head like I'm trying to rid myself of the memory. "I also helped her out a few days ago when her truck kicked the bucket. Gave her and the truck a lift to the shop and then home."

His jaw ticks, finally giving away to the anger simmering underneath.

"Is that right?" he drawls, turning his attention to Hallyn.

The bartender sets my beers on the counter, and I hand him my card to start my tab.

"You two have a good one." I wink, reaching for my beers, and turn to head back to our table.

Reed spots me coming, and he shakes his head.

"Why do I get the feeling you went over there for no other reason than to start some shit?" He snickers.

"Who? Me?" I feign innocence, and he scoffs.

"You do realize who that is, right?" he asks, taking his beer from me. "What the hell is he doing all this way anyway?"

"That's Ava's friend, Hallyn. She was at our place a few weeks ago for the party. I guess she's dating the QB for Keaton."

He nods, seemingly already aware. "Why the hell is she with him?"

That, right there, is the million-dollar question.

The two of them seem like an interesting pair. She's dressed like she's heading out and living the single life. Meanwhile, Freeman wears a polo and khakis like he's ready for a round of golf.

"Looks like trouble in paradise," he mutters, and we both glance in their direction.

Hallyn's fists are planted on her hips, her head bobbing from side to side. I've been on the receiving end of her sass. Whatever she's saying has her fired up.

Tanner holds up his hands and shakes his head. He motions to his friends, and the group finishes their drinks, leaving their empty glasses on the table before heading toward the door.

Hallyn spins on her heels and makes a beeline toward the bathrooms.

"Well, whatever happened, it looks like it didn't go over well."

I sip my beer and set it down on the bar. "I'll be right back."

My trip to the bar had nothing to do with wanting another beer, so I don't give a shit about leaving it unattended and full at our table.

Two bench seats line the hallway leading toward the bathrooms. An alcove across from the seating area has hooks on the wall where patrons can hang their jackets or coats. It's too hot out for it, though, so it's empty.

I lean against the wall and wait for her to appear. I notice her before she sees me. I reach for her wrist and pull her aside away from the crowd.

"Beckham?" Hallyn says, the door swinging shut behind her.

"You okay?" I ask.

Her eyes are red, and a part of me feels bad for causing her and Happy Gilmore to fight.

She shakes her head. "Were you waiting for me?"

She brushes her finger under her eye before stopping, standing up straight, and finding her resolve.

I grin. She's so damn stubborn that she won't dare let me or anyone else see her upset.

"Actually, don't bother answering. It doesn't matter. The deal you tried to make is not happening."

She storms past me, but I won't let her go, not yet. I reach for her hand and tug her back to me once more.

"Leave me alone." Her voice drops low, and she snatches her arm away.

"Why?" I ask, taking a step toward her. "All because your spoiled little rich boyfriend threw a hissy fit when I tried to introduce myself? Here, I thought I was being nice." I chuckle, and she curls her lip in frustration.

"No, you didn't. Don't fuckin' play these games with me, Beckham. You knew exactly what you were doing."

I take another step toward her, dropping the smile on my face.

"Who's playing games, Hallyn? Me?" I press my hand against my chest. "You want to try again?"

She purses her lips together, appearing to rethink her words. She takes another step backward until her back presses against the wall, and I follow her.

We're out of sight of the rest of the bar. Unless someone walks by and looks in here, they would never find us.

Her chest heaves as she forces a heavy inhale and exhale. I glance down at her chest and the hint of her cleavage on display at this angle.

I drag my lip between my teeth, flicking my eyes back up to meet hers. The anger on her face has been replaced with something else. Attraction? Defeat? I can't be sure which.

"I heard the two of you fighting when I stepped up to the bar to order my beers, so you can't put this on me."

She nods so subtly that I almost can't tell she moved. Her eyes flick up to mine from beneath her lashes.

"Why do you keep trying to act like you hate me?"

"It's not acting, Beckham," she retorts. "I do hate you."

I chuckle and shake my head, stepping close enough to where our hips touch. Her eyes flutter, and she snaps her mouth shut.

Her throat bobs, and I resist the urge to tilt her head back and drag my tongue over her salty skin.

She can try to tell me she hates me, but it's only to convince herself and not me. We both know if I take it a step further, she'll collapse like a house of cards.

I brush my knuckle over her skin and smile when goose bumps break out over her arm. She can't hide how her body reacts to me, no matter how hard she fights it.

"You want to know what I think of you, Halls?"

"Stop calling me that," she snaps.

"All right. Well, you want to know what I think?"

"Even if I tell you no, we both know you're gonna tell me anyway, so just spill it."

I laugh. "I think you feel this between us. I think you know you're attracted to me, and it pisses you off."

She rears back, her eyes flashing in anger. "Excuse me?"

"See." I graze my finger along her jaw. "I think the only reason you hate me is because wanting your boyfriend's biggest rival would make you what...?"

"Do you realize how arrogant you are?" she fires back. "You think because you're the hotshot quarterback, the big man on campus, that everyone will bow down to you. What, just because you're attractive and know how to throw a fuckin' ball, now every woman you encounter wants to drop their pants for you?"

"So, you do find me attractive?"

She tilts her head against the wall and squeezes her eyes shut, letting out a low growl.

I grip her throat in my hand, taking us both by surprise. She snaps her mouth shut and quiets her frustration.

Her eyes grow heavy, and the tension in the small space shifts to something else entirely.

I lean in, brushing my nose along her cheek. Her body shudders, and I grin, pressing my mouth against her ear.

"Say it, Hallyn," I whisper. "Admit it. I promise, I won't tell him. It'll stay between the two of us."

"Oh, like you promised you wouldn't tell him about giving me a ride?" She reaches her hand up to grip my wrist. "You're a cocky prick," she whispers.

"Try again."

My lips brush along her cheek until I pull back enough that our foreheads nearly touch. She tilts her head to the side and squeezes her eyes shut.

"Leave me alone. The deal is off the table. Do you hear me?"

"Do you lie to yourself about your boyfriend too? Or do you let it build up and reserve all this attitude for me?"

She shoots an angry glance in my direction.

"I hate you."

I shake my head. "No, you don't," I argue. "You don't hate me, just like you know this isn't over between us. We both have something the other needs, and as much as you want to, you don't believe any of the shit you're trying to convince yourself of."

I give in, leaning in to press a kiss against her cheek. When I push off the wall, her mouth falls open, and she narrows her eyes on me. I smile, watching the fire in hers burn.

"Suck it up, Halls. You know I'm right."

When I turn away and head back out to the bar, I hear her respond with a "fuck you." The echo of her growly voice makes me laugh.

I will, but only when she's writhing beneath me and begging for it.

CHAPTER 8

HALLYN

My neck aches, and my back screams when I slowly lift my head from the arm of the couch and blink my eyes open.

It was after midnight when I made it home from Whiskey Sinner's. Tanner took off after our fight, and I haven't spoken to him since.

He has an eight o'clock conditioning training this morning, so I knew he had to be back in Keaton. I suggested maybe he stay with me, but that idea quickly flew out the window.

No way would he agree to stay all night and wake up early to drive home.

All my texts since he left the bar, asking him to talk to me or if he made it home safely, went unanswered.

My phone vibrates on the glass coffee table, and the screen flashes with a text notification. I regret falling asleep on the couch when I push myself up and reach for my phone, immediately noticing the unknown number.

What if Tanner got pulled over on the way home? He only had one drink, which isn't enough to put him over the limit. Or what if he got into a car accident?

Worry coils like a knot in my stomach, but I force myself not to jump to conclusions. Ever since my grandpa's heart attack that led to his car accident, I can't help but immediately fear the worst possible scenario, no matter how many times I try to will myself out of it.

I swipe the screen, opening the message.

Unknown: Today is the deadline. Are you still refusing to accept our deal?

Beckham.

How the hell did he manage to get my number?

You gave it to him at the auto shop, Hallyn. Remember?

I squeeze my phone in my grip and grit my teeth, tossing it on the cushion next to me and stand. I stretch my arms above my head, hoping to loosen the muscles in my back, and shake my head.

Beckham will have to wait for now.

I broke a rule last night and crashed on the couch without bothering to change my clothes or wash off my makeup. I immediately head for the bathroom and turn on the shower until the steam from the water fills the small space. I shed my clothes and step in, hoping to wash myself clean of everything that happened the night before.

Including the memory of Beckham's hands on me when he pushed me against the wall.

Until we ran into Beckham at the bar, I was strongly considering his proposal. He had a point; we both had something the other needed. Deep down, I knew if push came to shove, I could ask to borrow money from Tanner. He's never known what it's like to struggle financially.

When he got a scholarship to Keaton, hell, even well before then, his parents promised to support him as long as he kept his focus on football and school. The cost of fixing my truck is pocket change to them.

It doesn't matter, though. I can't imagine accepting his money, even if I committed to paying him back.

He'd likely tell me to sell the truck to the junkyard and try to convince me to get a new car. Something brand new off the lot, flashy and unnecessary.

Never mind the history behind the truck and the sentimental value it holds for me.

So, when I steer my bike in front of the shop and hit the brakes, I've resigned myself to accept my hands are tied. Yes, I could hike around town on my bicycle for the semester while I save up. It still poses a problem when it comes to any tutoring session off campus or even traveling to away games for dance.

I tuck my hair behind my ear, adjust the straps on my backpack, and reach for the door handle.

The bell dings, announcing my arrival, and Beckham glances up from his phone behind the counter. A lazy smile stretches across his face when he notices it's me, and I try to ignore the way my stomach flips to his breathtaking grin.

I realize what other women see when he turns his charm on them. I can't help but feel annoyed at the revelation, and I resist the urge to raise my middle finger and turn back around.

"I was starting to think you were ignoring my text message," he says, bemused.

"That's because I was," I retort. "Take the hint."

His smile falls, and his eyes narrow on me.

"Isn't that against some privacy rule too? Stealing my number from your work and using it for personal reasons?" I wave my hand at the computer in front of him.

"Maybe..." He shrugs. "It's not like I couldn't figure out another way to get it. Some girls wouldn't mind doing me a favor."

The gleam in his eyes at the last part has me curling my lip in disgust. Of course, he'd be proud to announce his *connections*.

"I'm not here to listen to you brag about your hookups. Quite frankly, I couldn't give a shit less who you're dragging back to your place."

He nods slowly, his grin back. "Uh-huh." He drags out.

I press my lips together.

"Well, will you at least answer me then on our deal? If you want me to work on your pile of rust, I'm gonna need to order the parts."

I straighten my spine. He tosses his phone on the counter and crosses his arms over his chest.

The move distracts me momentarily, noticing the dirt and grease on his hands and the way his muscles clench. It's a stark contrast to anything I've ever seen from Tanner.

He wasn't one to get his hands dirty unless it came from a tackle. There's something so different, so rugged about Beckham. His messy hair and the calluses I felt on my skin. Like he isn't afraid to get down and dirty when necessary, and he sure as hell isn't scared of anyone who gets in his way.

He proved as much last night when he antagonized Tanner in front of me and his teammates.

I knew he was pushing his buttons, though, trying to find what made him tick and where to aim his shots so it hurt.

Beckham knows Tanner plays for Braysen's biggest rival, but he has no clue about the fact he took Tanner's spot as the quarterback for the Bulldogs.

If he knew and used it against him, it would land like an uppercut to the jaw.

"If I go through with our deal, we'll have to agree to some terms."

He tilts his chin up, and the cocky look on his face returns.

"All right, and what would that be exactly?"

"Well, for starters, I need you to back off and respect my relationship with Tanner."

His blank face is devoid of any emotion, so I continue.

"I also need you to promise me you won't tell anyone I'm tutoring you."

His gaze narrows on me, and he tilts his head to the side. "Why?" he barks out.

"You saw the way Tanner reacted to your antics last night. If he knew I was helping you, let's just say he wouldn't be very happy."

He chuckles. "You think I'm supposed to care about what makes him happy?"

"All right, fine then." I hold my hands up, accepting defeat, and turn to walk out.

I knew there was a chance he wouldn't agree to keep this between the two of us, and that was one stipulation I wasn't willing to back down from.

Although I know nothing is happening between us, Tanner wouldn't see it that way.

Hell, if anything, he'd rather I wouldn't help tutor him if it meant he failed his class. It could result in him not playing, and it would taste like sweet revenge to Tanner if he found out.

Still, as selfish as it may sound, it doesn't help me in the end.

It doesn't matter, though. I'll have to figure something else out and make do for a while.

"Wait, stop," Beckham calls after me when I push open the door and step outside.

I glance over my shoulder, catching him dragging his gaze up my body until they meet mine.

The look in his eyes, the heat in his stare. What I'm thinking about doing is dangerous, but dammit if I can't help but not care.

"You know, you're throwing out a lot of terms in this agreement. If I agree, do I get to counter with some stipulations of my own?"

I step back inside and let the door shut behind me. It pushes me on the ass, forcing me to take another step forward.

"That's fair. What are they, then?"

I cross my arms over my chest this time, waiting for him to come out with it.

"Well, for starters, if we're going to keep this a secret, we can't exactly meet somewhere public. I guess that means

I'll have to come to your place unless you want to come by mine?"

I clench my jaw and think about his answer. He has a point.

Even if we meet somewhere else in town, like one of the cafés down the road or even Rosey's, the small diner, someone will spot us out together sooner or later. And there's no controlling the rumors that would swirl from there.

"As long as you can agree to stop with the shit and respect my relationship with Tanner, I guess there isn't anything wrong with you coming to my place. Right?"

I'll have to figure out a way to explain this to Ava while reassuring her I'm not doing anything reckless.

Beckham doesn't answer me right away, and for a second, I wonder if he said something, and I was too distracted and missed it.

"So, you'll help me order the parts and repair my truck. No saying or doing anything to disrespect my relationship, and you promise not to tell anyone about us working together. In return, I'll help tutor you for the next, what, eight weeks? We'll meet twice a week at my place."

"Three times a week," he counters.

"Once a week, twice if needed for tests."

"Twice a week it is," he barters.

I roll my eyes and shake my head. I guess it's better than the three he was suggesting. The thought of dealing with him any more than those two days would drive me damn crazy.

"I guess it's a deal." I attempt to exhale slowly to release the anxiety squeezing my chest, making it hard to breathe. "Do Mondays and Thursdays work for you by chance?"

He nods. "Any time after seven."

That works perfectly since we have dance practice those nights too. It would give me a chance to get home, shower, and eat dinner.

"I'll get started on ordering the parts we need to fix your truck. Once they come in, I'll get to work. It should take me a couple of weeks, though, since I'll be working on it when I don't have school, practice, work, or hanging out with you."

"Not hanging out, Beckham. Tutoring."

"It's all the same, right?" He winks.

I shake my head, knowing there's no use in arguing with him. He'll find ways to poke at me, even if I warn him to stop.

I wave him off and turn, leaving without another word until he says something that has me stopping once more.

"Oh, and Hallyn," he calls after me. "You have a boyfriend, so I'll need for you not to fall in love with me."

I know I shouldn't entertain him any further, but I need him to get it through his thick skull that I'd never fall in love with him no matter what he says or does.

I glance over my shoulder, and my eyes lock on his.

"Hate to break it to you, Carver, but that's never gonna fuckin' happen."

For a second, I wonder what he sees when he looks back at me. The blank expression is back on his face, but it slowly transforms into his smug and amused smirk.

The one that makes me want to tell him to fuck off, the deal is off, and storm right out of here. The one that makes me want to smack the devilish grin right off his face because it's so infuriating to look at.

"I'll see you on Monday," I add.

"It's a date."

The fucker has the nerve to wink.

Without another word, I storm out the door and curse the universe for putting me on that road and in the path of Beckham Carver.

I have a feeling I'll regret agreeing to our deal, and something tells me he'll prove me right.

CHAPTER 9

BECKHAM

I was on board with her arrangement before she ever laid out all her terms, but the thought of having her alone twice a week was a deal I'd never refuse.

I'm still thinking about how pissed Freeman will be when he finds out.

I like stacking my odds when it comes to taking my competitors down. This was just another way I'd take him down a notch until we meet on the field in October.

"You goin' to The End Zone after practice? A bunch of the guys are going to meet up for a bite," Reed asks, running his fingers over the laces of the football, adjusting it in his grip before throwing a perfect spiral back to me.

Reed is one of our running backs. We've been practicing together more, building our on-field chemistry. I know the friendship we've forged off the field will carry over when we kick off the season.

Most of the guys already have a bond formed from playing with each other last year. I was worried it would take some time to find my place on the team, especially considering my brother played for Braysen last year.

Deciding to come to Braysen was one of my hardest, but in the short time I've been here, practicing with the guys, it's proven to be the right one.

Our offensive line coach, Coach Ferentz, has talked about Hayes's and my uncanny ability to read each other with a simple glance. It's about to make us an unstoppable force. Add on the fact Reed can run like a rocket shooting out of a cannon.

"No, I'll probably grab a quick bite from the cafeteria after practice. I have to meet up with the tutor helpin' me out."

I try to play it off like it isn't a big deal. Even though I told the guys about the warning from Coach to get my shit together, I never revealed that Hallyn is my tutor.

"You're actually goin' through with the whole tutoring thing?" Colter questions, stretching his arm across his chest before shaking it out, loosening himself up.

He's wearing gym shorts and a muscle shirt with his pads over top. His mouth guard hangs from his lip, and he chews on the edge, studying me with his brow raised.

"It's not like I have much of a fuckin' choice, do I?" I grunt, lifting my hands to catch the pass from Reed.

The two trade cursory glances, and I'm waiting for them to spit it out and tell me what that's all about. Clearly, something is on their minds.

"What's that look for?" I bite back.

Colter chuckles, kicking his cleat in the grass, and shrugs.

"I guess I just thought it was all talk. Just a warning to get your shit together and start focusing. I hadn't realized there was any credibility to it."

"Well, I'm not about to let it get serious either. Plus, I'm doing a favor for a friend who's paying me back by helping me get caught up."

"Friend, who's the friend?" Reed asks.

They are onto me already because I don't know many people in town, let alone well enough to consider them a friend.

"It's no one, just someone from one of my classes."

I pass the ball back to Reed, only with a little more force behind the throw this time. He jogs backward and catches it with a grunt, his eyes snapping over to me.

"You sure I didn't hit a sensitive spot?" he quips, and Colter chuckles.

"Why don't you drop it and focus on not dropping the ball, huh?" I bite back.

I've never been one to lie or hold myself back, especially when it came to a woman. I didn't particularly like leaving that part out, but it's also none of their business.

Plus, it's strictly business. She's helping me out, and I'm doing her a favor with her truck. End of story.

"It's too bad you won't be there. Leslie has been talking to anyone who will listen about you. Seems like the little show you put on at Whiskey Sinner's the other night has her thinkin' you two might be leading to something serious."

I exhale a heavy sigh. I shouldn't be surprised because I laid it on thick with her. I'm not one to use someone to make another woman jealous, but I guess that's what I did.

Something about the sight of Hallyn hanging on Freeman ground on my nerves until they were raw. I think she knew it too.

Strictly business, huh, Carver?

That's what I'm telling myself anyway.

Coach blows the whistle and calls for us to huddle together, effectively ending our conversation. I send up a silent thank-you because I was sick of being grilled by their incessant questions.

By the time practice is over, my shirt is drenched in sweat and my body is sore in only the best way. I end up showering in our locker room. It took me longer than I planned to get cleaned up and dressed, mostly because the guys kept pressuring me into meeting up with them at the local sports bar.

When I caught the time and realized I would be late if I didn't get my ass out the door, I threw my hand in the air and told them I had to go. They hollered at me, calling me names and booing, but I left with only my middle finger in the air.

It didn't take me long to get to Hallyn's place. She lives in a quaint little apartment on the edge of campus. The exterior is painted a light gray. She's sitting out on the patio in a chair when I pull up. There's a little side table and a pot of flowers near the sliding glass door.

It's cute and cozy, and it fits the vision I have of her in my mind. I've seen her around campus, usually coming or going from the coffee house next to the cafeteria. She typically carries a book in one arm and a coffee in her other hand.

I picture her sitting out on her patio in the mornings before she heads to campus for class.

She gets up to buzz me into the building. I don't realize I'm smiling at the thought of her until I reach the top of the stairs and find her waiting, leaning against her doorframe with a scowl on her face and her hand fisted at her waist.

"You're late," she barks, stepping back to let me through.

I glance down at my phone to check the time. "Only by a few minutes."

"I don't have all night, Beckham. We're scheduled for one hour together, and I want to make the most of it."

My eyes travel down her body to the Braysen U fitted tank top she's wearing and the blue cotton shorts. A hint of her stomach is showing. Her tan skin looks soft, and I realize I might find it harder to focus than expected if this is how she dresses.

She catches my attention drifting away and shakes her head, slamming the door behind her. She marches across the room and disappears into what I can only assume is her bedroom.

Am I supposed to follow her?

My fingers grip the strap of my bag, adjusting it securely. I consider following her before toeing off my shoes first and crossing the room toward where she went.

The door to the room is left halfway open, and I spot her standing in front of the closet before she plucks a hoodie from the mass of clothing.

Her shirt rides up when she pulls the material over her head, and my eyes stay trained on her stomach and the shorts sitting low on her hips. I only get a glimpse before she tugs the cotton sweatshirt down, covering her body, and I groan inwardly, wishing she would've gone without it.

Even if it means being distracted the entire time we're together.

She turns toward me and stops, her eyes locking on mine when she catches me watching her.

"What are you doing?"

I fumble, glancing around clueless as to how I'm supposed to respond.

"Was I not supposed to follow you?"

She grabs a book and a notebook on her desk next to her and shakes her head. "No, we'll sit at the dining room table."

"I thought you wanted to go somewhere private?" I wiggle my brows.

She exhales, stalking toward me. Only a few feet separates us when she reaches for the knob to close the door behind her.

"We're alone, aren't we?" She glances around, motioning to the empty space. "Can you stop messing around now, and can we get to work?"

She walks past me, dropping her stuff on the table before grabbing a bottle of water from the fridge. She holds one out to me and I force my feet to move to take it, studying her as she unscrews the cap and takes a drink.

I take a seat next to her at the table. If I had it my way, I'd be sitting across from her. She's fired up, which means I should probably put some distance between us.

I'm starting to like getting her riled up.

I flip open my book to where I stuffed my notes between the pages from the lecture earlier that day.

"Intro to Chem, right?" she asks, taking a seat next to me.

It takes everything in me not to glance down at her legs when she crosses them on the chair, perching her chin on her fist leaning over to study my notes.

"Yeah, with Professor Clein."

"I'm in the same class, except I go on Wednesday at nine. So that's a bonus. I'll be familiar with the material you're covering."

My eyes study the freckles dotting the apples of her cheeks and the way she drags her lip between her teeth. She tucks a loose strand of hair behind her ear when she flicks her gaze up and catches me looking.

"I was thinking we could spend some time talking about the lecture from last week and go over your notes, along with how you did on your previous exams. Then when we meet on Thursday, I'll give you a practice quiz to prepare you for the upcoming test. How's that sound?"

I nod. "Whatever works. You're the boss."

She smirks. "That's damn right. Remember it too."

I grunt, rolling my eyes. "Don't let it go to your head. This would be the only time I'd ever let you call the shots. I'm at your mercy here, though, so fine, what do you want to know?"

She takes the packet from our last exam. Her eyes roam over the papers, studying them. She jots down some notes I can't quite make out from where I'm sitting before setting it facedown.

"Okay, I'm going to begin by reviewing the questions you got wrong on the last exam. To start, what is calcium an example of?"

I rub my fingers over my forehead. Why did I think this was a good idea?

I have no clue what the hell she's talking about, and now she's looking at me, waiting for an answer. I'm about to make myself look like an idiot when I tell her I don't have the slightest clue what she's referring to.

"I gotta be honest. I don't have any idea. My first thought would be milk, but judging by all the shit I've heard in class, I know that's not the right answer."

She giggles, pressing her lips together, and shakes her head. "Sorry." She lifts her fingers, apologizing for her laughter before smoothing over her features.

"It's not milk, you're right. How about this, what type of metal?"

I lift my arms over my head, stretching, running my fingers through my hair, and tugging on the strands. I notice the subtle flick of her eyes before she trains her gaze back on me.

This is the first time since the night at Whiskey Sinner's she's given me that look. My brain goes blank, and the question disappears from my mind.

"Beckham." She says my name, and all I can think about is how it would sound when she's moaning it in my ear. "Will you pay attention and answer the damn question?"

I lean against the table, resting my forearms on top of my book.

"When was the last time you got off?"

Her mouth drops open. "What did you say?"

I resist the urge to smile. "You heard me. It's been a while, hasn't it?"

"I'm not talking to you about my sex life. Now answer the fuckin' question."

"You don't have to tell me because I already know the answer. If he was getting you off, maybe you could relax a little and wouldn't be so damn uptight. I can give you a hand if you want."

"If you don't focus on why you're here, I will ask you to leave right now."

"All right, all right. I know it might be a while until you get to see him, with him being at Keaton and all." I grin. "I promise to drop it, though, so I can get out of your hair."

Her face softens until she catches me studying her, and her cold exterior is locked firmly back in place.

I reach over and run my hand along the top of her forearm. She snatches her arm away and clenches her jaw.

"You could definitely use some relaxing." I wink.

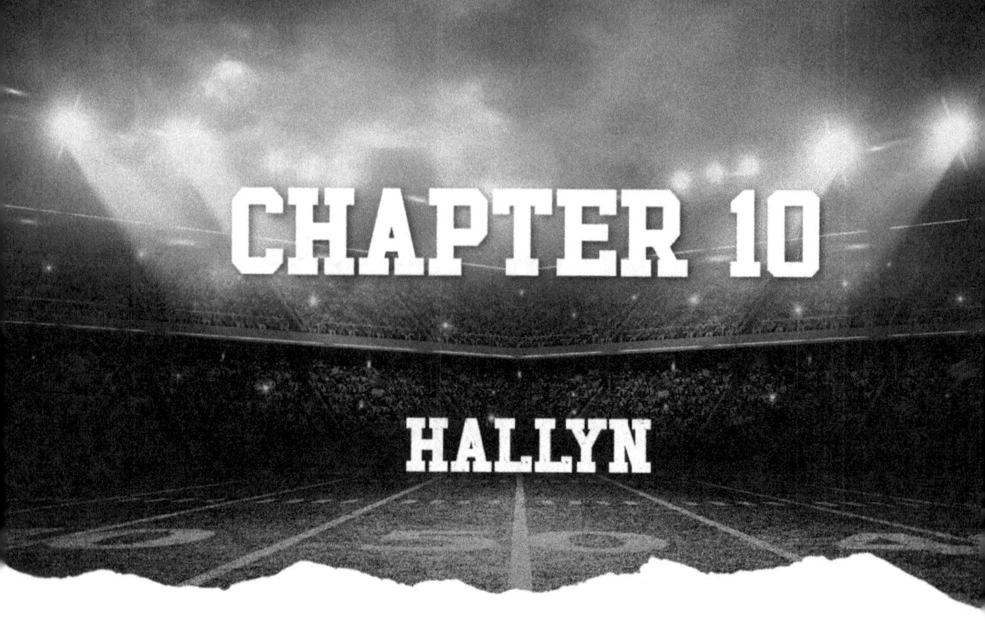

CHAPTER 10

HALLYN

By the time Wednesday rolls around, I'm dragging ass when getting up in the morning.

I snoozed my alarm four times before I forced myself out of bed. I have back-to-back classes, then a three-hour break before I need to be at the gym for dance practice.

While I wouldn't be late, I was pushing my luck. Sacrifices had to be made, and well, I chose to roll out of bed and show up the way I am as opposed to skipping my usual stop by the coffee house for my liquid fuel.

I manage to put on a few coats of makeup and throw my hair up in a messy bun before I dash out the door. I already decided before leaving my apartment that I'd be back to take a short nap and freshen up before practice.

I'm not a big fan of going out without putting myself together in some semblance. Although it wasn't like I was the odd one out. Many students in my class looked like they rolled out of bed with yesterday's hair and makeup, while others were like me and came to class fresh-faced and sleepy.

My face is buried in my chemistry book, jotting down notes about the lecture and my next tutoring session with Beckham. I'm so focused on what I'm doing that I don't even notice Professor Clein has stopped in the middle of his sentence until I hear his loud voice announce his presence right before someone claims the seat next to me.

"Mr. Carver, how nice of you to join us."

I inhale a strong whiff of his familiar cologne right when my mind registers his name, and I glance up to find none other than Beckham standing beside me.

"This seat isn't taken, is it?" he whispers, pulling out his book on the small desktop.

"What the hell are you doing here?" I chastise him, glancing around to see if anyone is looking in our direction.

As luck would have it, this is my only class with Leslie. She watches Beckham take the seat beside me before she flicks her gaze over to me. She levels me with a glare, her jaw clenching in frustration.

"Why don't you go sit next to Leslie? She has a spot open by her too."

"Why would I when I have my favorite tutor right here next to me?"

I shake my head, and he smirks.

"We're already like four weeks into the school year now. Why change your class all of a sudden?"

"My class conflicted with football. Besides, the guidance counselor thought it was a great idea when I suggested transferring to yours after I told her you've been helping me."

"Great idea, my ass," I retort, situating myself to focus on the lecture and my notes.

"It's good to see that attitude is still present, Hallyn. I wouldn't want your demeanor toward me to change just because we could be caught speaking to each other in public."

"I thought we were on the same page that our relationship was to be kept private."

"Relationship?"

"You know what I mean." I purse my lips and talk low, hoping no one else hears.

"I'm sorry, Hallyn. I'm afraid I don't. Can you elaborate for me?"

"Fine, partnership. Agreement. Deal," I emphasize.

"Oh, right. That. I have done my part to keep it a secret. Have you?" He raises his brow.

The only person I've told is Ava because she's my roommate. She's my best friend too, so I know she'd never tell a soul. Still, I needed her to know about it to keep the place clear whenever he came around.

The last thing I want is for her to come home and for him to start his antics with her present.

I'm trying to get through the next eight weeks without committing murder at the same time.

"The only person who knows is Ava."

His brows shoot up, and he grins. "Oh, so you've been talking about me to your friend, huh? What have you told her?"

"This is why you're going to fail this class, Beckham. You're not even paying attention."

"Well, maybe I could if you'd stop talking to me."

I clench my jaw and stare intently at Professor Clein. Even though my eyes are locked on him, I'm not listening or absorbing a single word he says.

My mind is a swirl of Beckham—every annoyingly handsome and frustrating inch of him. It's like whenever he's around me, I can't seem to think or focus on anything else. It's exactly why this is a problem.

I'm in a relationship with Tanner, the man I've been in love with since I was fourteen, and we're happy. Well, at least we were until we were separated, and he was forced to commit to Keaton instead of Braysen.

If it hadn't been for Beckham transferring and interfering with things, he'd likely be here with me now. See how he's ruining everything?

"You can try to pretend you're not enjoying every minute we've spent together, but we both know it's a lie."

I slowly turn toward him, but he keeps his face forward. There's a glimmer of amusement in his eyes. I could raise hell and force him to move to a different seat, but it would only bring more attention to us.

Attention I don't want. Attention would create rumors and a slew of questions I don't want to deal with.

I huff, leaning back in my seat. I don't even notice my incessant pencil tapping on my desktop until he reaches over and snatches it out of my hand, setting it down next to my textbook.

"Relax, will you?"

He sits back again, but something in the air shifts between us. Neither of us says a word for the remainder of the class until the bell rings.

"You know, you really need to stop losing your shit on me whenever we run into each other, or you'll raise some eyebrows. I'm sure you don't want people to think you're fighting your feelings for me, do you?" he says with an amused smile.

I shove my papers in my book and slam it shut, hastily thrusting it along with my pencil into my backpack.

"See, that's where you're wrong. I don't give a shit about what people think as long as it's clear that you and I are nothing to each other. There are no feelings. We're not friends. We're nothing. As soon as our arrangement ends, you'll go back to your life, and I'll return to mine. Now, let's just get through the next few weeks, ideally with you giving me as much space as possible except for those few hours when we need to work together. All right?"

He exhales a laugh, but it doesn't meet his eyes this time. I wonder if it's a defense mechanism.

The room clears out. Professor Clein stands facing his desk at the front of the room, his back toward us. The rest of the class has disappeared, leaving the two of us otherwise alone.

He leans in close until only a few inches separates us.

I try to calm my features, avoiding giving any signs or clues that his proximity affects me.

"Whatever you need to tell yourself. The sooner you can come to terms with the truth, the better you'll feel. You're still wound so tight. Clearly, you still need to find a way to relax."

His amusement is back, and I want to smack the smirk right off his face.

"I know you think you hate me, Halls, but there's a thin line between love and hate. Sooner or later, that line will blur, and you'll find yourself falling for me, just like I knew you would."

"You're so full of yourself. It's honestly the least attractive thing about you."

He chuckles. "What's the most attractive thing about me?"

I shrug my backpack over my shoulder and push myself to stand, stalking past him before throwing one last cursory glance his way.

"The rare moments when you shut the hell up."

He stands, brushing his finger on the skin of my shoulder, causing goose bumps to spread over my arm. A shiver runs down my spine, and it takes every ounce of me to hide it from him.

"You want to know the most attractive thing about you?" he whispers.

"No."

"Yes, you do. Don't lie to me."

I don't bother continuing this conversation, marching down the row of desks toward the door. Beckham is hot on my heels, following me.

As soon as I reach to open the door, he presses his hand against it, forcing it closed and stopping me in my tracks.

We're shut off from the rest of the room, hiding behind a wall near the door.

"There's two of them, now that I've had a minute to think about it."

"Beckham," I grit out, my voice low and annoyed.

"All right, all right. I'll tell you..." He smiles. "The first one is how you duck your head and avoid looking at me as if trying to force your attention on something else."

"I'm really just trying to avoid telling you to—" I say, but he holds his hand up, stopping me from continuing.

I was going to finish it with "fuck off" before he so rudely cut me off.

"The other is the way you smile when you think about something. I can't really be sure what it is. It's almost like you think of something, and you laugh, finding yourself funny. Your smile, it's one of the few genuine smiles I think I've ever seen from someone. Sometimes I wish I knew what you were thinking."

I'm almost surprised that he notices anything about me that doesn't have to do with the way I look or something sexual, so the fact he put so much thought into his response has me wondering if he's fucking with me or if he's thought about this before.

I glance at him, and he smiles, and I realize I was doing the very thing he just described.

He reaches for the handle, holding it open for me to pass through. I hate to admit it, but I think about what he said the whole way home.

It's not so much that I'm flattered by what he said, but the realization that Tanner never seems to notice the little things about me. In fact, now that I reflect on it, I don't remember the last time he said anything that wasn't calling me "sexy" or "hot," and even then, it's been months since he has.

It's no secret that the distance has taken a toll on our relationship, and it hasn't gotten any better these past few weeks since we got back together. Our schedules are full, and our lives have been busy.

I unzip the pocket on the front of my backpack and check my phone, noting an email from our dance coach about the upcoming Bulldog Fest. We'll dance at the pep rally and walk in the parade.

I have a couple of missed text messages—one from my mom asking me to call her later tonight and another from Ava telling me a box addressed to me was outside our apartment. She said she left it on the chair in my bedroom.

I drop my bag by the door and kick off my shoes.

My brows deepen. I haven't ordered anything, so I don't have the slightest clue what it could be.

I collapse on my fuzzy chair at my desk and pull out the small box cutter I got when I ordered a bunch of furniture for my room when we moved in.

Sliding the razor open, I cut into the packing tape and tear the box open.

A small note sits on top.

Every girl deserves roses. -BC

BC?

Beckham Carver.

What the hell? Why is he sending me roses?

My brain swirls with questions because this box is not big enough to fit roses.

I pull back the packing dunnage, revealing three white boxes. None of them have any sort of picture on the front, so I pop the top on the first one.

As soon as I pull out the contents, my mouth drops open.

"That asshole," I blurt out to only myself.

I hit the little button on the side, and the vibrator hums to life before I turn it off and drop it on the desk, opening the remaining two boxes.

Each of them is shaped like a rose, but according to the little sheet of paper on the inside, it reveals them to be a clit sucker, a tongue-licking vibrator, and a butt plug with a gem shaped like a rose.

You need to relax.

I know I said I was trying to get through the next eight weeks without committing murder. Now I'm certain it will happen.

I'm going to kill him.

CHAPTER 11

BECKHAM

We have conditioning practice this morning with Hayes and Reed. By the time we wrap up, I'm starving and ready to turn into a savage for some food.

Normally, I'll cut out early enough to head home and shower, but today, I decided to get cleaned up in the gym and hit up the cafeteria.

Since I live in a house with four guys, it's no surprise we go through groceries in no time. We walk through the seating area, and I spot Colter sitting with Ava and Hallyn, along with a few other girls I recognize from the dance team.

I managed to sweet-talk the guidance counselor into sharing Hallyn's schedule, so I know she doesn't have class for another forty-five minutes.

Okay, she may not have shared it with me. I may have glanced over her shoulder and snapped a photo of it on her computer screen.

Potato, pah-tato.

She's the only one at the table with her book opened and a notebook to one side while she furiously jots down notes. The rest of the group talks and laughs, but she's in her own little world.

"I'll take two cappuccinos, one with extra caramel drizzle. Thanks!" I say, stepping up to the counter at the coffee house.

"You're getting lunch and a coffee?" Reed asks, confused.

I nod, waving him off. "I'll meet you over at the table with Colter."

He glances over in that direction, spotting Ava and Hallyn with him. He turns back at me, smiling, but I ignore him.

After getting our drinks, I stop in the cafeteria and grab a couple of buffalo chicken wraps, a cup of fruit, two slices of pizza, and a sports drink.

I swipe my card to pay for it and tuck it back into my wallet, carrying the tray of food across the dining hall.

Ava bumps Hallyn's elbow and nods toward me before she pops another grape into her mouth.

Something changed the day I stopped her from leaving Professor Clein's class. She went from claiming to hate me to being indifferent when we're around each other.

Over the past week, during our tutoring sessions, she hasn't been the same.

She seems more relaxed and chill even though I still get under her skin sometimes. Neither of us has brought it up, but I'd like to think the little gift I sent her helped in the relaxation department.

I claim the seat at the end of the table across from Hallyn, then reach for the cappuccino I got and set it in front of her.

"What are you doing?" Her voice is low, and her brows deepen.

I take a bite of my pizza and chew it before I respond. "What do you mean?"

She rolls her eyes, and I smile before taking another bite.

"Don't start. What is this about?"

"Isn't today the day you have a full schedule?" I shrug. "I figured you could use a little something to get you through the day. Here." I hand her the other chicken wrap.

I can't forget the fact she has to put up with my ass during our tutoring session tonight.

She flicks her eyes at the rest of the table, and I notice the group has gone quiet. I've held up my end of the deal. No one knows she's helping me, aside from Ava, which was her doing.

I don't even know if Colter is aware. If he is, he hasn't said a word about it.

Hallyn closes her textbook and shoves it with her notebook into her bag before dropping it on the floor near her feet.

"Thank you," she mutters with a warm smile.

She takes a drink of the coffee, hesitant at first, before she hums. She seems taken aback by my kindness, and it makes me wonder how often Tanner treats her with coffee and lunch.

"Hey, Beckham," Leslie croons, and I glance up. She's staring down at my brother, waiting for him to acknowledge her. He flicks his eyes over to me, appearing confused.

Hallyn and Ava exchange a look before Hallyn bites her lip to resist laughing.

"Wrong brother." Hayes chuckles.

I almost feel bad when I catch the mortified look on her face. I shove the last bite of my pizza into my mouth before diving into the next, clearing my throat.

"What's up?"

Hallyn follows her as she rounds the table before she shifts her gaze back to her food.

"Are you going to Greencastle on Friday after Bulldog Fest?"

With this being my first year, I'm not too familiar with their traditions. Our homecoming game is on Saturday. Bulldog Fest is like a big pep rally with a parade and a bunch of food vendors lining the streets of downtown.

From what I've been told, everyone in town comes out and celebrates, cheering on the team before the big game.

I keep my eyes trained on Hallyn. She fidgets in her chair, and I suspect it's because she can feel my eyes burning into her, waiting for her to look at me.

"I'm not sure what our plans are," I lie. I hear Reed chuckle under his breath next to me. "I'm going out with my team-mates, though, so I guess we'll see where we end up."

Leslie brushes her hand along my shoulder, running it down my upper arm. I'd hate to be rude and embarrass her any more, but I still want to make it known I don't want her touching me.

It was all fine and well at the bar, staring at Hallyn from across the room with her prick of a boyfriend's arm around her.

Now, with her a few feet away, able to hear every word we're saying, something about it doesn't sit right.

I shrug my arm, hoping she gets the hint to move her hand, but if she does, she ignores it.

"Okay, well, what about tonight? You have any plans after practice? I have cheer, but I should finish up around maybe six if you're up for grabbing dinner."

I take one of the last bites of my other pizza slice and wipe my hands on the napkin, using it to buy me some time. Once I finish, I clear my throat, and that seems to get Hallyn's attention.

Her eyes glitter as if she's curious about how I'll respond. What am I going to tell her? It's not like I can be honest and admit about our tutoring agreement.

If I do, I know our friends will hear, and I'm not sure how to answer the questions that'll follow.

Hallyn raises her brows as if asking me, "*Well, what are you gonna say?*"

"I'm sorry, Leslie," I pull my arm away, and this time, she takes the hint and drops her hand by her side. "I have a date tonight after practice."

Hallyn appears caught off guard by that answer and gasps. She's in the middle of taking a bite, so she holds her fist in front of her mouth, coughing while she tries to catch her breath.

"Jesus, Halls. You good?"

Her watery eyes flash over to mine, and there's a clear warning in them. She's not too keen on the fact I've used her nickname in public, but I shrug. What does she expect?

"A date?" Leslie asks, interrupting the two of us.

Hallyn takes a drink from her water bottle and clears her throat.

"Yeah." I nod, flashing her with a sympathetic smile. "I've been seeing someone. It's new, but I'm not interested in seeing anyone else now."

There's a flurry of laughs coming from the end of the table. I guess the guys are surprised by this admission since it's news to them.

Ava, on the other hand, gapes at me as if she's both shocked and confused.

She mumbles under her breath to Hallyn, who shakes her head before leveling me with a serious glare.

"She's kind of feisty and possessive too. We've both been seeing other people, but something tells me she wouldn't be too happy if she knew I blew off our date for someone else."

Leslie glances over at Hallyn. Her eyes narrow as if she's trying to piece together what's going on between the two of us.

"I don't think she'd mind," Hallyn suggests. "You never did strike me as being a one-woman kind of guy."

"What?" I press my hand against my chest, pretending to be taken aback. "Are you trying to call me a hussy?"

She rolls her lips together, fighting off her smirk. "I was thinking manwhore, but either fits the bill, I guess."

I grin. "You sound kind of jealous. Don't you have a boyfriend, Halls?"

"I do." She nods. "I guess I just call it like I see it."

"And here I thought after buying you lunch and a coffee, I would've been working my way into earning your friendship."

She laughs. "You're getting there, but not quite, although you're right. Today is my full course day, so I probably wouldn't have been able to grab a bite until later."

Neither of us notices Leslie walk away, leaving the two of us to our bickering.

"You're welcome, too, by the way."

I drop my crumpled-up napkin on my plate and tilt my head to the side. Shouldn't I be the one saying you're welcome?

"For running her off," she clarifies.

"I guess it's my turn next." I grin.

Hallyn wears an oversized hoodie and leggings when she opens her apartment door. She was already waiting for me since I rang the buzzer and she let me inside.

Her hair is pulled up in one of those buns with strands framing her face. I think this is how I prefer her the best. Dressed in her comfy clothes with her hair pulled up so I can see her beautiful face.

I clench my jaw, mentally telling myself not to think about her that way.

This girl has been wreaking havoc on my thoughts since she first stumbled out of my bathroom a few weeks ago, and the more we're around each other, the harder it's become to force my mind off how badly I want her.

My dick seems to have a different idea, though.

I adjust my hoodie, hoping it does enough to conceal the hard-on in my pants. You know girls and their love of gray sweatpants, though.

She steps back, holding the door open, and gestures toward the dining table where we've been doing our studying.

"I'm sure you have high expectations when it comes to dates. Looks like it's you, me, and a couple of textbooks for tonight." She snickers from behind me.

She's wearing slippers on her feet, and I hear them tap as she pads along the tile floor, taking her usual spot next to me.

"I'd be the biggest idiot at Braysen if I was disappointed at this being the idea of a date with you."

Her mouth drops open before she quickly snaps it shut. I can't tell if she's shocked or questioning my sincerity.

She clears her throat and takes a seat, leaning to the side while she crosses her legs in her chair, getting comfortable.

"So how did you do on Professor Clein's test?"

Our grades were uploaded to the online class portal earlier today. I've been waiting to tell her how I did. I could hardly believe it myself.

"I got an A minus." I grin.

Her eyes light up, and she claps, bouncing in her seat. "See, I knew you could do it. I told you that you had this one in the bag."

Fuck, the smile on her face and the happiness in her voice hit like a punch in the gut. That fuckface of a boyfriend of hers has no idea how lucky he is. I don't think my parents have ever been this happy for me, not even when I won my first championship in high school against the three-time defending champs.

My chest swells with pride, and I thank her for her help.

"I need to cut back on doing so well, though. What am I gonna do when our tutoring sessions are over, and you start thinking I can get by without you?"

"I think you'll do just fine on your own." She giggles, shaking her head.

This seems different from our conversation earlier today at lunch. She seems calm, more relaxed even.

"That's the point, though." I pause, waiting for her eyes to lock on mine. "Maybe I don't want our secret little date nights to end."

She swallows hard, a look of guilt flashing over her face. I hate that my comment made her think of him.

"You know this isn't a date, right? Besides, if you still need help, it's not like I'm going away. You know where to find me."

She shrugs, holding her arms out to the fact we're in her house alone.

The time on the microwave behind her reminds me we won't be for long. Ava usually gets off work in about thirty minutes, meaning our time together will be cut short.

I nod, not sure how to answer. Maybe, in some sense, I want her to know I don't want this time with her to end.

How her jerk of a boyfriend doesn't deserve her, and if she gave me the chance, I could prove to her I do.

I've already pressured her enough, and she warned me she'd end this whole thing if I did. I guess if I have to, I'll shut up and keep my feelings to myself. I'll bide my time until he messes up again, and then I'll swoop in and make my move.

"You know if you ever need me, or you're broke down on the side of the road, I'd be right there too. Right?"

She smiles. "I don't know what you've done with Beckham, but I'm starting to wonder if you sent Hayes over here to try to fool me."

My face falls, and she throws her head back and laughs. She starts wheezing, barely able to take a breath between gasping out the words, "I'm joking. I'm joking."

"You better be because it'd be a cold day in hell before I'd ever share you with my brother too."

CHAPTER 12

HALLYN

My eyes flit across the page for the fifth time, attempting to reread the same sentence over before I give up and slam the book shut.

"Arrgghh," I groan, tossing it onto the rug in the middle of our living room.

I've been sitting cross-legged and hunched over, trying to study for the past hour, and I haven't made any progress. It's like I can't focus no matter what I do.

If I'm not stressing over school, figuring out how I'll get to and from where I need to be, or my financial situation, then I'm constantly arguing with Tanner over inconsequential things and dealing with Beckham just being Beckham.

I fall back on the couch, kicking my legs up with me, and fling my arm over my forehead. It covers up the soft light from the lamp on the end table, and for a few minutes, I let my mind drift off to nothing.

It doesn't last long, though, before I'm interrupted by the harsh sound of vibrating against the glass of our coffee table.

I lean over to reach for my phone, nearly falling off the sofa in the process. My chest pangs when I see Tanner's name on the screen and the photo of us together.

Seeing that picture from years ago, during our high school days, causes my chest to ache.

Back to when things were simple and easy between us.

Back to when I felt like we were truly in love.

I swipe the screen to answer the call, and the sound of music playing loudly in my ear has me holding the phone away from my face when I shout out, "Hello."

"What are you doing?" he greets, and I curl my lip in annoyance.

No *hey, hello, or how are you?*

"Studying, why?"

"I texted you this morning, and I never heard back."

I wince, guilt eating me up when I recall the message he sent earlier today asking about their homecoming this weekend.

It just so happens to coincide with our homecoming at Braysen. He was asking if there was any chance I could watch him play. Although he hadn't said the words exactly, he insinuated it bothered him I wasn't going to be there.

I read the text just as I was leaving my sociology class. The sun was bright when I stepped outside the lunch hall, and I could barely see my screen. I shoved my phone in my pocket, mentally telling myself I'd get back to him when I got home and completely spaced it off.

"I'm sorry, Tanner. I saw it earlier after I got out of class, and I forgot to respond."

He grunts, the line falls silent, and for a second, I wonder if he hung up on me.

I hold the phone up to check, to see the time still counting back at me before I say his name again.

"I'm here," he replies gruffly.

"You know if I could be there and didn't have other commitments, I would be."

"You could be here, but you chose to follow Ava to Braysen instead of coming here with me."

There it is. The very comment that's been hanging over our head since we found out Tanner didn't get the starting QB spot at Braysen, which meant he accepted the offer to Keaton.

I had two choices—follow my dreams of dancing with my best friend in college or follow Tanner where the offers were coming.

The last time he said this to me was when I told him I was going to Braysen.

Right before we decided to take a break and spend the summer apart.

"That's not fair of you to say, and we both know it."

"Even if it's not fair, it's still the truth."

"So, what, you just expect me to put my dreams on hold to chase you around while you pursue yours?"

He doesn't say a word. What's there to say?

"It's just gonna keep comin' back to this, isn't it? We're never goin' to move on and get past this?"

"Well, it's not my fault your choices are driving the wedge between us."

"What does that mean? We had always talked about us going to Braysen together. This was not just my dream but ours. How is it my fault?"

"I'm not talking about your decision to go to Braysen, Hallyn. Did you think I wasn't going to find out that you've been spending time with Beckham behind my back?"

My mouth drops open, and I shoot up from where I'm sitting, looking around the room as if searching for the answers as to how he found out.

"What are you talking about?" I play coy.

How does he know? The only person besides me and Beckham who knows is Ava, and she'd never in a million years tell a secret.

I trust her with my life.

Tanner chuckles, and it's not the kind of joyful laughter. It's cynical and maniacal, and frankly, it makes my stomach twist.

"You think I don't have eyes on you or other ways of finding things out?"

"What the hell, Tanner? Eyes on me? What does that even mean?"

"I'm just saying, you know I have friends at Braysen. People talk and rumors circulate, and of course they make their way back to me. Did you think I wouldn't find out that you have been inviting him over to your place?"

I attempt to swallow past the lump forming in my throat, but my mouth is dry. I swipe my tongue across my lips to wet them.

"It's not what you think."

"It's not? Really? So, you think I shouldn't believe that because I didn't get the spot on the team at Braysen, that you're not just moving on behind my back to the one that is?"

"You've got to be kidding me." I laugh, although this time, my laughter is more nervous and uncomfortable while searching for words to explain this to him.

The truth is, he has every right to be upset with me, even if my relationship with Beckham isn't what he seems to think.

"He's helping fix the truck, and I've been tutoring him in return. You know I've been tight on money lately."

"Tight on money, all over that fuckin' truck? Jesus, Hallyn. Will you let it go already?"

"No, I won't let it go."

He hates my truck. He doesn't care that it's more than a vehicle to me.

I would drive it until the wheels fell off, whether he liked it or not.

"I'm not tellin' you to get rid of the damn thing, but it's just not reliable. It's no wonder it's constantly breaking down. Any time I ask you to come down here to see me, you can't because that fuckin' truck is giving you hell."

It's not the truck he didn't like or issues with it breaking down that was the problem. It didn't live up to his expectations.

When I graduated from high school, I was given the truck as a gift from my grandpa.

When Tanner turned sixteen, his parents bought him a BMW and gave him ten grand. He's never known what it's like to struggle financially. That's the one thing his parents never gave him.

He wanted something, and it practically fell from the sky right into his lap.

I'm sick of feeling like everything I do or have isn't good enough for him. I certainly was getting tired of fighting over it too.

The door handle to our apartment jiggles, and the faint sound of keys on the other side follows before the knob turns and in bounces Ava. Her hair is down, styled straight, and she's dressed in a blue Braysen tank top and a pair of denim shorts with brown sandals.

She's smiling until her eyes land on me, and it falls from her face.

Whatever she sees when she looks back at me is evidently the reason for it.

"Tanner, I think we should break up."

Ava's mouth drops open, and she quickly drops her bag and purse on the chair next to me before circling the couch to sit at the other end.

She reaches her hand out for mine and squeezes it in a show of support. It helps ease my death grip on my phone and the tension coiling in my body.

"You want to throw two years down the drain for that fuckin' prick? It's because of him, isn't it?"

"No, Tanner!" I yell, at my wits' end. "What don't you get? This has nothing to do with him and everything to do with the fact that all we do is fight. You're constantly raggin' on me—about the fact I came to Braysen, what car I drive, that I'm on the dance team, or when I go out with my girlfriends. I'm sick of you constantly trying to control every little thing I do."

Ava squeezes my hand again, and I finally muster the courage to meet her eyes. She gives me a sympathetic smile, reassuring me it'll all be okay.

"You'll regret this, just like you did the last time."

"Maybe I will, or maybe I won't. All I know is I don't want to deal with this anymore. No matter what I say or do, nothing seems to get through to you. So I'm done."

"You're only doin' this so you can get with Carver. Sooner or later, you'll realize your mistake and be back, just like you were before."

"Who I'm with or what I do from here on out has nothing to do with you. You're free to do what you want, and I guess I am too. Goodbye, Tanner."

He doesn't say another word. The line clicks, and I stare back at my phone to see the call ended.

Ava exhales, scooching closer to me. She wraps her arm around my shoulders, pulling me in for a hug.

"You okay?" she mumbles into my hair, and I nod.

The tears hit me for the first time in months. All the pent-up anxiety and stress inside me releases, and it's like a dam breaking, flowing freely down my face.

Ava leans away, brushing her thumbs under my eyes to wipe my tears.

"It was time, ya know?"

She nods, and I wonder how long my best friend has been thinking about it but giving me the space and time to come to terms with it myself.

"Ever since the night we went out to Whiskey Sinner's, I've noticed the two of you have been fighting more."

I nod. "It just felt like it was all the time." I choke up, burying my face in my hands.

"You weren't the same happy and bubbly Hallyn, not since we got to Braysen. These are supposed to be the best years of our lives, right? Maybe it's time you focus on you and what makes you happy."

She wraps me in her arms again and tugs me to stand.

"He said something on the phone that has me concerned. He found out about me tutoring Beckham, and when I asked him how, he said he has eyes on me." My brows deepen, and I shake my head as I recall that part of the conversation.

"Eyes on you? What the hell kind of stalker shit is that?"

I nod. She's voicing my very thoughts out loud.

It makes me wonder how long he's been keeping tabs on me.

"Did he say who? I have to admit, that freaks me the hell out." Ava shivers.

"He didn't say." I shrug. "I don't think he'd do anything stupid and risk his scholarship. It still makes me wonder what the hell he's thinking."

"I'll talk to my brother," she reassures me. "What do you say we get out for a bit, maybe grab a bite?"

I glance in the mirror behind her, mounted on the wall. Mascara streaks run down my face. My hair is frizzy, and the strands I left down framing my face are turning curly. I either cried or sweat all my makeup off.

I have no business leaving the house.

"I think I'm gonna shower and try to get my head back into studying. I have a paper due tomorrow, and then we have Bulldog Fest and homecoming this weekend."

I shake out my hands and tilt my head back, thinking about all I need to get done. It's like everything is falling apart, and my thoughts swirl in my mind.

"Okay, fine, how about I pick us up some takeout, and you can shower? When I return, we'll both hang out here and study together, then maybe we can watch a movie before we crash."

She knows me and knows I don't need to be alone with my thoughts. It was the same way when we broke up over the summer. I ended up heading out of town early to stay with my grandparents, just trying to get away from it all.

Ava's letting me know I'm not alone, and I couldn't be more thankful for her.

I nod. "That sounds perfect." I give her a sad smile, and she grins.

She leans in and lands a hard kiss on my cheek. "I got you, sister. Everything is going to be okay. I'll pick up a pizza from The End Zone, and I'll be back. Get your ass in the shower, you hear me?"

I exhale a shuddered breath and nod, watching her pick up her keys and sling her purse over her shoulder.

She's right. Everything will be okay.

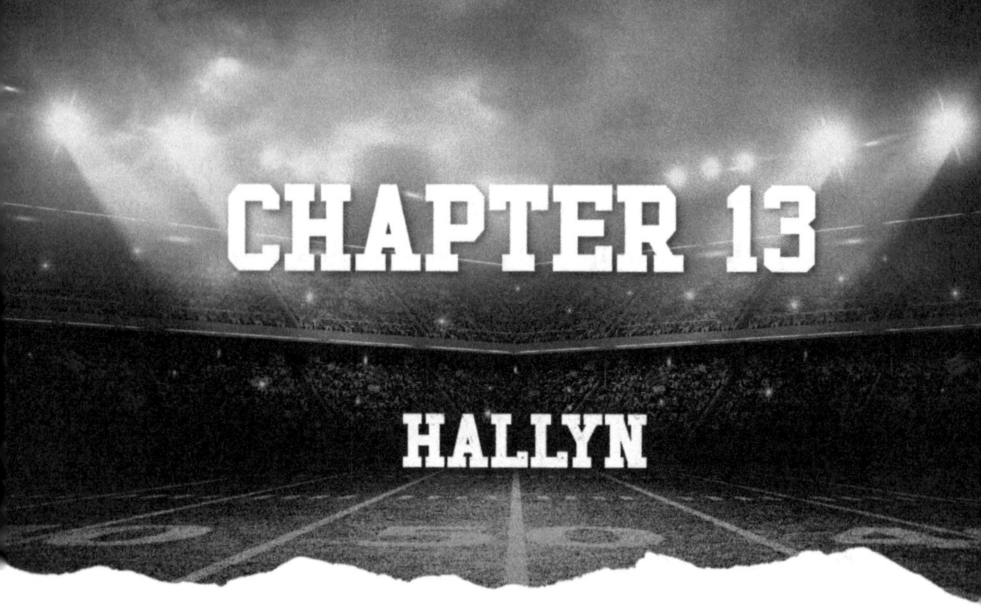

CHAPTER 13

HALLYN

The rest of the week passes by on autopilot. School. Dance practice. Tutoring. Study. Shower. Sleep. Wake up and do it all over again.

I don't know what has gotten into Beckham, or maybe he could sense I was in one of those "don't fuck with me" moods, but he has been easy to be around during our tutoring sessions. It's not like he doesn't have enough weighing on him too.

He managed to get an A minus on his last chemistry exam, which bumped his grade enough to get his coach off his back.

This past Thursday, as he was packing up to leave, he surprised me by telling me he had finished the repairs on my truck that morning.

I felt guilty when he mentioned he had been waking up at five o'clock to work on it before his conditioning practice. That, on top of making sure he's going to class, studying to bring up his GPA, and stressing over football.

When I asked him if he could give me a ride to the shop to pick it up, he dangled the keys in front of me and smiled when he said, "I had Hayes help me out. We dropped it off before I got here. It's parked outside."

I leaped out of my chair and jumped into his arms. He caught me, albeit at the last minute, and stared wide-eyed for a moment before his brows deepened. I pushed him on his shoulders, urging him to let me down, and took a step back, wrapping my arms around my middle.

For a moment, it's like we forgot who we were to each other.

As if I had forgotten I'm supposed to hate him and we're not supposed to feel anything more between us.

Except, the more time I spent near Beckham, no matter how hard I tried to tell myself I did, I knew in the back of my mind that he was right.

I lied to myself and him because I could never hate him.

The only reason I kept up with it was because of Tanner. Only now, he's not in the picture, so what does it matter how I feel about Beckham?

No one has to know about the butterflies I feel in my stomach whenever he looks at me. I'm not about to tell anyone, not even Ava.

I'm not trying to keep anything from her. It's more about the risk of admitting those feelings out loud. Instead, I'll keep them locked up tight and not tell a single soul.

The energy on campus shifted when Friday rolled around. Homecoming was here, meaning everyone in our small college town was covered in blue and teal.

I was thankful I didn't have any classes. Normally, I had a couple of tutoring sessions, but everyone was checked out for the week by the time Wednesday rolled around, so I wasn't bothered when both texted and asked to cancel for the day.

I decided to get my ass up and out of the house, stopping by the gym to get in some cardio before we met up to run through our game plan for the weekend.

Today was our big homecoming parade, followed by the Bulldog Fest pep rally, which really was a prelude to the party later tonight when the sun went down. Greencastle was at a pointe overlooking Sugar Bottom.

It all sounds pretty and serene, which it is when it's not packed with rowdy college students drinking their asses off.

Every time I think about it, I picture how dangerous it is when you consider it's a large pavilion with grass around us near the cliffs overlooking the beach.

There were kegs with bonfires going and music blaring. Everyone just hung out, having a good time.

Tomorrow afternoon is when the game will kick off. We're playing the Kolmont Kings, which should be a good game even though we're favored to win.

When we make it back home, Ava cranks the speakers in our apartment while we dance and sing, getting ready for the parade. We keep it simple, pulling our hair in an updo with a large blue ribbon and a temporary tattoo of the Bulldogs logo on our cheek.

I've never been one who knows anything in the makeup department, so Ava helps me do a blue, teal, and silver smoky eyeshadow look, pulling out the green hues in my eyes.

"Did you mention to Beckham that you and Tanner broke up?" she asks, adjusting the bow on my head, staring at me in our reflection in the mirror.

I swipe the lip gloss on my lips, pressing them together, and shake my head. "No, why would I?"

Her mouth curls on the edge in a smile, and she rolls her eyes, following up with an exasperated sigh.

"What's that look for?" I quip.

"You!" she shouts, playfully shoving my arm.

She holds the bottle of my Marc Jacobs perfume, silently asking if she can wear it, and I nod my permission.

She closes her eyes and sprays it a good five times. I wave my hand in front of my face before the grapefruit and rose scent hits me.

"Listen, I know you're still grieving after your breakup with Tanner. I wanted to give you time before I said anything because a part of me thought you didn't want to talk about it. Like maybe you felt you were disrespecting him for admitting it."

"What are you talking about? Admit what?"

She snorts. "Admit you want to jump Beckham's bones."

My mouth drops open, and I push myself up from my vanity, waving my hand at her as I stomp out of the room.

She follows me, grabbing her white sneakers from where she left them near the door. We're dressed in our blue skirt and halter top, with teal and blue splatter print on the front and the Braysen U Bulldog.

"Beckham has only been on campus for, what, six weeks? Maybe seven. I've seen him with three different women."

It's true. There was the girl the night of the party kicking off the season, the one that night at Whiskey Sinner's, and then another girl hanging all over him in the cafeteria not long after. I guess I don't know for certain they've hooked up, but they definitely seemed like they knew each other intimately.

"Only because he's trying to make you jealous," she adds. "Even though he's that way with girls whenever you see him, it doesn't mean he's taking them home. I've hung out at their house with Colter and even heard him say he doesn't let anyone in his room."

I guess that clears up why he was so pissed at me for using his bathroom and why he flipped out on me for being in his room.

I can't say I blame him.

Their house is where the football players go to hang out. At least that's the word on campus. After my run-in with him, I did my best to avoid their parties.

"Either way, it doesn't change my thoughts on him. So let's drop it."

She shrugs and lets out a low, "All right," as she sighs.

Ava blares music the entire way to the east parking lot near the stadium, where we're set to meet up with the rest of the squad. The parking lot is packed with cars, and floats line up for the parade, along with the cheerleading squad and dance team.

I tuck my poms under my arm, quickly swiping more lip gloss on my lips before handing it back to Ava who does the same.

A large group of football players are all dressed in their jerseys and jeans. I spot Hayes first, which makes me do a double take for a second.

He looks so much like Beckham that it always throws me for a loop. If you don't know them or see them often, it's easy to mix them up.

"If you don't want Beckham, you could always hook up with his brother." Ava giggles as a voice clears behind us, and my body tenses.

We both swing our heads to the side, and my eyes lock on Beckham's, who greets me with a knowing smirk.

Any chance of me hoping he didn't hear her is out the window.

"Well, this is news. You have a thing for my brother?" Beckham asks, his brow quirking.

His eyes flick down to what I'm wearing before quickly returning to meet mine. He drags his lower lip between his teeth, and I flare my nostrils, silently cursing Ava for opening her big mouth.

If she had dropped this like I asked, I wouldn't have to deal with this conversation.

"What happened to you and Freeman? Something tells me he wouldn't be too happy if he found out."

"They broke up," Ava interjects, and I turn my wild eyes on her. "Sorry, I think I just heard Mandy call for me." She grins, leaving us alone, away from the crowd.

"I've been trying to figure out how that dipshit managed to land you in the first place, but how did he lose you too?"

I glance over his shoulder, avoiding his gaze when I finally give in and look up at him. I suck in a sharp breath at where his hair falls over his forehead.

I dig my nails into my palm to resist the urge to move it out of his face, but I don't because that's uncalled for and weird. I don't think he'd like me touching him, either.

"I wouldn't mind if you touched me." He smirks, and I realize I said that last part out loud.

"It just didn't work out." I change the subject, reaching for my poms and gripping them. I'll do anything, I guess, if it means taking my mind off having him near me.

I take a step back, turning to search for Ava, when Beckham closes the distance between us. He leans in, and I could swear I heard him take a deep breath as if he's inhaling me.

When he says my name, the word comes out breathy, and it sends a shiver running down my spine.

"If you think for a second I'm gonna let my brother or anyone else on this fuckin' campus near you, you have another thing coming."

I tilt my head to the side and stare up at him from beneath my lashes. My words falter. Suddenly, every rebuttal I could've come up with disappears from my mind.

"And why is that?"

He grips the ball in his hand, clutching it against his side.

"I've already had to bite my tongue and hold myself back watching that fucker touch you when I know you were only doing it to get under my skin. I don't think I'll be so nice to the next person."

I chuckle and shake my head.

The last thing I'd call him and the way he reacted to seeing me with Tanner at Whiskey Sinner's is "nice."

"What do you care who I'm with or what I do?"

He steps back, tossing the ball into the air. It spins before it lands in his hand, and he does it again.

The cords in his forearms and the calluses on his hands are distracting. For a moment, my mind drifts to picturing him alone, feeling them skate over the most sensitive parts of my body.

He catches the ball, closing in on me again. He presses his lips to my ear and whispers, "I want you for myself, Hallyn."

I exhale a shaky breath.

It dawns on me I hear someone call my name from across the parking lot, but my eyes and mind cannot focus on anything.

My vision goes blurry from the adrenaline coursing through me.

"I want you for myself, and like I told you before, I don't like to share."

CHAPTER 14

BECKHAM

"It's about damn time you showed up," Reed hollers as I climb out of my pickup.

I wasn't sure if I wanted to come out tonight, especially with our game tomorrow. We didn't have to show up until eleven, giving us enough time to huddle up and warm up.

I'm a creature of habit and, as a QB, a bit superstitious. So I've always shown up earlier than everyone else. I'll head out onto the field, walk to the visitor goal post and back down to ours with my headphones in. Something about it helps me center myself and focus.

Then, I sit on the sidelines and take it all in before jogging back to the locker room and changing into my uniform.

It's something I've done since my high school days, and I've never looked back.

Reed holds his hand out to me, pulling me in to clap me on the back.

I can hear the crowd before I see them. The bonfire in the distance, past the sea of cars, illuminates the dark sky.

I've heard about the parties at Greencastle long before I transferred here. My brother has told me several stories about the trouble they've gotten into out here.

The sun is starting to set in the distance leaving only a glimmer of sunlight. We're both still wearing our jerseys and jeans, although I've traded in my sneakers for my boots.

It's what I'm most comfortable in anyway.

"Who all is here?" I ask.

"Uhh, your brother is here. Colter, Knox, and Zane are too. A few other guys from the team, along with some of the girls from the dance and cheer teams."

He shrugs, seeming to study my face.

"In case you're wondering, Colter brought that girl he's been hangin' with, and her friend is with her."

My gaze snaps over to him, and he curls his lip in a smirk.

"Okay, and? What makes you think I give a shit?"

He chuckles, shaking his head. "I saw the two of you talking before the parade. Looked kind of cozy. Isn't that the one dating that dipshit from Keaton?"

"She was, but the word on the street is they split."

He nods slowly, and I do my best to keep my face neutral. Whatever he's looking for as he studies me, he comes up empty.

"I mean, you always could pursue her and let the word get back to him. I bet it would make his head spin, especially if he found out right before we play 'em."

The thought did enter my mind, though I hated that she might think I was only in it to piss off Freeman. Yeah, there were perks, that being one of them, but if I went after her, it would be because I wanted her.

I've always been one to get what I want, and it wouldn't stop with Hallyn Rivers. Even if she's determined to prove she hates me.

Although I have to admit, a part of me felt the same when I got to thinking about how badly I wanted her.

"It doesn't matter, though. She's not my type anyway," I lie.

The words taste like vinegar in my mouth. Bitter and wrong.

The truth is she's exactly my fuckin' type. Every damn inch of her.

I've been fighting like hell to keep my mind off all the ways I'd like to explore her, just to see how perfect she is for me.

"If that's the case, then I guess I should tell you Leslie's here too. At least you know you won't be goin' home alone."

He chuckles, clapping me on the shoulder with a nod toward the crowd.

We weave through the vehicles parked in the grass lot toward where the sound of voices is coming from. Three logs form a circle around the large bonfire barrel. Past them, I'm going to guess, is where the kegs are, judging by the two sets of feet in the air and the chanting, "Go, go, go!"

Luke Bryan blares from a set of speakers sitting on the back of a tailgate. People mingle, dancing along and holding their drinks in the air.

I spot Colter with his arm around Ava. My brother is with them, along with Zane. He's tall and burly, so spotting him among the group is easy.

My eyes search the crowd until they lock on Hallyn's. She's sitting next to a girl I recognize from one of my classes. I can't remember her name, but I think it's Mandy.

Her face is bright, her eyes glistening from the fire. When she catches me looking her way, she bites the edge of her lip to fight off her smile.

Reed hits me on the arm, holding a red cup with beer from the keg. I told myself when I decided to come out that I was only going to have a couple, enough to make sure I could drive myself back home and wouldn't end up with a hangover in the morning.

"Hey, you," a warm voice croons.

I glance down at the girl standing next to me. She brushes her hand over my forearm. She stares at me from beneath her long fake lashes and flicks her tongue against her teeth.

It takes me a second to remember how I know her, then it dawns on me that she was the girl I hooked up with the night I first met Hallyn.

Yet somehow, when I try to recall her name, I come up empty.

I glance over at Hallyn, who's watching me from across the fire. Her eyes glitter as if she's tempting me, asking me what my next move will be.

Her gaze flicks to where her hand rests on my arm, reminding me of our conversation earlier today before the parade started when I told her I didn't like the idea of anyone touching her.

I smile down at the girl. "It's good seeing you again, Sophie," I say, finally recalling her name. Her face lights up, and she wraps her hand around my forearm. "I'm seeing someone now."

Reaching up, I free myself from her hold. She exhales heavily and steps back. When I look back over at Hallyn, she's pushing herself up from the log and taking off toward the kegs.

Reed clears his throat from beside me. I don't have the patience to answer any more of his questions.

"If you'll excuse me," I mutter, but Hallyn is already ten steps ahead of me.

At first, I think she's getting in line to refill her cup, but she tosses it into the large bin, throwing it away. I finish my beer, pitching my cup with hers.

"Hallyn," I holler.

I know she hears me because she picks up her pace, jogging past another group of people toward the nearby pavilion. Three rows of picnic tables and a bar overlook the park and the beach below the cliffs.

Her feet hit the pavement, weaving through the tables. A building off to the side of the overlook has a beautiful view during the day.

"Will you slow down and wait for me?"

"Go away, Beckham," she shouts over her shoulder.

"Not a chance in hell. Either you slow down, or I'll catch you, but I'm not letting you run away from me."

"You're an asshole."

"Yeah, well, you're a pain in my ass. Will you knock your shit off?"

She darts around the back of the building, but I go the other way. She doesn't see me coming, her head over her shoulder looking for me when she hits me like a brick wall.

I swoop my arms around her lower back, holding her to me.

"See, now that wasn't so hard, was it?" I grumble in her ear.

She presses her palms against my chest and thrashes, attempting to push herself off me. "Let me go."

"Not happening." I chuckle, slipping my hands lower over her ass. She sucks in a sharp breath, and I bend down, lifting her into my arms.

She fights me at first, pushing my shoulders and smacking me on the chest before she sighs, accepting defeat.

I press her against the wall, and she wraps her palm around my throat.

Her hands are small, almost delicate, and her eyes go hooded when I growl into her ear.

"So you get to go all territorial and say shit about not sharing and not letting anyone touch you. Let me guess, though, that doesn't work the other way around."

I slowly smile, and her nostrils flare when she sees the look on my face.

"Are you trying to tell me you don't want to share me either, feisty girl? If that's what you want, all you have to do is say the word."

She arches her back away from me, turning her head to stare off in the distance. She's fighting it, just like she keeps fighting me.

Just when I think she's giving in, she snatches her hand right back.

I lower her to her feet. She grips my forearm, and her body trembles when I press my mouth against her ear.

"Is that what you want, Halls?"

My lips brush along the shell of her ear, and her chest heaves as if she's struggling through every breath.

"You want to know what I think?"

She turns back to face me, lifting her chin to meet my stare. She seems to like it when I tell her what's on my mind.

"I think you got jealous back there," I say, testing her reaction.

Her throat bobs when she swallows, but she doesn't move or say a word to argue my point.

"I believe you've been fighting with yourself on it for a while. You keep saying you hate me and that I'm an asshole, but we both know it's only to convince yourself rather than assert it with me."

She narrows her eyes, her nostrils flaring.

When I press my cheek against hers again, she grips the front of my shirt, holding me to her.

"I bet if I were to lift that skirt and push your panties aside, you'd be wet and turned on for me. 'Cause you might think Freeman was the man for you, but you and I both know he never made you feel the way I do. You get off on fighting me, don't you? Like it's our very own form of foreplay."

"Beckham…" she mutters breathlessly.

I grip her chin in my hand, turning her to face me.

When our lips brush each other's, the moan that escapes her mouth has my dick so hard I could nail her to this wall.

Her hands drop lower to grip my belt.

She's goading me, and she knows it too. Her tongue brushes along the seam of my lips, and I let her in.

I groan, my hips thrusting toward her as our tongues duel, just like we have been for nearly six weeks.

Only now, neither of us is pushing the other away.

I debate making good on my word, lifting her skirt above her hips, and getting her off right here where anyone could come around the corner and see us.

I move my thigh between her legs, and she grinds on me. It's as if her body moves without her even knowing, desperate for her release.

Until I take a step back.

She sucks in a sharp breath and folds her hand over her chest.

"What? Why'd you stop?" Her brows lower.

"I'm waiting for you to admit I'm right and that this is what you want," I say.

I shove my fists into my pockets, needing to do something with my hands before I haul her over my shoulder and take her back to my place.

Even though she still fights it, we both know she wants this between us.

"When you go home tonight, and you're lying in your bed alone, I want you to think about me. I want you to remember my hands on your body."

"Why make me think about it? Why not just do it?"

I grin. "Where's the fun in that, feisty girl?"

She shakes her head, tucking a strand of hair behind her ear like she's searching for the words and frantically coming up empty.

I take a step closer to her again. Like the weak bastard I am, I'm unable to resist touching her.

"Or maybe I just want you to prove you do want me as badly as I want you."

CHAPTER 15

HALLYN

The scent of smoke still lingers on my skin.

It's after midnight by the time I stumble through the door. Tanner sent me a few text messages earlier. I hadn't been paying attention to my phone while we were out at Greencastle.

I just happened to notice them when I called for an Uber to pick me up and bring me back to our apartment.

I could've stayed longer and caught a ride with Mandy. Ava and Colter disappeared at some point. I still haven't quite figured out what's going on between the two of them.

She insists they're just friends, but I know we aren't friends like they are.

The apartment is dim since only the lamp in the living room is on. I drop my purse and poms near the door and quickly shed my shoes.

I don't bother sitting down or reading the text messages, beelining it straight for the bathroom to take the bow and bobby pins out of my hair.

Dragging my nails through my hair, I make sure I got every one, releasing a low moan at how good it feels on my scalp.

After I quickly shed my uniform and toss it into the hamper in the linen closet, I bend down to turn on the water before flipping the knob on the shower spray.

Fall weather is upon us. Once the sun disappeared into the horizon, it turned into a brisk night. The feel of the warm water on my skin sends chills breaking out over my arms.

I pull the curtain back and step into the tub, letting the water cascade down on me. Even as the scent of the bonfire washes away, I still can't rid myself of the feel of Beckham's hands and lips brushing along my skin.

My eyes close, and I tilt my head back, picturing the grin on his face when he'd take a step closer to me, the temptation in his voice every time he pushed my buttons.

I want you to myself.

I let my fingers roam over my arms and across my chest. My breath shudders when I pass over my nipples, hardening under the water as it pelts down on me.

I let my hands continue lower over my hipbone and down my inner thigh. An ache builds again. I've only felt it recently when I've been alone with Beckham.

I've thought about how I never felt this intense attraction for Tanner. When I close my eyes, I can almost picture what the two of us would be like together.

The thing about Beckham is that even my wildest imagination could never compare to what it would be like with him in real life.

He always seems to say and do things that take me by surprise, and I have no doubt the same would be true in the bedroom.

I reach for my loofah and squirt a generous amount of body wash on it, letting it suds up in my hand before I follow the same path with my fingers as if it were to cleanse my body but also my mind.

With each pass I make, I do my best to avoid the sensitive parts of my body, as if knowing it'll ignite the desire I've let remain dormant in me.

Pushing the shower curtain to the side, I lift my leg to rest my foot on the edge of the tub and run the loofah over my thigh. First one, then the other.

I let the water fall over me, rinsing the soap away, using my hand to help it along.

When I finally give in, I let my fingers brush over the neatly trimmed hair above my pussy and dip lower, rubbing over my clit and through my folds.

"Fuckkk," I groan, tilting my head against the wall.

When I squeeze my eyes shut, I let my mind drift to Beckham, picturing him kneeling on the floor in front of me. His large hands and those deft fingers skillfully brush over my clit, causing my body to tremble.

My breathing shudders, the heated water leaving me in a cloud of steam. My body trembles, and I quickly press my hand against the wall to hold myself upright.

All I can think about is the taste of his lips and the way he turned me on after muttering a few words breathlessly into my ear.

I hurry to wash the rest of my body, moving on to shampoo and condition my hair. Once I'm satisfied and successfully rid of the smell of smoke, I turn off the water and reach for the towel I set on the toilet lid.

The room is foggy. All my thoughts are on Beckham as I go through the motions of brushing my hair and teeth, until I finally hit the light switch and pad through the empty apartment to my bedroom.

The door is closed, and a shiver runs through me when I open it. I swear, it's like the vents don't do shit to circulate heat into my room.

I drop the towel wrapped around my body on the floor and open the closet door in search of something to wear. I grab a Braysen U T-shirt and a pair of sweatpants from the pile of laundry I left folded on the floor. My eyes land on the box of roses Beckham sent me a couple of weeks ago.

I debate for a moment before I give in, pulling out the boxes. Each one is shaped differently, with various features and vibrations. I stick with the small one. According to the front of the box, it's a clit sucker.

My thumb brushes over the power button before I let out a heavy breath. I push it a few times to go through each setting until the vibrations stop and it's powered off.

"He said he wanted you lying in your bed tonight, thinking about him," I whisper to myself.

I set the box back in the closet and pull back the comforter on my bed. My icicle lights line the walls, so when I flick off the light and climb into bed, I'm not left completely in the dark. I settle against my pillows and close my eyes, picturing we're back at the pavilion.

Beckham has me caged in against the wall as I run my hand over my breast, flicking over my nipple. It beads through the cotton of my shirt, but I continue my path lower.

My stomach trembles when my fingers pass my stomach, inching beneath the waistband of my sweats.

I skipped putting on underwear. Something about this feels risky, even if I'm home alone with no one around to hear me.

Back in my mind, Beckham's warm breath feathers against the shell of my ear. It sends a shiver down my spine as I inch lower to my pussy. A low moan escapes my lips when I rub a circle over my clit.

This isn't something I've ever done before. Even when I was intimate with Tanner, it was never anything like I picture it to be with Beckham.

I took the lead a few times, climbing on top of him and moving his hands over my body. The first time, Tanner looked at me like I grew horns on the side of my head, but when he saw I was serious, he seemed to pause as if he didn't know what to do.

Neither of us has been intimate with anyone else. At least, I don't think he was. Maybe it changed last summer while we were apart.

That was a question I never could work up the courage to ask.

My legs fall open, and I continue lower, dipping my finger inside my tight heat.

My chest rises and falls while my breaths come out in heavy pants. Wetness coats my finger, and I spread it over my clit, rubbing circles before I slip back down to fuck myself.

I continue to alternate between movements, slowly working myself up while I picture Beckham's face between my legs.

"*C'mon, Halls, what are you waiting for?*" He urges me on in my mind.

I imagine him brushing his lips along the inside of my thighs, pinning them down while his tongue and fingers follow the same path I'm making until I give in and reach over to the nightstand for my vibrator.

My thumb hesitantly brushes over the power button, turning it on before I slip it below my sweatpants.

I squeeze my eyes shut when I run the suction part over my skin before I give in and position it on my clit. The sensations are strong, too strong, and I clamp my legs together around my arm and moan, "Holy fuck."

The words echo around my bedroom, and I'm thankful Ava is gone on the night I decided to test this out.

I'd be mortified and embarrassed to think of my best friend in the room next to mine, hearing me alone while I got off to thoughts of Beckham.

I try to relax my body, but it feels impossible to do. The sensations are too intense, so I alternate between brushing over the hood of my clit and letting it off again.

Stars dance in my vision when I squeeze them shut, and my body tenses as a wave of pleasure crashes over me. One second, it feels like my body is wound up, and the next, I'm floating. It's new and unfamiliar, and I ride it out.

I manage to turn off the vibrator before my hand gives out, dropping it onto the bed beside me.

My body relaxes into the mattress, and my mind drifts off to this dream-like place. I nearly doze off when my phone vibrates from my nightstand, and I realize I forgot to turn it on silent before crawling into bed.

I peer one eye open and reach over, feeling with my hand for it until it vibrates again against my palm.

"Who the hell is texting me at..." I wince, the light from my screen nearly blinding me. "One thirteen in the morning."

Beckham's name flashes with a notification on the top of my screen with what looks like a picture, and I hurry to click on it, opening it to find him lying in his bed.

He's shirtless, with his arm tucked behind his head. His last name inked on his forearm is flexing, and I press my legs together again at the sight.

I never realized how big of a sucker I was for arm porn until I met him.

Beckham: Good night and sweet dreams

Beckham: Of me, of course.

I bite my lip at the mention of him wanting me to dream about him. I stare down my body, feeling the wetness coating my thighs, and my face heats.

If he had any idea I got off thinking about him, he'd never let me live it down.

My mind drifts off to picturing him standing at the foot of my bed, watching me. He's in those fuckin' sweatpants he likes to wear whenever he comes over after football practice.

His hand is inside them, leaving nothing to the imagination as to what he's doing.

Hallyn: Good night

I drag my lip between my teeth, debating whether I should add the rose emoji to it before I give in and do it, quickly hitting send.

He knew what he was doing tonight, letting things get heated up before he pulled away.

I guess, as the saying goes, "two can play that game."

CHAPTER 16

BECKHAM

"You're not even gonna tell him," Reed asks.

He keeps his voice low even though the noise in the stadium is nearly impossible to hear from where Hayes stands, running through plays with our offensive coordinator.

"Nah." I shake my head, catching the ball. My fingers run along the laces, adjusting my grip before I throw a perfect spiral back to Zane, one of our wide receivers. "You can't tell me the note wasn't for him. Especially today, of all days, when we're playing the Kings."

He grits his teeth, and his jaw ticks. "You're right. They did it to try to get in his head. Whoever it was doesn't know their head from their ass, if they mixed the two of you up."

I shrug, dropping back to catch the ball. "Better me than him, though, right?"

I showed up to the school before Hayes and most of the team. Turns out, someone must've broken into our locker room sometime since our practice yesterday because I found a note tucked in my helmet with the words "dirty-ass pussy" left for me.

My last name is printed above my locker, along with the rest of the team. Whoever was behind it clearly hasn't been keeping up with shit enough to realize that Hayes has a twin who plays for the Bulldogs.

It was against the Kings last year when my brother was trying to block for their QB on a play and collided with Osten, their cornerback. There's been a lot of talk and speculation about the play from everyone in college sports. The flag had been called, and the referees and everyone there—except for the Kings coaches, players, and fans—all seemed to think it was a dirty play.

It's part of the reason I decided to transfer to Braysen and play with him. Even though Hayes would never admit it, I knew my brother needed my support.

He hasn't been the same, and if he found out about the note, especially before the game, he wouldn't have been able to get his mind right to play today.

Maybe one day, after the season wraps up, I'll tell him.

I think he's still grappling with wishing he could've done something differently. Osten remains out of football almost a year later, and it's still up in the air whether he'll completely recover from his shoulder injury.

The clock in the stadium counts down to game time. We have ten minutes left until the teams take the field.

I jog over to Hayes, where he stands on the sidelines with a water bottle in his hand, taking in the packed crowd.

"You good?" I holler at him, clapping him on the back.

His eyes snap over to mine, and I know him well enough to know he's in his head right now.

"Yeah, bro, I'm good." He nods, aiming the bottle at his mouth and taking another swig.

"Listen, no matter what happens today, or what shit the guys on the field put in your ear, don't let them get to you." I pound my fingers into his head, shaking him by his shoulders.

He releases a heavy exhale and nods.

"It would be different if I knew I was looking on their defensive line and saw him playing, ya know? Sometimes I swear, I wish it would've been me."

"You can't think that way," I shout.

The band starts playing, and the crowd begins yelling and cheering with them. I wrap my hand around his neck and pull him in to me.

"You listen to me, Hayes. We both know the type of player you are. You fight hard, but you would never intentionally hurt an opponent. It was an accident. Don't let anyone convince you otherwise."

I pull back and shove him on his chest.

"You keep your fuckin' head up the whole game. I'll be aiming slingshots right at you, and I need you ready."

He nods again, bouncing on the balls of his feet.

My eyes flash over to Reed and Colter standing on the sideline, both looking in our direction. Reed shakes his head, the two of us exchanging a knowing glance.

"Through thick and thin," I shout, holding my fists out to Hayes, and he hits his gloved knuckles against mine, echoing the words back to me.

I push past him, heading over to the bench where the rest of our offensive line sits.

On instinct, almost as if I can feel her gaze on me, I glance down the sidelines to where the dance team is and lock eyes with Hallyn.

Now that I've had a taste of her sweet lips, I'm finding it impossible not to let my mind drift back to last night.

She catches me looking at her and purses her lips together, fighting off a grin. She's dressed in her Braysen uniform, showing off the flower tattoo on her upper back, centered perfectly above her spine.

Her stomach flexes as she bounces on her feet, and my eyes momentarily get distracted by the sight of her legs. Her tan smooth skin shines from here, and I wouldn't mind having them wrapped around my waist right about now.

She mouths along with her teammates the chant, and when I shoot a wink in her direction, she grins.

"Good luck, number eighteen," she yells when they're finished, and I smile back at her.

"All right, Carver. You two lovebirds can do your thing after the game. We need you to get your head on straight now."

I smirk at my QB coach. He sits next to me and hands me a tablet so we can run through the plays we came up with this past week in preparation for the game.

The first half blows by quickly. It was a tight game until they had the ball going into the second half. Their punt returner was able to make a fast break to their end zone, and they were near the fifty-yard line before their offensive line even went on the field. They managed to get the touchdown, putting them up by ten points.

The second half, you could feel the shift in the air. The tension was up, and the Kings came out even more aggressive than the first half.

We wanted to take advantage of the fact we had the ball at the start of the third quarter, and it was important for us to respond to their touchdown if we wanted a chance to stay in the game.

We put up a fight and get down to the red zone, when our coach called one of the plays we worked up specifically for today. It was designed to get the ball to one of our receivers, but I knew I wanted to get it into Hayes's hands. If he was able to make this catch, I knew it would get him out of his head and back in the game.

The guys huddle up around me, and I take a knee.

"All right, let's get it, boys," I holler, rattling out the play name.

My eyes lock on my brother, his face hard as stone, but he nods. He knows this one is coming for him.

I come up to the line, and we snap the ball. I take off running in one direction, before my eyes turn to the other side of the field and make the throw.

It's a perfect spiral, heading right for Hayes, until one of the defenders comes in from the side and hits him hard, taking him to the ground.

My heart races because it's hard to see exactly what happened or who might've been injured from where I'm standing. All I can hear is the sound of the fans near the field and their reaction to the play.

I stand there for a second, trying to see through all the guys to where my brother is on the ground and is slow to get up.

"What happened? Is he okay?" I holler to Colter, and he shakes his head, not able to answer me.

One of our teammates holds his hand out to Hayes and helps him up. He's clutching his side, but he looks in my direction and nods, letting me know he's good.

The next play, I let Zane know I'm coming for him. We run a similar play, only this time I drop back, looking to the right before I sail the ball straight into his arms as he crosses the end zone.

We're closing the distance, and that's all that matters.

We jog off the field as special teams come on for the point after.

"Everything all right?" I ask Hayes, who's wincing as the athletic trainers on the sidelines tend to him.

"Yeah," he grunts. "It's not anything I haven't had happen before."

He tries to wave me off, and Colter comes up right behind me.

"I guess one of their players made a comment about them coming for him every play."

On the outside looking in, especially from the ref's perspective, they're going to call it some harmless game taunting. It's what players do, and he's right, it's not anything that we haven't heard before.

Only I can't help but think about the note and wonder if they are looking to get even for what happened to Osten last year.

The rest of the game is more of the same. As the time winds down, you can practically cut the energy in the stadium with a knife. When we go up by a touchdown with six minutes left in the fourth quarter, it's clear the Kings players are growing desperate.

They have the ball, and their quarterback goes long, slinging it down the field. One of our cornerbacks is on their receiver. The two go up in the air at the same time, attempting to catch the ball, but he doesn't see us coming.

The offensive player tips the ball, and we manage to make the interception.

The crowd's reaction turns into a frenzy.

That play seals their fate. We managed to take time off the clock by running the ball. We make it downfield with less than a minute on the clock and score another touchdown, putting us up by fourteen points.

When the clock runs out and the Kings jog off defeated, the Braysen fans storm the field. I smile at my brother, the relief on his face is evident, until he raises his arm to clap me on the shoulder and winces, clutching his side.

"We did it!" I shout over the band and the fireworks going off. "We're one game closer to the championship."

He grins and nods past me. "I think someone wants to congratulate you."

I turn to find Hallyn staring between the two of us and wrap my arm around her waist.

"What the hell are you doing?" she cackles into my ear.

"I think you're my good luck charm. I'm undefeated when you're on the field."

She playfully shoves me away, and I grab her hand, pulling her into my arms. I lean in so only she can hear me.

"What do you say we go find somewhere to celebrate, just the two of us?"

"I say you're pushing your luck, Carver."

She might be denying me, but the smile on her face says otherwise.

I tug her close to me again. Her eyes flutter when she sees the serious look on my face. I push her hair away from her face and press my palm against her cheek.

"You say that now, but I'll have you begging for it one of these days."

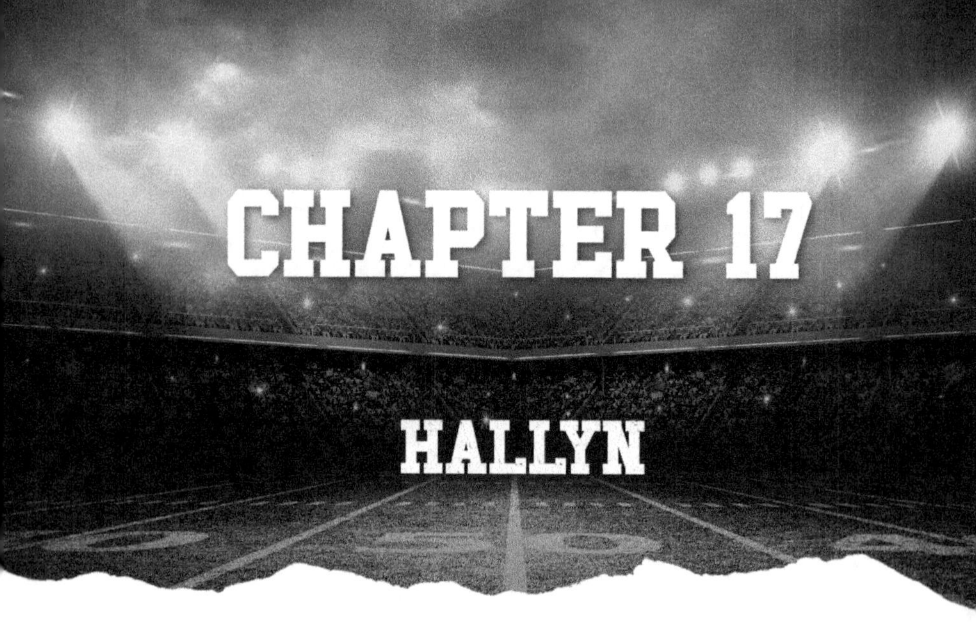

It's been two weeks since the breakup with Tanner. The first week was like going back to the summer when we took time apart. There was an aching pit in my chest that had me longing for the way things were between us when we first started dating.

The summer he asked me to be his girlfriend was right before we went into our senior year of high school. We spent nearly every day together. It's the first time since I became friends with Ava that we weren't tied at the hip.

She never batted an eye on the nights when I put off hanging out, understanding the feeling of dating someone and wanting to spend all your time with them.

When the time came that she got a boyfriend in high school, and even now with Colter, we still find time to catch up.

Two knocks hit the doorframe, and her face squeezes in the door's crack, darting her eyes from side to side while she sings, "Hello."

I turn over on my back and stare at the ceiling fan, watching the blades spin around.

"Heyyy," I sing back. "I'm surprised you're even home on a Friday night and not with Colter."

I have to admit, it's cute seeing the two of them. He's snuck in and out of our place a few times, thankfully on the nights when Beckham hasn't been around.

I'm still surprised he hasn't told anyone, although he's assured me when he makes a promise, he keeps it. I guess it doesn't matter now though, since Tanner and I are no longer together.

I think I'm more conflicted by the changes in Beckham since he found out about our split. He was continuously pushing my buttons before, but now it seems as though he's holding back. Not to mention, he was oddly quiet last Monday night during our tutoring session.

When I asked him about it, he shrugged it off and chalked it up to having a long day and coming straight to my place from practice. Then he slid into the seat next to me again on Wednesday during our chemistry class. He didn't say a word, aside from when he leaned over to set a coffee on my desk.

He lifted the corner of his mouth in a small smile, raising his cup in a cheers before taking a drink. I followed suit, pressing my fingers to my lips to contain my smirk when he got my other coffee order right.

"I asked the girl at the register your order. Guess there aren't many Hallyns on campus." He shrugged.

That was it, that's all he said for the entire ninety minutes until the bell rang and he told me to have a good one before disappearing into the hallway.

Is it sad to think I almost miss his antics? At least with them, it took my mind off the fact my relationship fell apart.

I can't help but wonder if the only reason he ever did it in the first place was never about helping me or needing my help in return, but about finding a way to get under Tanner's skin.

Braysen and Keaton are one of the biggest rivalries in our conference. I wouldn't be shocked to find out Beckham only did it as a way of digging the knife deeper and intensifying things when the two teams meet in a few weeks.

"Earth to Hallyn, are you there?" Ava asks, waving her hands above my face. I snap out of it, raising my hand to shield my eyes from the light.

"Are you okay?" she asks when I don't answer.

I nod. "Sorry, just a lot on my mind lately. I didn't hear what you said before."

She chuckles and shakes her head, holding her hand out to me. I take it and nearly fall over when she yanks me up and off the bed.

"That's what I thought. I'm not gonna let you sit around like a bump on a log anymore. Get ready."

"Get ready? Where are we going?" I question as she bounces out of the room.

I follow her to her bathroom, the door open as she unravels the cord wrapped around her curling iron.

"We're going out dancing. Get dressed up, put on those boots that make all the men's jaws drop, and curl your hair. You have forty-five minutes, then we're heading out."

She picks up her phone, and a moment later, Taylor Swift blares through the tiny Bluetooth speaker. She holds it up to her mouth, singing like it's a microphone, and shakes her hips in time to the beat.

Dancing with my friend is the perfect way to forget about everything. Add a few drinks into the mix and we have an epic night on our hands.

It ends up taking us a little over an hour to get ready. Mainly because I hadn't showered after practice earlier, and even though I wasn't going to wash my hair, I still wanted to freshen up before we left.

The lights are dim in Whiskey Sinner's when we step inside, and I'm surprised when I find it nearly packed to the brim. I recognize several of the students from school.

We slide up to the bar to order our drinks, and I let my eyes scan over the hordes of people, relieved when I find Tanner isn't anywhere in sight.

Since it's a relatively short drive from Keaton, it's not uncommon for students to head this way on a Friday or Saturday night, which has been known to cause a few fights here and there.

The whole turf wars thing.

I'm disappointed, though, when my search of the crowd doesn't show any signs of Beckham.

"Is Colter coming out for the night?"

The bartender slides our drinks over the counter, adding a tiny straw to both. I lift it to my mouth to take a sip. The taste of whiskey overpowers the Coke, sending a shiver down my spine and spreading warmth through my body.

"Yeah, he and Reed are gonna meet us here."

"No Beckham?" I ask, trying to downplay my question by taking another sip.

Ava quirks her brow at me and grins. I down the rest of my drink to avoid answering whatever questions might come my way.

I slam the empty glass down on the counter. The bartender, Kenny, grins at us, wiping his fingers on the towel hanging from his waist.

"Another?" he shouts over the music.

"Make it a double, two of them," Ava adds, finishing hers off, then sliding her glass next to mine.

Kenny nods and chuckles, filling them up again before I turn back to Ava.

"You know, if anything is going on between you and Beckham, you can tell me, right?"

My brows deepen, and she giggles.

"You can stop playing it off like you don't know what I'm talking about, too. Your secrets are always safe with me, Halls."

"I know they are, but nothing is going on. There never has been."

Kenny sets our drinks down, and we both reach for ours, lifting them to tap the glass together.

"How long have we known each other, Hallyn?" Ava asks. "Since we were, what, eleven years old? That's nearly half our lives, right?"

I nod. Sure feels that way. We first met back in the sixth grade. Most of my memories at school include her.

"You'd agree that we know each other better than anyone else does, sometimes even better than we know ourselves."

It's true. Ava has always had this weird sixth sense about people too. She's all about the vibes and picks up on them easily.

I've never had to communicate my thoughts or feelings with her. She just knows. Like tonight, for example, she knew I needed to get out of my head and our apartment, and if it hadn't been for her dragging my ass here, I'd still be back there lying on my bed until I fell asleep.

"There's no doubt you know me better than anyone." I agree.

She smiles. "So when I say this, you know there's a good chance I'm onto something, so remember that, okay?"

"Okay..."

She links her arm with mine. Kenny motions to the register behind him, signaling he's starting a tab for us, and we wave to him as we slip back into the crowd and claim a nearby high-top table.

"I know you loved Tanner, and you cared about him a lot. I don't doubt for a second you're still hurt over the split. I think you've held on to him because you feel guilty for the choice you made to come with me to Braysen after he accepted his offer to Keaton."

She's right. I felt like it came down to more than choosing a school. It was like I was choosing between my best friend and Tanner.

Even though I had already committed to Braysen, I still could have changed my mind, but I didn't.

I think a part of me felt to blame after all the plans we made, I didn't follow him to the school he went to. Maybe if I had, we would've been able to make it work.

I nod. "A part of me is still accepting the fact we were over long before it came down to what schools we attended."

She gives me a sad smile and reaches her hand between us to squeeze mine. She doesn't say anything, but she doesn't have to either. We both know I'm right.

I did everything I could to piece together what was broken in our relationship, hoping we could get back to how it was early on. The butterflies in my stomach, the giddy feeling whenever I saw his name flash on my phone.

Somewhere, over time, things changed between us.

Those feelings went away, and even when we got back together, they never returned.

"I know you've said you hate Beckham," Ava smirks, and I take another heavy sip of my drink at the mention of his name. "We both know the smile on your face whenever he's brought up, though, is not how you respond when you hate someone."

"What are you trying to say?" My eyes narrow, and I lean my arm against the table.

My heels are getting a little unsteady beneath my feet. When did I turn into such a lush?

"I'm just trying to say, if you like Beckham and want to explore those feelings, you owe it to yourself to do it. You're not hurting or betraying anyone either."

She smirks, her face lighting up when she looks past me, and I turn to see Colter and Reed slipping through the crowd.

She lifts her hands in the air and wraps them around Colter's neck, pulling him into her, and I smile.

You know, for someone who's pointing all the fingers at me for pretending nothing is going on between Beckham and me, I could say the same for her.

Hell, I don't think her brother has any idea she's been spending time with his rival either. Although Ava has never been one to back down to Alec.

She'd stand ten toes down, her fists on her hips, ready to throw down if he ever tried to get in her way of what she wanted.

They've always had a weird sibling relationship. The kind where you'd swear the two hate each other, but if anyone were to ever hurt his sister, Alec would be the first in line to slaughter them.

It's just the way it's always been.

I smile at the two of them, watching how Colter leans down and buries his face into her neck.

Reed grins when our eyes lock. "Sorry, I know I'm not the one you were hoping to see either."

My brows furrow, and I tilt my head to the side. How does he know about the two of us?

He chuckles. "He hasn't told me anything, but I've put two and two together after I saw a text message from you come through when he left his phone in my car."

I nod, finishing what's left of my drink. I raise it in the air to him before wobbling on my heels and spinning to bolt over to the bar.

I don't know how to respond to Reed, and I'm not about to say or do anything that could reveal my feelings toward Beckham.

Feelings?

Do I really have feelings for him?

Kenny is on the ball when he sees me saddle up to the bar. Maybe it's me, or maybe the liquor in my bloodstream is taking effect, but I swear this time around he put a little more Coke than whiskey in this one.

At least that's what I tell myself when I reach into my pocket and scroll through my contacts right before I hit the call button below Beckham's name.

When his smooth voice filters through the line, it sends a shiver down my spine.

Smooth like whiskey.

CHAPTER 18

BECKHAM

"Hallyn?" I holler, trying to hear her over the music blaring in the background. "Is everything all right?"

Hayes sits across from me, his long legs spread out on our sectional. We both decided to hang back at the house while Reed and Colter took off to the bar.

We have an afternoon game tomorrow, so it's not like we couldn't have joined. I tweaked my arm earlier this week at practice, though. I've been trying to relax, hoping it gets better before we face the Lions.

I can feel Hayes's penetrating gaze when I toss the remote at him and push myself off the sofa. He doesn't say a word, though, when I disappear down the hall, too focused on the rustling sound in the background.

"Can you hear me?" her throaty voice asks, and I swear my dick turns hard at the sound.

"Yeah, you good?"

"Everything is okay. Where are you? Why didn't you come out with Reed and Colter?"

The crowd's noise fades, but I can still hear the subtle sound of her breathing through the phone.

I sit on the edge of my bed, thinking about the first and last time Hallyn was here with me.

"I'm takin' it easy. Gonna call it an early night with the game tomorrow and all."

"Oh right, I bet you want to get to bed soon, huh? I'll let you go then," she rattles out.

"Whoa, hey, it's all good. I'm not crashing soon. I was just watching a movie when you called."

"I never did thank you for the, uh, for the roses you sent me."

I picture her face on the other end of the line when she says it, nervously tucking her hair behind her ear while she drags her lip between her teeth.

"Like I said, you deserve them." I clear my throat. "I thought you might like them, I mean."

"Beckham..." She exhales my name, and it comes out more like a sigh.

My brain may be short-circuiting, but I can't help but imagine her saying it that way with her legs draped over my shoulders while I slide deep inside her.

I squeeze my eyes shut, pressing my thumb and pointer finger to my eyes, but it doesn't help rid myself of the visual I've just painted in my mind.

"Yeah, Halls?"

The nickname flows so easily that it practically rolls off my tongue now.

"I used the one, the smaller one." Her voice cracks. "I've never done anything..." She chuckles. "I've never done it before. Hell, I was starting to think I was broken."

She laughs again, but it's one of those giggles like she can't believe she's saying it or confessing to it out loud. I have to admit that I'm shocked myself.

I squeeze my phone in my hand at the thought of her lying in her bed on top of her soft white duvet. Her toned and tan legs spread open while she skates one hand up and down her thigh and presses the tiny sucker to her clit with the other.

I cough, attempting to clear my throat.

She said she thought she was broken. I try to snap out of it, focusing on those words.

"What do you mean, baby? Why would you think you're broken?"

I don't even notice the term of endearment, and I'm grateful she doesn't protest me using it either.

"Well, um..." She hiccups, and I realize there's likely some liquid courage playing a role in her admission, but I wait, letting her continue. "Tanner, he never, um... he never was able to... you know."

My mouth drops open. Is she trying to tell me that fucker never got her off?

No wonder she balked at me when I suggested she get herself off to relax. She thought she was broken, and it wasn't something she could even do.

"Are you telling me you've never had an orgasm, Hallyn?"

She hums. "Yes. I mean, not until..."

Not until she used the rose.

My breath catches in my throat again, the vivid picture back in my mind of her spread open as if she's doing it for me. I picture the rosy shade of her cheeks and the way her legs shake, the moans she'd make when she realized what was happening right before she fell over the edge.

"Well... how was it?" I croak.

"Beckham..."

She's doing it again. The breathy way she says my name has me squeezing my eyes shut, thinking about her moaning while my fingers brush over her clit or while I fuck her until both of us come.

"Tell me," I urge. "I want to hear you."

"I pictured it was you..." she admits. "I wanted you to be there."

Dear Jesus, I know I was thinking it, and a part of me hoped maybe she had been picturing it too.

Hearing her admission, though, the throaty sound of her voice is nearly my undoing.

I reach my hand down and suck in a sharp breath, gripping my dick through the thin material of my athletic shorts. The urge to tug them over my waist and free my cock, getting myself off to the sound of her voice crosses my mind.

I don't, though. I force myself to hold off, knowing there will come a day, hopefully soon, when I'll get to experience it in person. It'll only make it that much better when I do.

"Hey, what are you doin' out here by yourself?" a deep voice growls. There's a rustling sound on the other end of the line.

"I'm on the phone," Hallyn answers, her voice changes.

Where is she at? Why did it sound like she was alone until this other guy approached her?

"Beckham, you still there?" she asks.

"I'm here," I mutter, hoping whoever it was has left her alone.

"Oh shit," she groans. "My battery. Dammit, I think my phone—"

The line cuts out, and I stare at the screen to see the call has ended.

I quickly hit her name again, redialing her number. It rings once before going straight to her voicemail. I hang up and try again, but I'm met with the same recording each time.

Something about the sound of whoever she was talking to sends a nervous chill down my spine.

I stalk toward my closet and hastily grab a T-shirt from the hanger, not paying attention to which one it is before tugging it over my head. I shove my feet in my shoes and take off down the hall.

"Yo, where are you goin'?" Hayes calls when he sees me barreling down the stairs toward the door.

"I gotta run somewhere quick. I'll be back in an hour."

"Go where? What's wrong?"

"I don't have time to explain right now. I'll tell you when I get back."

"Do you want me to come with you?" he asks, jumping up from the couch ready for whatever I'm about to throw his way.

He's my twin brother. We have that weird bond, so I don't doubt he can sense something is off by my tone alone.

I don't even know if there's anything to worry about, but my paranoid part argues you can never be too sure.

I shout to Hayes not to worry about it as I push through the screen door, letting it spring shut behind me, and jog down the steps toward my pickup.

It's a short drive to Whiskey Sinner's, but I end up calling Reed anyway, hoping he or Colter can find Hallyn and make sure everything is all right.

"What's up, man?" Reed answers, the pumping music in the background making it hard to hear him.

"Where are you?"

"I'm at Whiskey Sinner's, just ordering a beer. Why, what's wrong?"

"Are you with Hallyn? Do you see her?"

"No, I haven't seen her for a little bit. I thought she was heading up to the bar to get a drink, but I haven't seen her."

"Dammit." I clench my hand into a fist.

I hit the brakes, coming up to a stop sign, but there's no one around so I make it a quick one, hitting the gas to floor it through the intersection.

"What's goin' on?" Reed questions.

"I'll be there in a few minutes, but I need you to see if you can find her for me."

"Yeah, okay. Hang on."

I'm still about five minutes away. Whiskey Sinner's is on the opposite side of town, not too far from where Hallyn and Ava live.

The line goes quiet before I hear him again. "Beckham is on the phone. He's trying to find where Hallyn went. Have you seen her?" Reed asks.

It's hard to make out what the other person says with the background noise from the crowd and loud music.

"Leslie and Mandy just got here, and they said they saw her talking to that ex-boyfriend of hers outside. It sounds like they think she may have taken off with him. Have you tried calling her?"

"Ex-boyfriend, you mean Tanner?"

"Yeah, man."

There's no way that voice was Tanner. At least, I don't think it was. The way she responded, telling him she was on the phone, didn't sound like a response to someone she knew.

Maybe I'm wrong, though.

It feels like a punch in the gut thinking about her leaving with him, especially after her admission just before.

She'd clearly been drinking, though. She wouldn't leave with him, would she?

Of course, she would, Beckham. He was her fuckin' boyfriend.

I pull into the parking lot and jerk the steering wheel, making a sharp turn into the first spot I find. My hair is a mess, having pulled on my baseball cap after showering.

I quickly swipe the black hat on the passenger seat and put it on backward, jumping out of my truck. I point my key fob over my shoulder while I jog toward the door, hitting the lock button.

"Wait, where are we going? I don't wanna leave yet." The words are muffled, and I stop, spinning around trying to figure out if my mind is playing tricks on me and if it was Hallyn.

Where is she?

"Hallyn?" I shout.

My chest heaves, and I tighten my hand into a fist, already on edge.

"No, I said no. I don't wanna leave." Her voice grows louder this time, but it's still hard to make out where it's coming from.

I stand on the curb overlooking the dimly lit parking lot, but I know it's her. I'd know that voice anywhere.

"Hallyn," I shout. "Hallyn, is that you? Where are you?"

There's a grunting sound. My head snaps to the corner of the lot, where a tall and burly dark-haired man's head sticks above the hood of a pickup truck.

I'd miss him if it wasn't for the fact I'm standing on the curb. The parking lot is on a slope, giving me a better vantage point from where I'm at.

I take off running in that direction, my feet pounding the pavement. The sound of rocks crunch beneath my shoes.

When I round the back of the pickup to the beat-up silver Honda parked next to it, I spot the man with his arms wrapped around Hallyn's shoulders, attempting to shove her into the back seat of his car.

"Yo, hey," I growl, grabbing the collar of his shirt in my fist to pull him off her.

He barely budges. He's wearing a red baseball cap, so it's hard to see his face when he slowly turns to face me, his eyes leveling me with a death glare.

"What are you doing? She doesn't want to leave with you."

"How do you know what the fuck she wants? As a matter of fact, she does want to leave. Ain't that right, sweetie?"

His hand grips her upper arm, and she whimpers, attempting to tug her arm away from him.

"Release her arm," I say, spit shooting from my gritted teeth.

"Or what? What are you gonna do? She's with me, so why don't you turn the hell around and go back to wherever you came from? This one is mine."

Hallyn's wild eyes dart over to me, the panic clear on her face. A sob escapes her throat. The moment he glances at her, I jump on him, rearing back and landing a hard blow to his jaw.

It's enough for him to let her go, and she ducks, attempting to back away.

"Run, Hallyn," I yell, right as he lowers his shoulder and hits me, slamming me backward.

I'm thankful for the car parked facing his, knocking me back on the hood, otherwise I would've hit the concrete. Either way, I know I'm going to be in a world of hurt in the morning, judging by the shooting pain from my hand splitting up my forearm.

I don't know how Colter and Reed know where we're at, but I hear them before I see them. Reed stands over me, and I don't doubt Colter, by his sheer size alone, sent the prick running.

Reed holds his hand out to help me stand. Ava and Hallyn huddle together across the parking lot, arms wrapped around each other.

Tears stream down her face, leaving black streaks in their wake.

"You okay?" I gasp, crossing the space between us.

She nods, releasing her hold on Ava to slip her arms around my waist.

"Thank you," she whispers against my chest.

I wince, lifting my arm to wrap it around her shoulder, holding her to me.

I don't know how I'm going to play tomorrow. The throbbing pain from earlier in the week has intensified, and now I have a hand injury to add to the list.

It doesn't matter, though. All I care about is Hallyn and knowing she's safe.

Safe and in my arms.

CHAPTER 19

BECKHAM

After the altercation, the dude got in his car and flew out of the parking lot. At first, Hallyn seemed anxious and scared, especially as the reality of the situation set in. She appeared to relax when she wrapped her arms around me.

I offered to give her a ride on my way home. She has her arm draped over the center console, her head resting on my shoulder.

I park my truck in an empty spot and glance through my windshield at the balcony outside her place. Her blinds are shut, but you can still make out the muted lighting, giving the appearance someone is home. Ava decided to stay at Whiskey Sinner's after much reassurance from Hallyn.

My fingers brush over the soft skin of her forearm, and I grin when her body shivers and a light moan escapes her lips.

"Halls, wake up."

She groans, stretching her arms out and tilting her back against the headrest. Her eyes slowly blink open, locking on mine, before she jolts herself upright.

"Well, hello, Sleeping Beauty."

She glances around, disoriented, trying to figure out where she's at before I answer with, "We're outside your place."

My body misses the loss of her touch when she pulls her arms away.

"C'mon, I'll walk you inside."

If I thought maybe what happened outside the bar sobered her up, the sight of her stumbles when she climbs out of my truck confirms that's not the case. Not enough, anyway.

The alcohol drops her inhibitions enough not to over-think when she links her arm with mine, gripping my fore-arm while I lead her to the front door and upstairs.

"Is anyone else staying with you and Ava?" I ask, grasping her forearm.

She's slow to respond, staring down at each step until we reach the top, then she raises her head to look at me.

"The door," I clarify, pointing at where it's been left open. The door looks like it was kicked open from the crack in the frame. Anyone walking on the second floor has a free shot inside.

"No, just me and Ava?"

Her voice cracks, the panic evident in her tone.

"Give me your keys."

She unzips the small purse slung across her chest and pulls out the Braysen U lanyard with her keys attached.

I peek my head inside, noting nothing appears out of place from my recollection.

A blanket is flung across the back of the sofa, and I notice her lava lamp next to her TV is on. I gave her shit about it the first time I came over, telling her she was stuck back in the '90s. The small lamp in the corner of the living room is on, which explains the light I noticed from outside, along with the one above their stove.

I reach for the door handle to pull the door closed. It takes a couple of tries before it stays shut.

"Wait, what are you doing?" she questions, holding her hand out to stop me.

"You're coming back to my place. You can stay with me for tonight."

"What, why?"

I don't bother stopping to have this conversation in the hallway. It doesn't feel safe to leave her here alone, especially after a few drinks.

I'm still trying to get over the fact I saw the Keaton logo on the front of the guy's shirt back at the bar.

What would they be doing all the way in Braysen? Much less, what is their reason for pinpointing Hallyn?

"It's not safe for you here tonight. C'mon, let's go."

I'm not trying to scare her, but the whole thing sends alarm bells off in my head. If this has anything to do with the note I found in my locker, the last thing I want is for Hallyn to get dragged into this.

She doesn't fight me any further when I slip my hand in hers and help her back down the stairs, which I have to admit I'm grateful for. She never pulls her hand away or acts shocked when I continue holding it during the drive home.

I don't think I'd be able to explain my need to touch her, even if I tried.

Everything about tonight has me on edge, and I won't feel good about it until we're back at my place where I know she's safe.

No one with half a brain would try coming through our door, not with the four guys living there.

Hallyn dozes off again on the drive home. When I pull into the driveway, I quickly fire off a text to Colter, explaining to him what we found and telling him not to let Ava go home by herself.

I doubt either would protest spending the night together even though they're still intent on fighting whatever is going on between them.

"Where are we?" Hallyn asks when I gently shake her arm to wake her up.

"You're staying with me tonight," I remind her.

"I thought I'm not allowed in your bedroom?"

Her eyes brighten, the dashboard lights illuminating her face. I chuckle, turning the key in the ignition and reaching for the handle to climb out.

"That was before…"

Her hand is warm when I open the door and help her down again. She sucks in a sharp breath when she feels me brushing my thumb over the top.

She's unsteady on her feet, so I use the opportunity to wrap my arm around her waist, holding her to me. She gasps again, pressing her palm over my heart, and I wonder for a second if she can feel how hard it's beating in my chest.

I can stand tall in the pocket with a packed stadium in overtime and the game on the line, but it still wouldn't compare to what I feel when I have her in my arms.

Something about that realization still freaks the hell out of me.

"Before what?" She lifts her eyes, her hair falling away from her face. It takes me a second to piece together what she's saying, until I remember my comment when I got out.

"Before I've gotten to know you."

She presses her lips together to suppress her grin. I wait for it, though, fighting like hell to resist the urge to kiss her.

Her fingers grip the front of my shirt, holding me to her. If only she knew how I didn't want to let her go.

"Let's get you inside," I whisper, and she nods.

She stumbles over the first step leading to the small porch out front and giggles. It's a reminder that no matter what she said on the phone earlier, no matter how tempted I am to kiss her, it can't happen tonight.

I don't want our first time together to happen under a cloudy haze of alcohol.

No, I want her to remember every second as I bring her to the brink of her orgasm, then pull her back again before she finally falls over the cliff.

I want to be there to catch her when she does, and I want my face to be clear in her mind and not that fuckin' prick Tanner.

Hayes sits on the couch holding an Xbox controller when he sees us walk through the door.

"What the...?" he questions, glancing from Hallyn and back to me.

He knew I helped her with her truck because I spent mornings at the shop working on it before practice or class. He has no idea about the tutoring sessions or how we made a deal in exchange for her payment.

That was the only terms of our agreement I've abided by.

Regardless of what I thought of her stipulations, I wasn't about to break the rules she laid out, no matter how bad I wanted to rub it in her little boyfriend's face.

It didn't matter, though, considering they've broken up.

Now she's here with me, about to fall asleep in my bed.

I hold my hand up to Hayes, staving off the questions I can read written all over his face. I shake my head, answering the big one, that I'm not hooking up with her.

Not tonight anyway.

Hallyn rests her head against my forearm as I lead her down the hall to my room. She releases a heavy sigh when I shut the door behind us and lift the strap of her purse over her head.

She closes her eyes as if she's lost in her own world.

"It smells like you in here," she admits when she slowly blinks her eyes open.

I quirk my brow at her in question. "Oh yeah. What do I smell like exactly?"

She giggles and shrugs. "It's like a mix of your cologne, the smell of clean laundry, and I don't know... *you*."

I take a step closer to her, eliminating the distance between us, and she gasps when I brush my finger along her jawline, lifting her chin until our eyes lock. We stand there like that until I finally break contact, my gaze flicking to her lips and back up again.

She tilts her head back as if she's waiting for me, tempting me to kiss her.

"Are you going to kiss me?" she asks, voicing her thoughts out loud. It reminds me of our conversation in the parking lot the night of Bulldog Fest.

I brush her hair away from her ear, leaning in to her. She drags her nails over my chest, taking a step closer to me, and I hiss when she brushes her hip over the front of my pants.

"Is that what you want, Halls? You want me to spread you out on my bed and run my tongue over every inch of you?"

"Beckham..." she whispers.

"I wanna hear you say it."

"Do you?" she asks, hesitating to answer the question as if she fears I'm teasing her with no intention of following through.

Maybe I am, just a little, but I have every intention of following through on my word.

I always do.

"I asked you first." My lips skate along her jaw up to her ear, and she trembles against me.

I could keep going all night, finding every way to elicit a response from her.

"I-I want you to kiss me."

The desire glistens in her eyes when I pull back, her tongue darting out to drag over her lips, wetting them like she's priming them for the moment I inevitably break, and one of us gives in.

Nothing is wrong with a little taste though, right? Just one kiss, enough to hold me over until the next time we're alone and can take it further.

I grip her chin between my thumb and forefinger, lifting her eyes to meet mine and lean in, pressing our lips together.

Her moans vibrate against me, and I release a groan of my own, using my other hand to grip her hip and hold her body to me.

I'm not sure if I'm trying to prevent her from touching the front of my pants again, or if I'm trying to restrain myself from lifting her in my arms and carrying her over to my bed.

When her mouth opens and her tongue seeks entrance, the taste of whiskey brings me back down from earth, and I force us apart.

"Wait, why'd you stop?" she asks, running the back of her hand over her lips.

The hurt marks her face, and I can see the regret that follows for voicing her thoughts.

"I'm sorry, I shouldn't have—"

I take another step toward her, and she steps back, her legs hitting the edge of the bed before she gives in and takes a seat.

"Hallyn, whatever's swirling around in that pretty little head of yours, knock it off."

"Well, then why'd you pull away?"

I turn toward my closet, plucking a shirt and shorts from one of the shelves and tossing them onto the bed beside her.

She crosses her legs, pressing her fingers to her mouth while she stares at the floor, lost in thought.

"Hey," I mutter, trying to get her attention before repeating it a second time.

She falls back on my mattress, turning over onto her side.

"Tell me what you're thinking."

She shakes her head.

"Why not?"

"It's nothing. I'm not thinking about anything."

"Bullshit. You might get away with it with other people, but it won't work with me. Tell me what's on your mind."

The hurt on her face is back, and I wonder for a second if my comment touched on a sensitive spot.

"It's just—" She stops, shaking her head. "No one has ever looked at me the way you do. I've heard all about the other girls you've been with."

She winces, squeezing her eyes shut.

Fuck. What the hell did she hear about me? I've only been here for going on two months.

Yeah, when I visited my brother last year and during the summer when we moved in at the start of practice, I got out and mingled with other women, and I went home with a couple.

I hadn't realized word got around.

"Let's just say the girls talk, and I've heard all about how you're not selfish or one to hold back in the bedroom..." she admits.

"Who the hell have you been talking to?"

"It doesn't matter," she says, pushing herself back up. "The point is, you keep holding back, so I guess it must be something about me."

I shake my head, but I'm fighting and failing to find the right words to tell her the truth.

"Hallyn, the only reason I'm holding back with you is because when I finally get my hands on you, I don't want a single thing in our way. I want you, and I know now you want me too, but I want to hear you say it when you haven't been drinking."

She stands, and I reach for her hand, pulling her back.

"You're not broken and were never broken. I promise there will come a day when I'll show you."

CHAPTER 20

BECKHAM

Hallyn sits on the edge of my bed, wearing my T-shirt and shorts, when I step out of the bathroom the following morning. I'm shirtless with a towel tied around my waist.

I may have done this intentionally in hopes she'd be awake.

Her mouth drops open, and her gaze burns into my skin, dragging her eyes down my body. She pauses where my dick grows hard beneath the cotton material before snapping up to meet my gaze again.

Yeah, it was worth it, all right.

"You sleep okay?" My voice goes hoarse, and I cough to clear my throat.

She swallows and nods. "Too good."

She asked me to sleep next to her, and I selfishly agreed. I woke up in the middle of the night to her sleeping, or at least I thought she was, until she arched her back and pressed her ass against my groin. I damn near bit my lip off, trying to suppress my groan.

What I wouldn't give to have her bent over the side of my bed now, her delicious ass on display for me.

"How are you feeling after last night?" I ask, raising my brow.

"I'll be honest, a little shaken up after what happened. I'm glad I wasn't left home alone after, so thank you for letting me stay with you."

She tucks her hair behind her ear, pushing herself to stand, and grabs the clothes she left folded on top of my dresser.

Her eyes widen, and she gasps when she catches sight of my hand before I pull it away.

"What about you? Are you going to be okay?"

I nod. "I woke up early to ice it. I think it looks worse than it is, but we'll see how today goes."

She winces, a look of guilt passing over her face.

Without thinking, I reach out to reassure her, and my knuckle brushes over the edge of her jaw. Her breath hitches as I slip my fingers into her hair, and she tilts her head back. I graze my thumb over her lip and give in, leaning down to give her a hard, punishing kiss.

She moans, and I screw my eyes shut, attempting to control myself and ignore her sounds.

Never mind the fact I'm still strung tight after she spent the night torturing me.

The conversation we had on the phone—her admission about Tanner never getting her off and the fear of being broken—still plays through my mind.

I don't think I have it in me to keep denying this between us, and I don't think she wants me to either.

She steps into me. Her fingers slide over my pecs, making their way down my abs. She stops above where I've cinched the towel at my waist.

Our lips break apart, and I press my forehead to hers when she whispers, "How long until you have to leave for the game?"

Every thought in my mind—the worry from last night and how my hand will be during the game—escapes me.

"I have about an hour still," I respond.

I think I have an idea why she's asking.

"That's enough time, don't you think?" She lifts her head, her hair falling over her shoulder.

Her nipples bead through the thin fabric of my T-shirt, and her cheeks turn pink. I find myself giving in.

Bending down, I lift her into my arms, careful to use my good hand to hold her. She yelps, looping her arms around my neck and her legs around my waist. She giggles when I drop her on the edge of the bed, bouncing as she falls back onto the mattress.

"You jerk," she balks.

I grip her ankle, tugging her toward me. She sucks in a sharp breath when I lean over her, our chests pressing together, and kiss her again.

She circles her legs around my waist again, holding me to her. There's not much keeping this towel in place. So when she thrusts her hips up and grinds against me, I don't pull back when its hold loosens.

I slide my hand over her waist and brush my thumb over her nipple. She exhales my name, her eyes growing heavy.

Damn, my girl wants it just as bad as I do.

My girl?

I shove that thought from my mind when she rotates her hips again, desperately seeking more friction. I drop my head and flick my tongue over her nipple through her shirt. She drags her nails along my scalp, sending a shiver down my spine.

I want to take it slow, drag it out, and tease the ever-loving fuck out of her, but we don't have long.

I'll have to save that for next time.

I slip between her legs to kneel on the floor. She props herself up on her elbows, staring down at me. When I lift her leg and brush my lips along her inner thigh, she trembles. Her reactions alone make my dick harder.

"Beckham," she exhales as I continue my path higher, slipping my fingers along the edge of her shorts.

My shorts.

She doesn't stop me, lifting her hips for me to drag them down her legs and blindly toss them over my shoulder.

She's wearing a pair of black underwear. The fabric is dark, but the damp spot between her legs reveals her wetness.

I drag my nose over her clit and inhale her scent. She's fuckin' intoxicating.

I tug the material to the side, revealing her pussy.

"Mmm," I hum. "Look how wet you are for me already."

I stare up at her from between her legs, and she snaps her mouth shut. She's not sure where she wants to look, but I take the question out of her mind when I flick my tongue over her clit. Her eyes close, and her mouth drops open, lost in the sensations.

She grips my hair, holding me against her. I slowly drag my tongue through her center, flicking over her swollen bud before sucking her clit into my mouth.

My arms curl under her thighs, tightening my hold on her.

Judging by the rapid rise and fall of her chest, she's close. She drops down on the bed, her fingers digging into the sheets.

"Oh fuck, that feels so good." She grits her teeth, lifting her hips to grind against my face.

"Let me taste you, Hallyn," I groan.

Her movements grow erratic, her moans echoing around my small bedroom. Dear God, I wasn't prepared for how turned on I'd be watching her chase her release.

Just knowing her prick of an ex never gave her this has my dick swelling.

I slip my finger inside her, curling it up to brush over the bundle of nerves.

"Holy shit," she huffs, and I flick my tongue over her clit one last time.

Her body sags, and I pull my fingers out, moving her panties back and pushing myself to stand.

"Mmm," I groan, tasting her desire on my fingers. She lazily stares at me from beneath hooded eyes and gasps as she watches me enjoy every drop.

My dick is bricked up beneath my towel. I loosen the knot and drag my wet fingers over my length, using it to coat my skin before I wrap my fist around me.

The move sparks renewed energy in Hallyn. She scoots toward the end of the bed, reaching toward me.

"Next time, beautiful." I shake my head, reaching for my boxer briefs.

"Why isn't it my turn?" she huffs.

I grin. She's cute when she doesn't get her way, which is exactly why I like pressing her buttons from time to time.

"This wasn't about me. It was for you. When I get the chance to be with you, I don't want to rush it. I want to take my time fuckin' you."

She smiles. "Fine." She crosses her arms over her chest in protest, and I smirk.

There's a pounding on the door, followed by my brother's annoying voice.

"You two about done in there? Or do you wanna drive yourself to Gridiron?"

Gridiron is the stadium near campus where Braysen plays their home games. The parking lot will be full of fans and students tailgating. We talked about riding together to avoid the chaos of finding somewhere to park.

Hallyn stands. She looks mortified at the thought of them hearing us, her face turning red before burying it into my chest.

She may have gotten a bit carried away and forgot about my roommates. I have to admit, I wasn't thinking about them either.

It's not like they haven't and won't do the same to me sometime in the future.

"I should get going. Ava will probably head back to our place soon. I can catch a ride with her."

"I talked to Colter. He's gonna give the two of you a ride to your place to get your stuff."

She nods and turns toward the door, but I stop her, tugging her back into my arms, and kiss her one last time.

My nostrils flare when she groans against my mouth, tasting herself on my lips.

"Don't worry about changing. Just keep the clothes."

She grins. I don't tell her I like the thought of her wearing my clothes out of here and having them at her place.

Hallyn stays in my room for a few minutes, watching me change into my suit, and helps me with my tie before she leaves.

The next time I see her is when we walk out of the tunnel. I'm carrying my helmet, standing alongside my teammates as we gear up to storm the field.

She's with the rest of the dance team and cheerleaders. When I see her, all I can think about is how she was spread out for me on my bed with my face buried between her legs just a few hours ago.

My eyes trail down her body, taking in the sight of her and the glimpse of her stomach flexing as she jumps up and down, cheering. She waves her poms in the air but stops when her eyes lock on mine.

Like the twisted asshole I am, I grin before I drag my tongue over my lips like I just finished the best damn meal I've ever had.

Her mouth drops open, and the pink hue is back on her cheeks. I smirk, reaching out to squeeze her hand as I pass by before tugging my helmet on.

The moment I step on the field, it's game time.

I don't think about anything else but winning.

No rivals. No suspicious notes. No crazy pricks outside of bars.

The stress of Hallyn's apartment will have to wait.

I can't forget the reason I'm here to begin with. Winning is my priority, getting us closer to the championship.

No matter what it takes.

CHAPTER 21

HALLYN

Colter dropped us off at our apartment before the game. I don't remember much from the stop at our place last night, but I guess word got back to Ava, and she filled me in on our drive here.

"Stay here," Colter says, holding his hands up to us.

I wrap my arms around my middle and nod, watching as he goes from room to room to check them before returning.

"If it weren't for the doorframe being cracked and beat to shit and Carver mentioning the door was left open, I wouldn't have thought anyone was ever here," Colter announces.

I adjust my purse, hanging across my body at my hip, and reach inside for my phone. "I'll call our landlord to see if someone can come by and fix the door."

"Don't worry about it. Beckham took care of it this morning," Colter adds.

My brows deepen. "He did what?"

Colter shrugs, reaching for Ava's hand and linking their fingers together. My mind is all over the place, so it's hard for me to focus on the fact they're showing affection around me, which is something they haven't done much of until now.

All I can think about is the fact Beckham took care of it.

"He mentioned knowing your landlord. Guess he's a customer over at Kavlik's."

Colter drapes his arm around Ava's shoulders, and she buries her face against his chest. I would've felt anxious getting ready here alone, just the two of us.

There's a knock on the door.

We all exchange looks before Colter drops his arm and reaches for the handle. Craig, our landlord, stands on the other side.

He doesn't bother with a greeting, his eyes surveying the damage on the exterior. Knowing he was here to fix it made me feel better.

"I gotta take off to the stadium," Colter says, glancing back at Ava, and she nods. "I'll see you both at the game. Text me when you get there."

He's trying not to alarm us, but it's his way of saying, "I want to make sure you're safe and alive."

Ava must sense the impending doom I feel crashing over me.

"Knock it off." She reaches for my arm. "Don't think the worst, or it'll bring bad energy."

I chuckle and shake my head. I don't know how she can always be so chill and go with the flow. If I don't know what's going to happen, I swear it makes me more stressed. To her, I'm just ruining the vibe.

I wish I could let things go and let whatever happens happen.

"Let's get ready so we can get the heck out of here, all right?"

We leave Craig to do his thing. It takes him a while to finish his job. At one point, I heard the commotion coming from the hallway, and I found him with our door leaning against the wall while he replaced our frame.

By the time we reached for our shoes to leave, he went over the new locks he installed, fitted with a keypad and two keys, one for each of us.

This one was more elaborate than the one we had before, and I have to admit it did make me feel better.

We rode together to the stadium. Ever since my truck got fixed, I haven't had the need to drive it too much. As happy as I am to have it back, I'm relieved I don't have to put too many miles on her.

I tuck my poms under my arm, adjusting my ponytail with a bow.

Four tunnels under the stadium seating lead to the field. Two are from the locker rooms—one for Braysen and the other for the visiting team. The media, the dance team and cheerleading squads, and anyone else who may be hanging out on the sidelines use the others.

The energy in the stadium is electric. The seats are packed, and the crowd cheers and chants the Bulldog fight song.

There are still about fifteen minutes to kickoff as the team starts lining up to swarm the field. "Enter Sandman" blares in the stadium. Ava and I stand near the entrance with the dance team lined up on both sides, forming a path.

Beckham leads the team. Hayes flanks him on one side, with Colter and Reed on the other.

He grips the front of his helmet between his fingers. Our eyes lock, and he makes a show of licking his lips. He grins, and my face heats, wondering if anyone else caught him or our exchange.

To anyone who saw him, they may not have picked up on it.

To me, on the other hand, his message is loud and clear. He's making it known he can still taste me on his lips, and desire pools in my belly at the memory of him between my legs, watching me while he had me melting in the middle of his bed.

Reed and Colter jostle him on either side as he lifts his helmet, sliding it over his head.

The guys line up, holding hands, and as the beat of the music amps up, they jog out onto the field while the announcer introduces them.

The crowd is so loud you can barely hear your own thoughts. The dance and cheer teams wave their poms in the air.

"It may have been a secret before, but I think it's safe to say the cat is out of the bag now." Ava tucks her mouth against my ear and shouts over the crowd.

My eyes fly to hers, my brows deepening. She nods across from us to where Sophie, Mandy, and the other girls stand.

Mandy seems clueless, linking her arm with Sophie, whose eyes darken on mine. She probably put two and two together after he rejected her at the bonfire, then chased me down.

I shrug and turn back to Ava. "I have no reason to keep it a secret anymore anyway."

We jog along the field after them as three of the guys from the cheer team make their way toward us, waving the flags spelling out Braysen with the Bulldog logo at the end.

We line up on the edge of the field and, throughout the game, dance to the music and amp up the student section.

We're tied at seven for most of the game. After the third pass attempt misses our receiver, Ava leans in close enough so only I can hear and whispers, "Did he say anything this morning about his hand?"

My stomach twists. I only remember bits and pieces from last night. I vaguely recall talking to him on my phone before it died, the guy approaching me, trying to convince me to go home with him, and then Beckham was suddenly there.

And he was livid.

"He just reassured me he was okay..." I glance back out on the field. He is down on one knee, ready to call the next play on a third and goal.

We're playing the Lake Ridge Lions, and no matter what we do, we haven't been able to make a solid play when it comes to rushing. Almost all of our yards have been from passes, which the injury to Beckham's hand isn't working in our favor.

Ava presses her fingers to her lips, and I glance back, watching intently as they run their last play. Less than a minute is on the clock before halftime, and we need to get ahead while we have the opportunity.

Beckham calls the play, and Reed weaves through two defensive players into the end zone. Beckham tries to fake right before dropping back, throwing the ball toward him.

He overshoots the ball, though, and you can practically feel the energy from the crowd as we all exhale a heavy sigh.

Beckham slaps the side of his helmet in frustration. I watch him jog off as the field goal unit comes on.

"We were a little distracted this morning, and I was in a post-orgasm haze. We didn't talk much more about it."

I smirk at her, and her mouth drops open. "I'm sorry, you were in a what now?"

It's no secret my relationship with Tanner left me sexually frustrated.

I purse my lips together, fighting off my grin and nod. "Mm-hmm."

We manage to add another three points to the scoreboard before halftime. The team jogs past us, Beckham along with them, toward the locker room. I stand along the sideline, watching them, hoping Beckham would glance my way, but he never did.

He has a lot on his mind right now, and I can only imagine his injured hand being at the very top of the list.

"Word on the street is you're the reason we're bombing this game," Leslie says, flicking her tongue against her teeth.

The marching band lines up with the color guard to take the field. Halfway through, we'll join them for our performance.

I don't even bother to give her my attention. She's clearly jealous at the thought that he doesn't want her.

She was pulling the same bullshit with Sophie after she caught them talking in the cafeteria.

"Leslie, go back where you belong and get out of my face." I roll my eyes.

She's getting on my last damn nerve, and I'm starting to lose my sense of humor with her.

"Rumors are spreading all over about how you got drunk and were trying to go home with another player from Keaton. You made a scene, and Beckham came to your rescue, only to end up in a fight with the guy."

My face falls, and I narrow my eyes on her. "I don't think that's how it went down, but you were there, right? You would know?"

She curls the edge of her mouth in a snarl. "Don't you have a boyfriend?"

She bites her lips, glancing around the group of girls, twirling a strand of her hair around her finger.

"I don't see how it's any of your business who I'm with or what I do, but since you're so interested, no, I don't."

She rolls her eyes and smirks, clearly loving getting under my skin.

"As a matter of fact, why don't you ask Beckham what he thinks about you spreading lies about some supposed fight the next time you see him."

I'm playing it off like it's all a lie when even I, in my drunken stupor, know it's not.

"Since you're so worried about who I'm with and what we're doing, you can also ask him who was in his bed last night."

I should feel a twinge of shame at the pride I feel seeing her arrogant smile transform into a painful wince.

I should, but I don't. Not in the least.

She's made it her mission to use every opportunity to hang on Beckham in an attempt to stake her claim and make me jealous.

He may have let her in the beginning. Hell, we both were trying to get under each other's skin.

Not anymore, though.

It has to sting even more to know Beckham isn't one to bring girls back to his room. Word has it that he never has.

Something about him letting me sleep in his bed with him, only to wake me up the way he did, gives me a small sense of hope that maybe this does mean more to him than the others.

SJ hollers for us to get into formation. Leslie acts like she doesn't hear her, standing on the sideline with her arms crossed over her chest. When she doesn't move, SJ intervenes and points her finger down the field, warning her to join the rest of the cheer squad.

I exhale when she spins around and stomps away, clearly having a tantrum at the thought of someone else playing with her toys.

If only she knew how Beckham woke me up, she'd probably fling herself on the ground, kicking and screaming.

"You do realize the rest of the school is gonna know the two of you are together before we even make it to class on Monday, right?" Ava snickers.

Did I care? Not really.

The only question is, would Beckham?

CHAPTER 22

HALLYN

We managed to beat the Lions by the skin of our teeth.

We were scoreless for most of the second half. I could tell with each third and out play that Beckham grew more and more frustrated. It wasn't until the final few minutes of the fourth quarter that we scored, tying it up and sending us into overtime.

When it came down to it, our defense pulled out the stop, preventing the Lions from scoring, and we beat them by a field goal.

Beckham: You mind if we study at my place today?

It's Sunday afternoon. I spent most of the morning vegging on the couch.

Despite us winning, it left Beckham in a less-than-stellar mood. When I texted him after the game, congratulating him on his win, he thanked me before saying he was laying low for the night.

I was hoping he'd ask to see me, especially after the way we started the day off, but I was still recovering from the long week and a rough night before. I took advantage of the opportunity to hang out at home.

Ava ended up dipping out early to meet up with Colter, which left me alone for the night.

I used the time to focus on self-care. Something I've been desperately needing over the past couple of weeks. I've kept myself so busy between dance, school, and tutoring that I didn't have time for much else. On one hand, I was glad because the last thing I needed or wanted was to be in my head.

It wasn't that I was still trying to process the breakup. I hated thinking I was jumping from one relationship to the next because even though Leslie liked to make it out like I was, I knew I was choosing to focus on what made me happy.

Six weeks ago, if you had asked me if I saw Beckham in my future, I would've laughed in your face.

Now, I can't say one way or another, but I'm hoping he is.

It rained overnight, dropping the temperatures down into the low sixties. I pull on a pair of my blue sweatpants with my Braysen U hoodie. My hair is down, curled loosely, and I opt to keep my makeup light with some tinted moisturizer and mascara.

When I pull into the driveway behind a black sports car, I spot Colter and someone who looks like Beckham bent under the hood.

"Hey," I say, adjusting my backpack on my shoulder.

Hayes glances up at me and smirks when he realizes my mistake.

"I don't think I'm the one you're looking for, baby, but I won't tell him if you don't." He winks just as Beckham kicks the door open, sending it flying against the side of the house.

"I don't know what bullshit you're saying, Hayes, but she's off-limits to you."

He exhales a humph and flashes me a smirk. That look right there makes him look nearly identical to his brother, and it's dangerous.

"He doesn't realize that threatening me by saying you're off-limits only makes me want you more."

Hayes reaches into his back pocket to pull out a rag and wipe his hands off. Beckham jogs down the steps toward us and shoves his brother on the shoulder, then reaches for my hand.

I don't notice until he links our fingers that his hand is wrapped, covering his knuckles and around his palm.

"He has to let you out of his sight at some point," Hayes calls after him.

He doesn't mean it. It's only some brotherly banter.

At least, I don't think he does.

"Shut up, fucker, or I'll drag your ass out back."

"No, you won't, or you'll end up with a broken hand, and you'll be dead." He cackles, and Beckham grunts, muttering, "Asshole."

"I guess it's safe to say the word is out on our tutoring arrangement." I laugh as he leads me down the hallway to his bedroom.

"I think he knew about us when he saw you arrive home with me the other night. The point was solidified when you came out the next morning, looking as sexy as you did."

Beckham shuts the door to his room behind us, leaning against the wall and crossing his arms over his chest.

The mention of that night and the subsequent morning shifts the energy in the room. I shrug off my bag, dropping it near his nightstand.

He pushes off the door, stalking toward me. He lifts his hand, brushing the back of his finger along my cheek and tucking the hair away from my face.

Tilting my head back, I expose my neck to him, and he sucks in a sharp hiss when he leans in to skate his nose along my skin.

I blindly reach out to grip his forearms, more in an attempt to steady myself than anything.

"Do you know how fuckin' intoxicating you are?" he whispers. "All I can picture is you staring down at me between your legs. It's taking everything in me not to drag you over there and do it again."

I moan, rolling my eyes closed, and he inhales sharply when I dig my nails into his skin.

"Is that what you want, Halls? You thinkin' of my face buried between those soft thighs?"

The words run through my mind like a soundtrack to the thoughts playing out like a highlight reel.

I'm picturing every sound he makes, how his rough fingers feel on my body, his strong arms banding my legs open, holding me firmly against the bed until he gives in and lets me wrap them around his head.

"Mm-hmm," I say, coming out more of a sigh.

Reaching beneath my hoodie, he holds me by the waistband of my sweats and drags me to the edge of his bed.

He takes a seat on the side, guiding me onto his lap.

I reach between us for his hand, holding up his battered one, and press my lips to his fingertips.

"How's your hand?"

"Fine now," he mumbles, and I give him a small smile.

"You didn't have to do it, you know? Not for me."

His eyes narrow, his face turning serious. "Do it? Do what exactly? Protect you from a man who was putting his hands on you?"

I nod, clenching my teeth. I can tell it's the wrong answer, though, judging by the way his face transforms from concern to his jaw ticking in anger.

"How much of that night do you remember?"

His words are clipped. I hate how, in a matter of minutes, we went from him ready to haul my ass on his bed and bless me with orgasms to this.

"Not a lot. Only bits and pieces."

He nods, his nostrils flaring. "Then let me remind you again that when I found you, the front of your pants were unbuttoned and he was shoving you into the back of his car. You were three sheets to the wind, Hallyn, and he was trying to take you God knows where. I can't even bring myself to think about what he'd planned to do when he got you there."

I try to swallow past the lump forming in my throat.

"The icing on the cake was when he tried to tell me you wanted it. Like this was all some sick plot, and you were on board for it every step of the way."

I shake my head. "I'm sorry. I-I-I don't even remember that part of it. Some parts are a little fuzzy."

"Honestly, I'm glad. The last thing I want is you tortured with the thought of that disgusting prick trying to take advantage of you."

I press my palm against the side of his face, and if only for a second, it seems to calm him.

"He didn't, though, all thanks to you."

He exhales heavily, and I lean in to press my lips softly against his, still holding his hand between us.

His lips are firm at first, but he relaxes when I brush my tongue along them, opening his mouth for me, our tongues dueling before he pulls away.

He catches me off guard when he grips my chin, forcing my eyes to meet his.

"What about our phone call earlier in the night? Do you remember that part?"

"I, uh, remember thanking you for the roses you sent me." I smirk.

His face brightens. "If I remember correctly, you also told me you used it too."

Heat slides up my neck and over my face. He studies my reaction before leaning in, pressing his mouth against my ear.

"You also admitted you thought of me when you did."

His warm breath against my skin sends a shiver down my spine. I loop my arm around his neck, holding him against me.

"Would it make you feel better to know the whole night, while you were asleep next to me, all I could think about was wanting to watch you get yourself off for me?"

"Beckham," I sigh, grinding my hips against him.

He's hard. I can feel him beneath me, and when he moans into my ear, it only spurs me on.

He grips my hips, helping to set the pace.

"Do you want to hear how I've lain in this bed and jacked off thinking about you? Back when you weren't mine, and I had no right to picture you with me."

My chest heaves, my breathing growing labored with every word.

I bury my head into his shoulder, pressing my lips against his collarbone. He drags his hands under my ass, rolling us over until he pins me beneath him.

"I told myself I wasn't going to rush things. That I'd take my time and enjoy it, but I don't think I can wait anymore."

I hook my feet around his waist, holding him against me.

He smirks, staring down at me.

"What do you want, Hallyn? It's whatever you want. You say the word."

"I want you," I whisper.

He brushes my hair back away from my face. "You already have me. You're gonna have to be a little more specific, baby. Tell me."

I drag my tongue across my dry lips. He's asking me to spell it out for him, and I don't think I can.

That's not something Tanner and I ever did.

He was as vanilla as it gets in the bedroom. Anytime I hinted at us spicing up our calls or texts, he always made me feel weird and uncomfortable for bringing it up.

"Don't make me say it, Beckham."

"Why?" He leans back, pushing the sweatshirt up to reveal my stomach. Bending down, he presses his lips ever so lightly against my skin.

My body shudders, desperate for him to continue.

I drag my fingers through his hair, tugging on the strands, urging him on. He pulls away, though, shaking his head.

"Not until you tell me."

I fling my arm to the side in frustration. "You know what I want."

He pushes off me, standing at the foot of the bed, and drags his shirt over his head.

The sight of his arms and abs flexing makes my mouth water. He doesn't stop there, though. Reaching for the button of his jeans, he reveals his black Calvin Klein boxer briefs before he shoves them along with his jeans over his hips.

He wraps his left hand around his hard length, and my mouth drops open before I quickly snap it shut.

"Is this what you want?" He oozes confidence in a way that makes me feel silly and inexperienced.

What could he possibly want with me when he could have anyone he wants? Who knows how many others there were before me? Like the foolish girl I am, I'm about to add my name to his list of conquests.

If that's the case, I'm at least going to make this one to remember me by.

I turn over and crawl toward him. The closer I get, the more the smile on the edge of his lips grows.

It dawns on me that I came over here for our tutoring session, but Beckham, doing what Beckham does best, has managed to throw me off. All I can think about now is how bad I want him.

I take us both by surprise when I don't answer his question. When I'm close enough to him, practically lining us up perfectly, I lean in and flick my tongue over the head of his dick.

"Oh shit," he grunts.

He releases his hand, gripping my chin, tilting my head back until my eyes lock on his.

"If I'm going to come, it's gonna be with my dick buried in your sweet pussy. I bet you're already wet and ready for me."

"Then do it," I taunt. "But hurry because otherwise, I'm gonna take you in my mouth."

He groans, stepping back to drop his pants and his briefs to the floor.

"Take your fuckin' clothes off, Hallyn. Do it slowly, though. I want to savor this moment."

I'm relieved he's taking control and calling the shots. It's what I need right now because this side of him is new and intimidates me.

"Where is the smart-mouthed Hallyn I met in the beginning?" He chuckles, and I shrug, tossing my shirt on the floor near my bag.

I don't know how to answer the question without acknowledging that I'm entering unfamiliar territory.

It's one thing for me to throw sass his way, but it's another thing to put my foot down and call the shots in the bedroom.

"Don't worry, baby. I got you." He climbs up the bed toward me. I spread my legs open for him, just like he wanted.

When he positions himself at my entrance, I loop my legs around his hips again, urging him forward until he's buried deep inside me.

"Mmm," he moans in my ear. "Is this what you want, Hallyn? You want me to fuck you hard and fast, or do you want it soft and slow?"

As much as I'd love to see Beckham take it slow, it's not what I want. Not right now.

"I want you to fuck me so hard, Carver, that I can still feel you when I walk into class tomorrow."

He growls, pulling his hips back before thrusting into me hard and deep.

With our hands linked, pinned above my head, he fucks me like it's our first and last time together.

Like he owns me, and he's staking his claim.

When he leans back, reaching between us to brush over my clit, it sends a jolt through me, and I throw my head back as my release hits me.

If I wasn't sure before, he solidified it now.

I'm his.

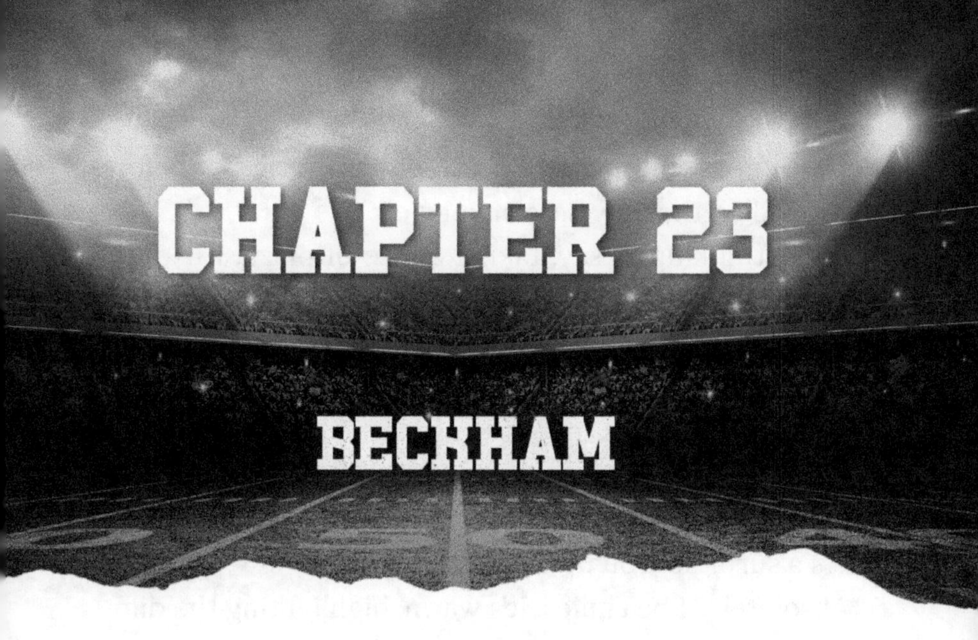

CHAPTER 23

BECKHAM

Hallyn has hung out at my place every night this week. Each time, it's harder and harder to watch her leave.

We haven't done the whole sleepover thing since the fight at Whiskey Sinner's. Although we've agreed to stick to our normal tutoring sessions, she's coming over for pizza and a movie tonight while we have the place to ourselves.

Hayes is working, and I have no idea where Reed and Colter are.

"I hope you don't mind. I ordered sausage and pepperoni," I say, opening the cabinet to grab a couple of paper plates.

It's the only way the dishes stay out of the sink. None of the guys bother to keep it clean. Not unless I threaten them.

"Sounds good to me." She grins, her eyes widening when I lift the top. "It's been forever since I've had pizza."

My face falls. "Are you kidding me? That's like a staple. It should be its own food group."

She shakes her head, leading us over to the kitchen table before I nod to the living room. We talked about a few movies—an action film she heard about on Netflix before we landed on the new *Scream* movie.

"I was thinking," I say, taking a bite of pizza. I use the napkin to wipe my face and swallow before I continue. "What would you say if I told you I wanted to take you out this weekend? On a real date."

She purses her lips together, using the back of her hand to cover her mouth.

"What do you have in mind?"

"It's a surprise. You up for it, though?"

"Absolutely." She smiles. It's warm, highlighting the dimple on her cheek.

I lean across the couch and kiss her.

"I should get out of practice around six on Friday. I'll be by after, around seven or seven thirty, to pick you up."

"I have dance until five thirty, so that'll be perfect."

My phone vibrates in my pocket. I don't bother checking it until after we finish. I take our plates and step away into the kitchen before I check it.

Unknown Number: Did you think you can get by without consequences? Your time is ticking, Carver.

My stomach drops. Could it be another message from the fucker at Kolmont who left the note for Hayes? Or could it have something to do with the fight outside of Whiskey Sinner's?

What are the chances one of the guys from Rixton tracked me down and are lookin' to get even for what happened last year?

"Everything okay?" Hallyn asks, and I snap my head up to find her standing in the doorway.

She leans against the doorframe, wrapping her arms around her middle, studying me intently. Her eyes narrow on my face before glancing down at my phone as I quickly pocket it.

"Yeah, it was just my coach texting me about some plays he sent over earlier," I lie.

She nods slowly, and a pang of guilt feels like a stab in the chest. She must sense I'm not being truthful, and I hate it.

I shove the thoughts out of my mind and cross the room toward her.

"Hey," I whisper, raising her chin to look at me. "I'm not thinking about football or school, or anything else but being here with you."

She grips the front of my shirt, pulling me closer, and I lean in to kiss her. She turns, pressing her back against the entryway, and I pin my forearm above her, lifting her mouth to mine.

"Mmm," she hums, sliding her hands down my chest, dipping beneath the material to drag her nails over my stomach.

I groan, holding back the hiss when she slips her fingers into the waist of my shorts.

"Hello?" a familiar voice hollers, followed by a series of heavy footfalls on the steps leading upstairs to the living room. "Anyone fuckin' home?"

I sigh, squeezing my eyes shut, and tilt my head down to press against Hallyn's.

"Could you cockblockers get fuckin' lost?" I grunt, pulling away and linking my fingers with hers.

"Listen, you have a room for a reason. Judging by the sounds I heard coming from it a few nights ago, it's one you two have no problem using. If you want to be alone, go right ahead."

Hayes grins at Hallyn, leaping over the back of the couch and taking a seat. He reaches for the remote before I snatch it out of his hand, leading Hallyn over to the loveseat on the other side of the room.

"I got dibs on the TV. We're watching a movie, so get lost."

"This is the living room," Hayes says, shedding his shoes and lifting his foot to rest on the coffee table.

Reed comes around the corner, holding a slice of pizza in his hand, claiming the spot next to him.

So much for the two of us being alone.

"We can go into my room if you want to watch something in there instead?" I whisper into her hair.

"Oh, c'mon, Hallyn don't mind. Do ya?" Hayes winks at her.

He's only doing it to get under my skin, and he knows if it were anyone else, I would've laid his ass out. I should've after the first time I saw him flirting with her at Kavlik's, only she was still trying to convince me she hated me, and well, I didn't want to give her any signs or clues her attitude only made my dick hard.

"I don't mind, but hopefully, you'll keep your mouth shut so you don't ruin it for the rest of us." Hallyn snickers, and Hayes has the nerve to act wounded, pressing his palm to his chest.

The throw blanket I brought from my room is draped along the back of the loveseat. Shortly after the movie starts, Hallyn reaches for it and covers us both up while she tucks herself against my side.

There's not shit for space, and I'm tempted to suggest we go back to my room and finish it until we're about twenty minutes into the movie, and her hand brushes over the front of my gym shorts.

I clench my jaw and keep my eyes focused on the TV.

My arm is wrapped around her back, and her long, fit legs lie across my lap. She turns to rest her head against my shoulder. I tried to tell myself it was an accident.

She was only trying to get comfortable, right?

Wrong.

I knew she was dead set on teasing me the second her hand skated across the front of my shorts again. This time, she continues her path underneath my shirt, raking her nails over my stomach.

I flick my gaze over to Reed and Hayes, who are enraptured by the movie. The music is growing intense, and they're engrossed in whatever is about to happen next.

When I'm confident they're not paying any attention to us, I glance down at Hallyn. Her soft expression conceals any sign she's aware of how she's teasing me beneath this blanket.

I mentally tell myself to relax and watch the movie until her deft fingers slip beneath my underwear.

She's not going to do this right now, with my brother and Reed sitting only a few feet from us, is she?

"What do you think you're doing?" I whisper into her hair.

She drags her lower lip between her teeth, a devious smile curving the edge of her mouth.

"Shhh." Her warm breath is hot against my ear. "I'm enjoying the movie."

Her attention turns back to the TV, but only for a moment. Her hand beneath the blanket has a different idea.

I'm thankful for where the couches are positioned, making it easy to use her body draped over mine to conceal her movement beneath the fabric.

She tugs on my shorts, and I lift my hips enough to help her without making it too obvious. I clench my jaw, waiting while she rubs her hand over my front, trying to find the hole in the front of my boxer briefs before I reach down to help her.

It takes everything in me to keep my eyes on the screen. Despite my eyes being trained on it, I can't tell you what's happening, having lost all thought the moment she started tempting me.

My hand grips the base of my dick, and her delicate fingers wrap over mine.

When she brushes her thumb over the tip, I hiss through gritted teeth. I'm ready to pull my shorts up and haul her ass into my bedroom.

Where's the fun in that, though?

"I'm going to enjoy getting you back for this," I mutter low enough for only her to hear me.

She quirks her brow.

"If you think for a second I'm gonna let you make me come in your hand, with my brother and best friend sitting a few feet away, and not in your mouth, you're sadly mistaken."

"I guess that means I'll have to give you my worst or, in this case, my best."

Like the little temptress she is, she turns her gaze back to the TV and slowly drags her fist up my hard length.

All I can think about is wishing there was some way I could get her pants down and drag her ass into my lap, so I could at least be inside her when I finish.

My body is tense with each stroke of her hand. When she lightly brushes her thumb over the tip, my balls tighten, and I grit my teeth to stave off my release for as long as I can.

"Shit, Hayes, I forgot to ask you. My timing belt on my car is making noise again. You mind lookin' at it before it gets too dark?" Reed bumps him on his arm.

The blinds are still open, but it's nearly pitch-black outside. The only light comes from the lamp across the street.

I glance over at Hayes as he smacks his hand down on his knee before flicking my gaze back to Reed. It isn't until Hayes agrees, shoving his feet back into his shoes and pushing himself to stand, that I notice Reed's subtle wink before he ducks his head and jogs down the steps behind him.

"Hallyn," I warn as soon as I hear the front door shut behind them. Her fist tightens around me, and I growl.

I slip my arms underneath her legs, sliding out from underneath her.

I quickly lean over the loveseat, parting the blinds to see the two of them pop the hood of his car for the second time in a week.

No way is he having issues with his timing belt again. Not when Hayes just helped him fix it.

I make a mental note to return the favor to Reed the next time the opportunity comes up.

"It looks like luck is on my side, and I'll get to feel that hot mouth around my dick sooner than I expected."

She drags her tongue along her lips, wetting them before dragging one between her teeth.

I push my shorts and underwear down my hips and wrap my hand around the base of my dick. This time, when she flicks her tongue over the tip, I use my other hand to slide my fingers into her hair and urge her forward.

"Goddamn, Halls, you're perfect."

She moans around me, tears forming in her eyes when she watches me.

"You like hearing me tell you how good your mouth feels?" I ask, and she nods subtly.

She brushes her tongue along the underside of my dick, and I groan, wrapping my hand around her chin, holding onto her.

"Relax your throat, baby," I moan, "and look up at me. I want to see tears in those pretty eyes while I fuck your mouth."

Her throat constricts when I test how much she can take, fucking her deeper and deeper. Her grip tightens on my hips, her nails digging into my ass, and I moan at how perfect her mouth is.

"I'm close, baby. It feels too fuckin' good, and I can't stop. Get ready."

She exhales a heavy breath through her nose, her lips tightening around me, sucking me hard, and I throw my head back and groan.

She hums when I pull out, a satisfied smirk taking over her face.

"I think I've created a monster," I growl.

CHAPTER 24

HALLYN

I was late leaving dance practice Friday night. Tomorrow is our away game in Englewood against the Panthers. They have a few buses traveling north with a bunch of Braysen students.

The football team will be leaving earlier than we will, arriving about an hour before the game kicks off at two thirty in the afternoon.

SJ ran through our plans—everything from our uniform for the game, arrival time, and all the other need-to-know details she could've sent in an email.

I quickly type in the lock code on our door and kick off my shoes when I step inside, making a mad dash for the bathroom.

Ava was behind me since we drove separately, and I know when she gets home, she'll be anxious to jump in the shower next. Before practice, she talked with Mandy about meeting up at The End Zone for drinks.

She may have intentionally let it slip about my date with Beckham. I was all too keen on making Sophie and anyone else around listening aware that Beckham is off-limits.

We may not have solidified our relationship yet, but I know that much is true.

I tie my hair up in a bun before I step into the shower, letting the water wash over me while I lather up my body. I don't have the time to blow-dry and style my hair, so I'm skipping the washing step to save me some time.

After I've exfoliated, shaved, and washed myself thoroughly, I hop out of the shower and quickly towel dry, wrapping the material around my body.

My laundry remains stacked in a basket from my trip to the community laundry room three days ago. I grip my towel in one fist while I use the other hand to sift through my clothes to find the off-the-shoulder sweater to wear with my distressed jeans.

It's not until I'm bent down when a strong gust of wind blows the sheer curtains in my bedroom, sending a shiver down my spine, that it clicks.

"Why is my window open?" I mumble out loud to myself.

I drop the clothes in my hand, pushing the curtains to the side and pulling the string to the blinds up to review the crack in my window.

It's barely open—maybe enough to stick my fingers in, but the part that has me stopping in my tracks is the fact the screen is popped out of the window.

I don't bother trying to figure out what to wear. After grabbing and slipping on the first pair of panties and a bra from my dresser, I pull on lounge shorts and a T-shirt, shove my feet into my sandals, and fly down the stairs.

It dawns on me when I'm racing through the grass, about to turn the corner at the front of our apartment building, that I probably shouldn't be doing this alone.

It's dangerous, and if I'm worried someone tried breaking into my place through my window, the last place I should be is outside searching for them or any clues to their plan.

I don't care, though. Anger and frustration over the whole break-in a couple of weeks ago is the only thing fueling me.

Sure enough, the screen to my apartment isn't lying haphazardly on the ground. I mean, if it were, I could try to reason it away that maybe the wind or the storm the other night did it.

Even though I know it's crazy to believe.

The fact it's leaning gently against the side of the building has my heart beating wildly in my chest, dropping to the pit of my stomach.

I reach in my pocket for my phone. At least in my frantic attempt to come down here, I did think to bring it with me. Without hesitating, I press the button on Beckham's name and race inside while the call rings.

"Hey, I'm about to head your way in about five, maybe ten minutes," he answers.

"Okay," I exhale. My breathing comes out heavier, a mixture of physical exertion and anxiety.

"Everything all right?" His voice turns serious.

"Yeah, I'm fine. Everything is fine," I rush out. "I just..." I glance around my bedroom, my brain all over the place while trying to sort out my thoughts and what to say. "I got home from dance and got out of the shower, and I noticed the window in my bedroom was open, but Beckham, I never opened the window. I've never once had it opened since I moved in here."

"What?" His voice deepens.

"It was only barely open, though. Cracked about an inch or so. The thing is, I don't know how long it's been that way."

"Well, it couldn't have been long," he quips. "I made Colter check when he left that morning after he brought you and Ava back to your place. He assured me it was locked up tight, and even mentioned checking the windows outside before he left."

My stomach churns. Who could've possibly tried breaking in through my bedroom window, and what could they be searching for?

"I'm leaving right now." He must sense my worry through the phone. "I can stay on the phone with you, if you want. Otherwise, I'll be there in just a few minutes."

"I'm fine. I'll let you go and see you when you get here. I need to finish getting ready."

After we hang up, I double-check that both windows in my room are closed and locked. The one that was cracked open is on the side of the building with very little light from the streetlamps.

The other is on the front, directly above the entry door. It would be impossible to sneak through that window without drawing attention to yourself.

My mind is still all over the place as I'm coasting through finding the outfit I planned on wearing and sitting down at my vanity to do my makeup.

Beckham arrives at the same time Ava gets home from dance, and I hear the two of them talking when she opens the door.

She pokes her head in, Beckham standing behind her. He's dressed in a pair of khaki shorts and a black button-up top, with the sleeves rolled up to show his tattoo.

He crosses his arms over his chest, listening intently while I tell Ava what happened. I try not to focus on his intense stare or the way his muscles cause the shirt to pull taut over his forearms.

She loops her arms around my neck, pulling me in for a hug.

"Maybe I'll ask my dad about getting one of those cameras. We can set a couple up on our windows and throughout the main areas of the apartment."

Her dad is everything I wish my dad had been for me.

Kind, loving, protective, consistent.

Present.

"If you don't mind," I mumble against her neck, glancing over her shoulder to see Beckham nodding in agreement.

"Of course, I don't mind. I haven't told him about the door," she admits, and I step away.

She shrugs. "You and I both know if I did, he'd be in his truck flying down here, threatening to haul my ass back to Beaufort."

We both laugh because it's the truth.

"The only way he would've compromised is by getting a camera."

"See." She walks toward the door, letting Beckham pass by. "I'll even let it be his idea too."

Ava leaves the two of us alone, mentioning how she needs to get cleaned up before she meets up with Colter.

Beckham closes the door behind him, pulling me into his arms.

"Are you sure you want to go out tonight? If you'd prefer, we can stay in instead."

I shake my head, raising my eyes to meet his.

"No, I want to go. I just need a few minutes to finish getting ready," I reassure him. "I don't want to let whoever is fuckin' with me ruin our night."

He nods, but his face changes, and I'm trying to pinpoint what he's about to say.

"When is the last time you spoke to Tanner?"

I pull away, taking a seat at my vanity again to put the finishing touches on my makeup. The mention of his name has guilt twisting in my stomach. Maybe a part of me feels guilty about how quickly I jumped into things with Beckham.

"He texted me a couple of days ago, saying he heard we're together."

I study Beckham's face in our reflection.

"How does he know?"

I recall our conversation when he brought up hearing about us hanging out when I was only tutoring him. "He told me he had eyes at Braysen, and the word got back to him."

It didn't take long after the last game against the Lions for people to start talking. It's not like I hadn't helped it by mentioning to Sophie, Leslie, and the rest of the dance and cheer teams that we were seeing each other.

"I didn't realize he had any other friends in town that would relay the information back to him."

I shrug. I've stopped underestimating the lengths Tanner will go to prove he's right.

"He was convinced we were messing around when he found out I was tutoring you. For all we know, he's still running with that same thought."

Beckham takes a seat on the edge of my bed, his hands linked together with his elbows pressed to his knees. He doesn't say anything or nag at me to hurry up like Tanner used to do.

Instead, he just watches me as I touch up the curls in my hair from earlier today. When I try waving him out of my room to change my clothes, he smirks and reclines against my pillows as if he's preparing himself for the show.

"Would it help if I told you to take your clothes off?" His eyelids grow heavy, studying me.

I think back to the first night we were together and how nervous I was. Something about the way he's looking at me now and the confidence it gave me, watching his reaction when we were viewing the movie together the other night, makes me want to take the lead.

Even if I do like it when he calls the shots.

I reach for the hem of my shirt and lift it, tossing it near the clean pile of clothes since I only had it on for a short time.

Beckham's eyes trail down my body, pausing on my ample chest hidden behind the light pink lace bra before continuing his path to where my hands grip the waistband of my shorts, eagerly waiting for me to continue.

He grows impatient, clearing his throat as if to urge me on. When that doesn't work, he adds, "Hallyn."

His low, throaty voice sends a shiver through me.

I don't know how he does it, but he can somehow lure me in until all I can see, hear, and think about is him.

I give in, pushing the cotton material over my hips, and let them drop to my feet. He sits up quickly, moving to the edge of the bed, and reaches his hand out for mine, pulling me between his legs.

"You sure you don't want to skip our plans for tonight?" he mumbles, dragging the back of his knuckle along my inner thigh.

My legs tremble, and I grip his shoulder. His chest rises and falls quickly, and it makes me feel good to know I'm not the only one feeling the intensity between us.

"And miss the chance to be the first girl at Braysen to go on a real date with Beckham Carver?" He lifts his eyes to mine. "Not a chance."

"And only," he adds, and my eyes narrow.

"You said first, and I said and only. The first and only. I won't ever go on a date with anyone else. Only you."

I press my palms to the side of his face and lean forward to kiss him.

He drove me crazy and got under my skin when we first met, but somehow, he's the only person who can have my stomach fluttering with butterflies after only a look or a few simple words.

His lips are soft, and he reaches for my hips, urging me onto his lap when I shake my head, pulling away.

He never takes his eyes off me while I tug on my pants and my top.

"You're tryin' to drive me fuckin' crazy all night, aren't you?"

"Maybe..." I smirk. "We still have a long night ahead of us."

He reaches down, gripping his dick through the front of his khakis. There's no disguising it either in his shorts.

"I still have to work out a plan to get you back for the movie night."

I bite my lip, turning to face the mirror while I clasp my gold necklace around my neck. We lock eyes in the reflection once more, and I smile.

"I look forward to it too."

CHAPTER 25

BECKHAM

I keep my hand on her thigh during the entire drive to the beach. I play it off like I don't notice how her other leg bounces or the subtle way her chest heaves.

She leans over when the song on the radio changes and turns the volume up to disguise her voice while she sings along.

She's doing it to shift her focus to something else. When I brush my finger along her pants, she folds her hand over the top of mine, linking our fingers together to stop me.

Sugar Bottom is the local beach not far from the South Carolina-Georgia border, where the Savannah River meets the ocean. Nearby is Black Rock Cove, the spot my brother took me cliff jumping after moving to Braysen this past summer.

It was the first time I hung out with Colter, Reed, and some of the guys from the team.

It's one of my favorite spots. I came down here after our last game to sort out my mind. I was feeling a bit hard on myself for the way I played. Injury or not, if it weren't for our defense, we wouldn't have won.

That's a weight I carry on my shoulders because the team looks at me to show up at those moments, and I let them down.

We pull in, and Hallyn glances at me, then back to the beach. The sand is white, and the waters are beautiful, especially now, as the sky turns a mixture of pink and orange as the sun sets in the distance.

"What do you have up your sleeve, Carver?"

I don't know why it turns me on when she calls me Carver. Maybe it's because she's the first girl I've ever spent time with who I truly picture giving my last name.

What the hell is wrong with me?

I called earlier this week to order takeout from Rosey's, a local diner. It's a small mom-and-pop spot that reminds me of the restaurant I used to go to growing up with my parents.

"Let's go." I grin, pushing the door open. I open the back door and pull out the insulated bag I brought with me when I picked up our dinner.

Her brows dip when she circles the back of the pickup, finding me standing there with a blanket slung over my shoulder and the bag in my hand.

"Here, let me take this from you," she says, reaching for the basket with our drinks in it.

The beach is quiet. A couple throws a Frisbee with their dog, but they appear to be walking in the other direction, leaving the two of us alone.

I set the bag down and unfold the blanket, spreading it out for us to sit on.

Hallyn kicks off her shoes and takes the seat next to me. She's biting her lip and subtly shakes her head, her eyes searching mine.

"What's that look for?"

"You just surprise me is all."

"Oh yeah?" I chuckle, unzipping the bag. "Well, I hope you like smoked turkey and bacon wraps. I also got us pasta salad and a small char-coochie board."

"Char-coochie?" She throws her head back and laughs.

It wasn't long ago when I showed up at her place, and she was riddled with stress and anxiety. I almost felt bad for following through with our plans tonight, but she was right.

We couldn't let it ruin our night even though my mind spins as to who could possibly be fucking with her. Not once, but twice now. Is it Tanner, and is it connected to the text message I got the other day?

She opens her wrap, her tongue flicking across her lips subconsciously, and takes a bite. She hums around it and nods. "So good. So, so good."

If it weren't for our athletic trainers riding my ass about what I'm eating, I'd be like every other college student and getting by on frozen pizzas and microwaveable noodles.

"You went to school in Tennessee last year, right? What made you go there and then transfer to Braysen?"

I take another bite, thinking through her question.

"The truth? Well, I wanted to go to school where my best friend, Talon, plays hockey. The truth is it was a move to tick my dad off."

He still calls me before and after every game, but accepting the scholarship to Tennessee meant I was out from under his thumb.

"My dad has always ridden Hayes and me hard regarding sports. After we won the championship back home in Charlotte, it still felt like it wasn't enough. He couldn't even let me celebrate the win. He was already thinking about the next thing—college, what top schools were offering me the chance to play. I was offered the QB spot at Braysen back then, too, but I didn't accept it. A part of me wanted to rebel, go against the grain, take the route everyone least expected. Rixton isn't known for being a football college. Their hockey team is what has made a name for them, so when I turned in my acceptance and told my dad that's where I was playing, part of me felt like I was sending a message. He couldn't control me anymore."

She crawls toward me, and I open my legs to her, wrapping my arm around her shoulders.

"Well, then what made you come to Braysen this year? Why not stay at Rixton and play there?"

"Hayes." I clench my jaw and stare down at her hand holding mine. "He needed me. Even though he said he didn't, and everything was fine, I knew better, ya know? He's my brother, my twin, and no matter what he says or does, I'll always know when he's not being honest with me."

She nods, not even needing me to explain the circumstances any further. His reputation is something that has been talked about all over campus. I know he hates that he can't seem to shake it.

"Before our game against the Kings, someone left a note in my locker. They meant to leave it for him, though. He doesn't know, and I won't tell him until after the season ends, if I even do."

"What did it say?" she mutters.

"Some bullshit, calling him a dirty player."

Her face softens in sympathy, and she nods. "Don't tell him. It's not gonna change anything but make it harder to move past."

She has a point there, and that's exactly why I've been wrestling with telling him at all.

We finish our food, and I pack our stuff in our bag before pulling out the homemade brownies I had Rosey throw in.

She grins when I unwrap it, holding the warm and gooey treat to her mouth and taking a bite. Chocolate coats her lips, and she laughs, swiping her tongue across her skin.

I shake my head when she covers her mouth as if trying to hide herself every time she eats. It makes me wonder what other things she's self-conscious about doing and how I can strip away all those worries and fears to reveal the confident and self-assured woman she keeps hidden.

Without thinking, I lean forward and crash my lips on hers.

She moans against my mouth, holding her hands back to avoid getting any chocolate on me. When I pull back, I hold her hand to my mouth and drag her finger over my tongue, first one and then the other.

Her eyes blaze as she stares at me. We both take one more bite of our brownie before she crawls into my lap, straddling me, and wraps her arms around my neck.

"I think we're alone out here," she mumbles.

I push myself up to my elbows, and the couple who was farther down the beach is gone. She looks in the opposite direction, then back at me with a mischievous glimmer in her eyes.

"What do you have on your mind, naughty girl?"

I circle my arms around her waist, rolling her until I'm on top of her now. She yelps and giggles, but abruptly stops when I lean in and trail my nose over her cheek to her ear.

"Hmm?" I hum. "Are you thinking about me pulling these jeans off, pulling those pretty little pink panties you're wearing to the side, and fucking you right here where anyone could see us?"

She doesn't answer, only grabs the side of my face and pulls me into her, crushing our lips together. She hooks her legs around my waist, and I grind my dick against her.

"Are you wet thinking about me fucking you out here?" I groan, and she nods.

I pull back and drag her into my lap again. My fingers skate along the edge of her top, slipping my hand beneath the material.

My hand is cool against her skin from the night sky falling over us, the temperatures dropping as the sun disappears.

Her stomach trembles against my palm. Her breaths grow labored as I run my fingers under her breast before tugging the material down and brushing my thumb over her nipple.

She arches her back into me, and her eyes grow heavy.

"You fit so perfectly in my arms, in my hands, like you were made just for me."

"You mean it?"

I lean away from her to look at her face. "Have I given you any reason to believe I would be lying?"

She shakes her head and swallows hard.

"Tell me what you're thinking," I say again. Only my tone is serious this time, and I pull my hand away.

She quickly folds her hand on top of mine over her shirt, stopping me.

"You want to know what's on my mind?"

I nod.

"I'm thinking about the way you make me feel. Like your touch sears into my skin, and your gaze burns into me, stripping away any doubt, making me feel beautiful and wanted."

"I want you," I agree. "I want all of you, every fuckin' inch." I move my hand over her heart. "I want in every dark corner and thought of your mind, every part of you that has been touched by anyone else and make you mine."

"I am yours."

My fingers tangle into her hair, gripping the back of her head and pulling her into me.

"C'mon," I urge, pulling my hand out of her shirt and reach for hers.

She pulls back, her brows deepening. "Where are we going?"

"Back to my place. It's late, it's dark, and I need you in my bed tonight."

She presses her lips together and nods. She hurries to pack up our drinks while I shake the sand out of the blanket, and we head back to my truck.

Our hands are linked together, and her lips tease me, brushing over my cheek, my neck, forearm, and even the back of my hand during the entire drive to my place.

The light in the kitchen is on, but judging by the empty driveway, no one is here. I hadn't expected anyone to be, though. The guys planned to go to Whiskey Sinner's tonight even though we need to be up and out the door early for our away game tomorrow.

I lead her up the stairs and down the hall to my room. We didn't even bother to unpack the stuff from the beach when we got home.

Most of the food is gone, but everything else can wait until tomorrow.

She spins on her heels the second the door clicks shut. I lean in, pressing my lips against her mouth.

"You can find a pair of my shorts and a shirt to wear if you want," I whisper against her lips. "I'm gonna use the bathroom quick."

She smiles and nods while I step away for a minute. This isn't the first time she's stayed over with me, and I half expected her to do what I said: find one of my T-shirts and a pair of shorts while she waited for me on my bed.

Yet Hallyn always has a way of throwing me off my game.

When I step out of the bathroom and flick off the light to find her wearing my jersey I left hanging on the back of my chair, my footsteps falter, and I gape at her.

"Come here," I order, and she smirks, crawling across the bed.

I can't quite tell if she's wearing anything underneath, and the thought catches my breath in my chest.

"Turn around, Hallyn."

She drags her hair over her shoulder. My jersey falls past her mid-thigh. She glances at me, and then down to where my name is printed in block letters across her back, a devious smile curling her lips.

I reach into my pocket and pull out my phone, snapping a few pictures of her as she stares back at me before tossing it onto my desk.

I take a step toward her, molding her back to my front, and reach down for the hem, pulling the jersey up to check if she's still wearing her panties.

She's not, and the sight of her bare pussy concealed by nothing but my jersey has me rocking my dick against her.

I wrap my arm around her waist, holding her against me like a rubber band, and lift her onto the edge of the bed. She's thrown off guard when I push her chest down, lifting her hips so she's lined up perfectly with my waist.

"Mmm, fuck, I can see how wet you are."

I drag my finger over her clit, up to her pussy, and dip the tip into her tight heat. She clenches around me before I quickly pull out.

Her hands fist the sheets, and I make a show of holding my finger up where she can see me and sucking it into my mouth.

She sways her ass in the air, and I quickly land a hard slap on her ass, earning me a delicious moan.

"All you've been doing is teasing me," I mutter. "I think it's time I do some teasing of my own, don't you think?"

I fall to my knees behind her, burying my face between her legs. I flick and suck her clit before trailing my tongue to her pussy, stopping to fuck her, then continue my path to flick over her ass.

She releases a loud and throaty groan.

"You like that, baby? My naughty girl." My dick hardens at the sound. "You wait. One of these days, I'm going to fuck you there too."

I turn her over on her back, pressing her thighs against her chest. When I slowly brush my thumb over her clit, my finger slowly entering her, her mouth drops open, and her eyes roll shut.

She tightens her pussy, clenching me like a vise. My dick strains hard at my zipper, desperate to break free and feel her tight pussy around me.

"Tonight, though," I murmur against her. "Tonight, I'm going to prove to you, you were never broken. You were just waiting for me to show you that you were mine all along."

I curl my finger inside her, brushing over the bundle of nerves, and her hips come off the bed. She reaches her arms out wide, digging her fingers into the mattress, desperate for something to hold on to.

"See, baby," I croon, smacking my fingers against her pussy. She cries out. "Come on my fingers and let me taste you."

I latch my lips onto her clit and suck, and she clenches her thighs around my head, rocking her hips while she grinds and fucks my face.

I moan, my lips adding vibration to her clit. It isn't long before she starts chanting that she's coming, and her body goes tense as the wave of her orgasm rocks through her.

When her body grows lax, I stand and push my jeans off, quickly shedding my shirt in the process before I climb over her.

I brush the tip of my dick through her wet folds, and my eyes roll shut as I slowly slip inside her.

"Oh my God," she groans, and I bury my face into her shoulder until every inch of our upper bodies melt together.

The last time, it was fast and rough, but it's passionate and unhurried this time.

When I lean back enough to brush my finger over her clit and we finish together, it's my name on her lips.

As if to say she knows she's mine.

And has been all along.

I've been living with my head in the sand for the past few weeks. Between football, Hallyn, school, and fitting in work, I completely forgot about the text message I got from the unknown number.

Even though I tried to push it out of my mind and live in the present with Hallyn that night, the first chance I was alone, I called up Talon to ask him about it.

The fall is super busy for us both—him with hockey and me focusing on football—which made it hard for either of us to get the other on the phone.

"I'm tellin' you, man, you have nothing to worry about. I haven't heard shit about what went down, and we both know it would've been me if they were on the hunt for anyone," he grunts.

He has a point there, but still. We were both there that night and had a hand in what happened.

It all started when Talon and his cousin, Kolt, got wind of a couple of hockey players starting shit with Talon's sister.

She downplayed it at first as immature teasing, but then the truth started to come out.

They should've known who they were fucking with the moment they started messing with them. We weren't about to let them get away with it too.

There were rumors going around after we confronted them that the fight left their star player, James, with a broken shoulder, forcing him out for the rest of the season.

Sorrows. Sorrows and prayers.

We left him messed up good and threatened him that if anything came out about the fight, we'd make sure to hit him back ten times harder. The dirt we stirred up on this fucker made sure he'd be good on his promise.

Or I guess, so we thought.

"I still don't know who it could be fuckin' with me. Unless it's my girl's douchebag of an ex, but something like this doesn't seem right. Why send some ominous message? When I tried calling them back later, the number was disconnected."

It wasn't adding up.

"Probably one of those text apps. Hell, brother, it's probably just someone fuckin' with you. You know how people are in college, man. The pranks run wild."

I pull up outside of Kavlik's and put my truck into park.

"Yeah, you're probably right."

He had a point, but still. Something wasn't sitting right with me, and I couldn't quite put my finger on it.

"How's Tatum?" I ask him, glancing out the window. "Have things settled down around there?"

"She's okay. I'm starting to wonder if staying here is holding her back, though. Maybe we all need a change of scenery like you."

"Our door is always open. You know that."

He answers with a muffled, "Yeah."

We end our conversation there when he lets me know he just got to the gym for conditioning. He promises to hit me up later this week after my game.

I arrived at work a little early, hoping to talk to Hank before my shift starts. He's bent over his keyboard, his elbows pressed to his knees, studying his laptop screen. I knock on the doorframe to get his attention, but he doesn't bother to look up from his computer.

"What's up?" he says absentmindedly.

"I was hoping I could talk to you for a minute about my upcoming schedule," I say, clapping my hands together.

He leans back in his chair, his gaze finally meeting mine.

"Sure thing. What's goin' on?"

"Well, I told you how I've been stressing over my grades. I picked up tutoring sessions and managed to bump it up enough to get Coach off my ass."

He crosses his arms over his chest and nods.

"Well, we're halfway through the season now, and shit is only getting more challenging. Several of our remaining games are against top-ranking teams. I was hoping maybe you could bump me from the schedule through the end of the year. At least until we know if we have any prayer of making it to the national championship."

"I figured this was coming." He chuckles. "That brother of yours was in here asking me the same thing yesterday."

He mumbles under his breath something about, "What the hell am I gonna do with all you fuckers dropping like flies?"

He's a grumpy old man, but even I know he's only messing with me.

"I'll tell you the same thing I told him. Give me a week to sort out how I'm gonna fill your spots, but we'll make it happen. All right?"

"You got it. Thanks, Hank, I appreciate it."

He nods toward the door, his silent way of ending the conversation. I tilt my head and step out. The front is empty, which it often is by this time.

Whoever was scheduled before me must've cut out of here as soon as the time hit five o'clock.

I run through the list of shit leftover from the day shift, along with our closing duties, when the doorbell to the shop dings.

It takes me a second before I drag my eyes away from the notepad. He looks different than he did the first time I met him at Whiskey Sinner's, so I don't recognize him at first. That night he was dressed like he was about to sit down for a business meeting, fitted with a pair of dress slacks and a polo.

Today is more of the same, although his once slicked-back hair is unkept and messy as if he couldn't have been bothered to style it.

His khakis are wrinkled, and I wonder if he dug them out of his dirty clothes hamper and pulled them on. Same with his polo, the Keaton logo on his chest.

It isn't until he slips off his aviator sunglasses, revealing the dark circles under his eyes, that it finally clicks.

Tanner.

"May I help you?" I ask, skipping the pleasantries and getting straight to the point.

He folds his glasses, hanging them from the V-neck of his shirt.

"Oh good, so you do remember me." His words come out low, mumbled. For a second, I start to wonder if he's had a few drinks before he waltzed in here.

I don't bother entertaining his question, though, and just nod at him, waiting for him to spill it.

"Well, since you remember me, and I'm sure you can figure out why I'm here, I'll cut to the chase. I'm here to pay for whatever is owed on the repairs for Hallyn's truck."

He reaches into his pocket and pulls out a leather wallet, flipping it open to display the credit cards, namely the black American Express card on top.

I chuckle and shake my head. "That won't be necessary. The balance has been paid in full."

His nostrils flare, and he shakes his head. "No, I think you're missing the point. I know about the little arrangement the two of you have. I know she's still helping you. So tell me, what does she still owe you? I'm here to pay for it. Whatever the two of you have, it's done."

I press my palms flat against the counter and lean into him.

"I don't know what's not sinking into that dense fuckin' skull of yours, but let me say it to you again. She doesn't owe shit. Not me, not you. You hear me? So you can tuck daddy's credit card away, pick up your pride off the floor, and get the hell out of here."

I can feel my pulse beating wildly. I clench my jaw, waiting for the moment he pushes me further.

"Now that's where you're wrong, Carver. Hallyn and I have a long history together. We go back years. She belongs to me. She loves me, and the two of us have a future planned together. I refuse to let you come in, treat her like another one of your one-night fucks, and throw her to the side," he growls. "You hear me? She's mine."

I push off the tabletop and step back, releasing a loud, throaty laugh. It's forced, fake. I cut it off, turning to saunter around the counter, coming toe-to-toe with the little prick I plan to take down on the field in just a couple of weeks.

"You see, that's where you're wrong. She's not yours. I'd wager she hasn't been since the moment she stepped foot in Braysen and first met me."

"You think you know her? You think she won't see through this bullshit eventually? I've heard everything about you, Carver. You've only been in Braysen for, what, a couple of months now? Yet somehow, you've assembled quite the roster of hookups."

"I don't know what you think you know or what you've heard, but just because I've spent time with women doesn't mean I've hooked up with them. It doesn't matter, though. You seem to think you have this claim over Hallyn like you own her. That's where you're wrong," I growl. "You don't know a damn thing about her or her wants and needs."

"You think you do?"

I grin wildly. I'd love nothing more than to detail all the ways I know exactly what Hallyn wants and needs.

Except I refuse to diminish or demean what I have with her. Just because I know how to take care of her in and out of the bedroom doesn't mean I'm going to twist it to dig the knife in deeper.

"Let's put it this way, Freeman. I took your spot as the Bulldogs QB, just like I took your girl. Before you embarrass yourself any further, get your punk ass out of this shop and Braysen. The next time I see you, it'll be when I take your chance at a conference championship too."

He curls his lip in a snarl and backs up from me. He swipes his wallet and shoves it in his back pocket, then stalks out of the shop.

"You know, you sure can be an asshole when you want to be?" my brother says from behind me.

I turn my head, glancing over my shoulder at him.

He has a rag in his hand, leaning against the doorframe with an easy smile. His relaxed demeanor makes me think he stood there, taking in the show the whole time.

"Like you aren't?" I grunt.

"Cut from the same damn cloth." He grins.

He's always been the jokester between the two of us. I got called to the principal's office for starting fights, but he got into trouble for messing around.

He orchestrated our senior prank when he turned the two main hallways at school into a giant slip 'n' slide. He was suspended for three days, which wasn't much punishment, considering those were the final days of school.

"Do you think he's behind the break-ins at their place?" Hayes asks, his tone turning serious.

"I wouldn't put it past him."

A part of me is still trying to work out why, though. If it's not him, is it somehow connected to her relationship with me? If so, what does the text message have to do with it?

"All I know is if I find out he is, or if he lays a hand on her, I'll do more than end his football season."

I'd make sure he never knew peace if he ever tried to hurt her.

I've taken two of the most important things in his life. I won't even hesitate to take away football too.

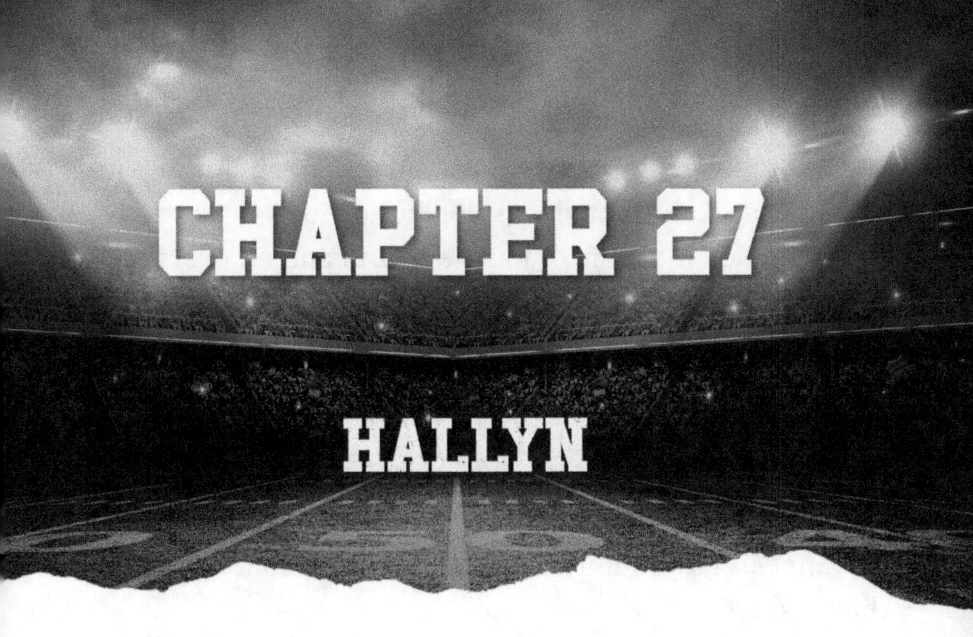

"When Erica's family hadn't heard from her after twenty-four hours, they contacted the police to report her missing."

My face is buried in my chemistry textbook, and I'm jotting down notes from our lecture today, making some test questions for Beckham and my other tutor students while another true crime documentary plays in the background.

I'm zoned out, so it takes me a second to differentiate whether the two knocks on the door are coming from my apartment or the show.

I glance up and freeze, my eyes flicking back and forth while I listen for any noise or movement from the hallway. The remote sits next to me on the arm of the chair, and I hit the volume button to lower the sound when two knocks follow.

The time on the digital clock in the entertainment center reads after seven. Beckham is working at the auto shop tonight. We didn't have plans to see each other after, but maybe he got off early and decided to stop by.

"One second," I holler, shuffling the book and notepad from my lap to the couch cushion beside me.

I'm dressed in a pair of lounge shorts and an oversized top hanging off one of my shoulders. I quickly hurry toward the door, eager to see Beckham, but I see another familiar face when I glance in the peephole.

Tanner.

My fingers reach for the door handle, flipping the lock and opening it.

"Tanner?" I say, but it comes out as a question. "Is everything okay?"

His eyes almost appear frantic as he glances past me into the apartment and back to my face. How the hell did he get into our building?

"Can I come in?" He exhales, rubbing his hands together.

His hair is longer than it was the last time I saw him. His normally clean-shaven face has stubble growing in, and the look in his eyes reminds me of the time we took a trip up to Seattle after graduation.

It was our first time traveling together, a graduation gift from his parents to both of us. I had never flown before, and the flight coming home was hell. After being delayed twice, we didn't get back to our place until the next day. By that point, it had been over twenty-four hours since we'd last slept.

I nod and take a step back to let him in. He pushes the door open farther, causing it to slam against the wall, and I jump.

"Jesus, Tanner, what the hell?"

"I guess I just didn't think I'd have to drive all this way to have a conversation with you. I've been trying to get in touch with you for, what, almost three weeks now? You can't seem to remember how to work your phone now or what?"

I cross my arms around my waist. Something about his tone doesn't sit right with me.

We've gotten into fights before. Heck, I've lost count of how many arguments.

Those times were different, though. Even when he got mad or upset and raised his voice, he didn't slam things, and he didn't have this cold and sinister tone he has now.

"We broke up, Tanner. I told you it was best if we had space. I was giving us what we both needed, and that was time apart."

He nods slowly, running his hand along the back of the couch, his eyes scouring every inch of my apartment as if taking in every detail.

"I stopped by that car shop you told me about, the one you took your truck to, and talked to your boyfriend." He chuckles, a wide grin stretching across his face. "Did he tell you?"

My throat bobs at the mention of Beckham and the reference to him being my boyfriend.

"Tanner, what is this about?" I ask, skipping straight to the point.

He tilts his head to the side and chuckles. "He may have gotten my spot on the team, but did you really think I would let him have you too?"

My mouth drops open, but I snap it shut, my eyes narrowing on his.

"Excuse me?"

He takes a step toward me, then another, closing the distance between us.

"You heard me, Hallyn. Did you really think I was gonna believe that you two were only helping each other out? That he fixed your piece of shit truck, and you returned the favor by tutoring him? Did it ever dawn on you to let the fucker fail the class? Maybe he deserved it. After all, his spot on the team should've been mine to begin with."

The mention of him referring to the quarterback position as being his, as if he owned it, was the tipping point for me.

Just like he felt it should've been handed to him, like it belonged to him.

"Tanner, our entire relationship consisted of you ordering me around, fitting me into this mold of what you wanted your girlfriend to be. When I didn't follow you to Keaton, you did everything you could to drive me out of Braysen and back to you. You fail to realize that's exactly what drove a wedge between us and why we aren't together now."

I shake my head, stomping toward the door.

"For the record, did it ever dawn on you that maybe you didn't get the spot on the team because of your self-entitled attitude? You don't get to march around here, commanding people to fall into line because it's what you want. Just like respect, you have to earn a spot on the team. You aren't owed anything."

I open the door and step back, motioning with my hand for him to leave.

He shakes his head, and I think he's going to leave for a second, but he stops when he reaches me. He stares down his nose, and his eyes and the cruel curve of his smile leave an uneasy feeling in my stomach.

How could I have been so blind to who he truly was?

"I don't know what has gotten into you, but we both know that spot on the team was supposed to be mine. I'm a man of my word. I won't let him take you from me too." He shakes his head. "It'll be a cold day in hell before I let it happen."

He stalks out the door and turns, disappearing down the stairs leading out the front entrance.

My mind is wild, trying to wrap my head around what he said before I snap out of it and quickly slam the door shut. I flip the lock, racing across the living room to the sliding glass door leading to the small patio overlooking the parking lot.

I push the blinds to the side, waiting for him to leave. It's hard to see in the darkness with the lights on behind me until a pair of headlights flash on, and I drop the blinds and step back.

My phone sits next to the remote on the couch, and I reach for it, scrolling through my messages with Tanner over the past week. I muted the notifications after the fifth day he reached out.

I would've responded eventually, but I have to admit, I didn't know what to say to him. Each time I saw a text from him, I felt more guilty.

Why did I feel guilty, though?

I think in some sense it's because I knew my friendship, relationship, whatever was going on with Beckham would eventually make its way back to him. He would be crushed, but I did it anyway.

I also believed that no matter what was going on between us, our relationship ran its course. As hard and as hurtful as it was to accept, the only way to fully heal and move on was by cutting off communication.

When I went to stay with my grandparents last summer after we broke up the first time, the only thing that helped me was getting away from home and all the reminders of him.

I think that's what being here at Braysen has been for me too. Although we planned to attend college here and pursue our passions, this place was new and untainted by our memories.

I scroll through endless messages from him. There were a lot more than I realized, several each day, all of which have gone unanswered.

My finger hovers over the photo of us saved as his contact name, and I remove it. The couple in the picture is so far from who we are now. Then I scroll down to the bottom and click on block right as Beckham's face appears on my screen.

"Hello?"

"Halls, you okay?" Beckham asks, skipping a greeting. "I'm just pulling up outside. I'll be up in a minute."

"Wait, you're here?" I answer.

I barely have a chance to stand before he replies, "Open the door for me."

I hit the buzzer to let him in the entrance. Somehow, Tanner seemed to get past it. I peered through the peephole again. At this point, I'm paranoid that maybe Tanner saw him coming and turned around to come back.

For the first time in twenty minutes, I exhale a heavy sigh and open the door to him.

He ends the call, slipping his phone into his pocket, and reaches for me as he steps through the threshold. His hands find their way to my hips, continuing lower to my thighs, and he lifts me into his arms.

"Tanner was here, wasn't he?" He glances around the room.

I loop my arms around his neck and lean back to look at him.

"How did you know?"

He doesn't bother answering, carrying me with him through the dining room to my room. The door is cracked, but he uses his shoulder to push it open before kicking it shut with his foot.

He sits on the edge of the mattress, and I adjust my position, my legs straddling his lap and still holding on to him.

"He came by Kavlik's. When I tried calling you and you didn't answer, I took off and headed this way."

"You called?" I ask, my brows deepening. I hadn't even realized my phone was on silent nor did I notice a missed call.

"What did he say to you?"

I shake my head, massaging my fingers into my temple. "He just kept going on and on about how you took his spot on the team, and he wasn't going to let you have me too."

Beckham tightens his lips and shakes his head. "I figured. I may have let my temper get to me and told him you were mine, just like I took his QB spot."

My lip curls, fighting off my smile.

"I'm yours, huh?"

"That's the part you're choosing to focus on?" He smirks.

I shrug. "Say it again."

He leans in, brushing his nose along mine. His eyes stay locked on me, and I can feel the warmth of his breath on my lips.

"You're mine, Hallyn Rivers. There's not an asshole in this town, or hell, this country, who I'm going to let hurt you or take you from me."

"Say it again."

He chuckles, rolling us over until I'm pinned beneath him. I hook my arm around his neck and pull him closer, only this time he doesn't tease me or lean away. When our lips crash together, he moans against my mouth, and I tremble when he drags his hands along the sides of my body.

How does he somehow make me forget the fact my ex-boyfriend was here not long ago, crazed with jealousy and making threats?

I don't care, though, because when Beckham tells me he isn't going to let anyone hurt me or take me away, I believe him.

In the beginning, I never thought I would, but I do.

He breaks his kiss and tilts his body away from me, trailing his hand over my stomach up to my chest, folding his palm over my heart.

"One day soon, this is going to be mine too. I promise."

Warmth spreads through my body, and I blink through the tears forming in my eyes at his sincerity.

I don't know what this feeling blooming inside me is, but it's different from anything I've ever felt before.

Maybe it's love. I don't know, but if I know one thing for certain—if that's all I have to give to him, it's his.

He can have all of me.

CHAPTER 28

BECKHAM

When Halloween rolled around a few weeks later, everyone talked about a party out at Greencastle.

A lot has changed between Hallyn and me since the last one out here. Tonight will be our first time showing up to a party together, making it known to everyone we're more than friends and damn sure more than a hookup.

"Are you ready?" I ask, leaning against the doorframe of the bathroom.

A shot of arousal spikes when she turns to face me, and my eyes trail down her body, taking in her referee uniform. She's wearing a black miniskirt and a black-and-white-striped top with a whistle hanging around her neck and black lines across the apples of her cheeks.

"Who are you refereeing tonight, baby?" I grin, reaching for her hips to tug her body toward me.

"You." She returns my smile, and I moan. "I guess that means I'm callin' the shots."

I quirk my brow as she trails her nail over my chest, eliciting a low hiss.

After what felt like an hour, Ava finished painting the skull on my face. The level of detail in her work is impeccable.

Yet I'm willing to risk messing it up before I ever step foot out the door when I drag her ass into my room and let her do just what she's promised.

"We can blow this party if you want."

She giggles and shakes her head. "Ava would come in and haul your ass outta here if she knew you were wasting all her hard work. Plus, I plan on giving it some time, dragging it out before I have my way with you."

She trails her hand lower to the black denim jeans and the obvious bulge forming beneath the zipper. I inhale a sharp breath when she cups her hand to wrap around my length and thrust against her hand.

My fingers tangle in the strands of her blonde hair, tugging on them enough until she tilts her head back, her eyes meeting mine.

"I'll have no problem lifting that sweet little skirt of yours in the middle of that damn field and fucking the innocent smile right off your face."

Her eyes lower in a daze. She moves to nod, but my grip on her hair is tight, making the movement subtle.

I release her, turning her to spin around, facing the mirror in front of us.

My fingers brush over the glimpse of her stomach beneath her breast, along the lace of the corset top she's wearing underneath, and wrap my palm around her throat.

She tilts her head against my shoulder, the low groan vibrating on my hand.

"You're going to torture me all night, aren't you?" I mutter.

Her eyes gleam, and I flare my nostrils. She knows where to dig her nails to drive me crazy every time.

"I have to test the limits somehow. See what makes you tick."

I clench my jaw and grind my dick against her ass. She grips my arm, arching her back to give it just as good as she gets.

"Are you two ready to leave, or should I tell the guys we'll meet you there?"

I drop my hands to my side and step back. I didn't even hear Ava enter my room, which is saying a lot, considering this old-ass house creaks with every footstep you make.

"We're ready," Hallyn answers for both of us. "Beckham was just telling me how excited he was for the party tonight. Ain't that right, Carver?"

She flashes a devious smile, patting her hand against my chest as she follows Ava down the hall.

We'll see about that, won't we?

Hallyn rides with me to the party, so we're alone again until we arrive. The last thing I want is to be stuck out in a field with a bunch of drunk fuckers without a way home.

Not to mention, I wanted an escape route for the moment she pushes me too far, and I'm ready to drag her ass out of there.

I may have underestimated the number of people coming out to Greencastle tonight. If I was ready to ditch the party before, I sure as hell am now.

She waits for me to climb out of my truck and circle to her side to open the door and help her down.

Rob Zombie blares off in the distance. Hallyn slips her hand into mine, leading us through the rows of vehicles parked before I stop. She takes another step, not realizing I've halted my movement, stopping her mid-step.

I tug on her arm and pull her back to me, wrapping my arms around her waist. She giggles when I lift her chin, our lips a hairbreadth away.

"You're beautiful, you know that?" I murmur.

Her eyes blink slowly.

"And you're sweet when you want to be," she replies.

"Only with you." I brush my lips over hers, wrapping my palm around the side of her face.

She deepens the kiss, her tongue seeking entrance, and I open up to her. I haven't had a taste of alcohol all night, yet I'm somehow drunk on her.

"Let's get this over with so we can get out of here."

When we eventually make our way to the crowd, she spots her friends huddled in a circle near the fire and jogs ahead toward them.

The temperatures are cooler tonight, but it's surprisingly warm for the end of October. It's the perfect weather for playing football, and I hope it sticks around tomorrow when we face Keaton.

There's been a lot of anticipation for this game, and I must admit, I want nothing more than to go head-to-head against Freeman.

It's put up or shut up time, and this win will be the one to knock them out of the race for the conference championship.

Both teams have a lot riding on this game, but the thought of taking this from Tanner would make that victory oh, so sweet.

Colter spots me, two beers in hand, and I notice he has one shoved in his pocket too. We all agreed to take it easy tonight. We'll have enough to loosen up and have fun, but we know what's at stake tomorrow.

We're not about to fuck it up.

"How're you feelin' about tomorrow?" Reed asks, staring intently at the fire.

Every couple of minutes, my eyes find their way back to Hallyn a few yards away.

She's dancing with her girlfriends, and at times, they all throw their hands up and their heads back to sing along. It's the most relaxed and carefree I've seen her since we've met. Even though we haven't spoken much about it since the night Tanner showed up, I think the finality of him leaving and where we are now has brought a sense of peace.

"Honestly, I'm feelin' great. We're locked in. I know I am, anyway. Practice went well today. We got this."

I eye Colter, trying to get a read on his thoughts. He nods, lifting his beer in cheers, but he's too busy staring ahead at the girls.

Ava wears a shimmery white tank top and a pale pink and green tutu. I mistakenly assumed her iridescent makeup meant she was going for the mermaid costume.

She corrected me on it, clarifying she's actually a fairy before motioning to the wings draped over the side of the couch.

Somehow, that seemed more fitting for her.

"Beckham," a high-pitched voice says from behind us, and I turn to see who it is.

Leslie's eyes light up when I spot her, taking the liberty of stepping into my side and wrapping her arm around my waist to greet me with a hug.

"I almost didn't recognize you with all that makeup on." She giggles. I hold my arm up, not returning the gesture, and she leans back to stare at me beneath her long fake lashes.

I release a low growl at how she took it upon herself to touch me, especially when I have no doubt Hallyn saw. What didn't she get after the last time I talked to her about seeing someone, even if it was all bullshit about a date?

My eyes quickly dart over in Hallyn's direction, but I don't see her anywhere.

"Can I help you?" I growl.

"It's been a while, and I've missed seeing you around. How have you been?"

I step back to give us some distance, and she begrudgingly drops her arm.

"We got Rivers flowing in at two o'clock." Colter holds his beer up to cover his mouth, speaking low enough for only me to hear.

It takes me a second for it to click in my mind, right about when Hallyn steps between us, taking her spot at my side.

"Hey, Leslie, nice to see you slithering around," Hallyn snickers.

Leslie's mouth snaps shut, and I press my lips together to keep from laughing. She knew what she was doing when she came over here. I don't know if she thought I'd entertain her or if she was trying to get under Hallyn's skin.

If so, I think it's safe to say it worked even though I know Hallyn won't give her the satisfaction of finding out.

I lift my beer and take a heavy swig. When Leslie doesn't move to leave, her gaze darts back and forth between us, analyzing our connection.

I don't know what I expected to happen when Hallyn reaches up, slipping her hand around my neck and pulling me down until our lips crash together.

Surprisingly, I manage to keep ahold of my beer when I loop my arm around her waist, her body molding to mine. When I break the kiss, I finish off what's left of my drink and reach for her hand, tugging her behind me.

She yelps and giggles, and I look back to catch her jogging just to keep up.

"Forgive me, Leslie. I think my man here has some things to take care of. Have a good night," Hallyn retorts. I grin, watching her gingerly wave her hand in the air.

The crowd thins out the farther away we get, and I slow my pace but keep my focus trained ahead.

"We aren't leaving, are we?" Hallyn whisper-shouts at me, but I don't bother answering her.

I honestly don't know, but I have one thing on my mind, and one thing only.

We weave through the parked cars until we get to where my truck is along the line of trees leading into the brush. It's secluded enough that although we can see the party perfectly from here, we're hidden from everyone else.

Which is exactly what I want.

She takes a step closer when I stop near the back of my pickup and glances around to make sure no one is around. There isn't, though. I made sure of it.

"Turn around, Hallyn," I growl, my voice deepening. She sucks in a sharp breath and nods.

I skate my hands down over her arms to wrap around her wrist, positioning her hands to grip the bumper of my truck.

"Is this what you wanted?" I press my face into her hair, my warm breath feathering over her ear. Goose bumps break out across her skin, and she tilts her head to the side, giving me better access.

My hands trail over her side, along the hem of her skirt, finding her thin lace panties underneath. I kick her foot out to widen her stance and brush my finger along the edge of her underwear.

Frustrated the material is getting in the way, I kneel on the ground and lift her skirt. I bite her ass, earning me a yelp right as I tug on her panties, tearing the material away from her body.

Her mouth drops open. "I can't believe you..."

"Are you really surprised?" I quip, brushing my finger up her inner thigh before swiping through her folds.

She gasps, her tongue quickly darting out to wet her lips.

I lift her skirt, and the cool breeze on her backside sends a wave of chills over her heated skin.

"Put your hands back where they were," I order, and she quirks her brow. "Now."

She sighs, but I pull her hips toward me, pressing my hand to her spine to arch her back, positioning her ass in my face.

I nip, lick, and suck on her cheek, dragging my finger over her clit before moving lower to slip into her tight heat.

"I think you like to get a rise out of me. This is exactly what you wanted, isn't it?" I ask, right as I land a hard slap against her ass.

She moans, pushing back toward me, and I shove my finger inside her, adding a second this time. She's practically dripping for me.

I push myself to stand, unhooking my belt and flick my button, shoving my pants down enough to free my dick. I drag her wetness over the tip, using it to coat my skin before I line myself up at her entrance.

"You better hold the fuck on," I warn her.

My face presses against the side of hers, my chest molding against her back.

"Give me what I want already."

She wiggles, earning a low groan before I slam deep inside her. She presses her lips together, attempting to contain her whimper.

"Mmm, good," I croon. "So fuckin' good."

I grip her chin, tilting her head back against my shoulder.

"You're gonna walk back to the party after I fuck you with my cum dripping from your pussy, coating the inside of your thighs."

"Beckham," she exhales my name with a breathy moan.

"Who does this pussy belong to, Hallyn?" My lips are pressed roughly against the side of her face.

"Y-y-ou," she stutters, her body trembling.

I band my arms around her, one slipping into the V cut low on her top and into her bra. The other to the front of her skirt, rubbing circles over her clit while I thrust into her in hard and fast pumps.

"Say it," I mutter. "I want to hear you say it."

"Y-you." She shudders. "You, Beckham. It's yours."

She squeezes her eyes shut as her pussy clenches around me, and I moan into her ear, my heavy pants blowing her hair away from her face.

Despite the cold temperatures, perspiration dots my skin. I can only imagine what my face will look like after.

I pinch her nipple at the same time I smack my fingers over her clit, causing her body to tense, and she releases a loud, throaty groan.

"Good girl," I mutter. "Take this dick, Hallyn. Let me feel your pussy squeeze me like a vise."

My name comes out in short pants as her release takes over. I roll my eyes shut when her pussy tightens around me, and I'm right behind her.

"I don't know how I'm ever gonna get enough of this, of you. You've fuckin' ruined me."

Beckham was up long before me the following morning. I slowly blink my eyes open, squinting through one to see him sitting at his desk, flipping through his playbook. It's something I often find him doing before games.

"Good morning," I mumble, tucking my arm under my head.

He turns in his seat, resting his elbow on the back of the chair. "Mornin', sleepy."

"What time is it?" I ask, a yawn escaping my mouth.

He smirks and shakes his head. "Just after eight. I have to pack up and head to the school in about forty minutes."

I push myself up, letting the white sheet fall away to reveal my bare breasts.

Over the past few weeks, my comfort level with him has grown, and I don't bother to cover myself like I would've before.

His nostrils flare, and I relish the sight of him taking in my body. It's slow, as if he's enjoying every inch. Something about the way he drinks me in is exhilarating.

I've never felt this way before, not even with Tanner.

"I need to get dressed and head home. Ava and I are riding with Mandy to Keaton. She'll be there to pick us up around eleven."

He nods, still distracted. With a snicker, I tug the sheet away, swing my legs over the edge of the bed, and reach for my clothes from the night before.

Beckham mutters a low, "Nuh-uh," and motions for me to come to him. I do without question.

He drags his hands over my body, positioning me to stand between his legs as he flicks my nipple into his mouth, his large palm grabbing my ass.

"We both know there's no way you'll make it out the door on time if we start this now."

"I think you're wrong." He chuckles. "In fact, I happen to remember the first morning I woke up to you in my bed, I enjoyed you spread out for breakfast right there."

I drag my fingers through his hair, tugging on the strands until he tilts his head back and meets my eyes.

"You have a big game today. Don't they say it's bad to have sex before you play?"

His face turns serious. "I guess that just means I'll have to make up for it after we win."

I hold his face in my hands and kiss him, straddling his lap.

"You're teasing me again," he mumbles.

"And you love it."

He smacks my ass, and I push off him before sliding on my discarded pants.

Ava knocks on the door and shouts that she'll see me back at home. I finish getting dressed and shove the rest of my stuff into my bag, slinging it over my shoulder.

"Good luck today," I whisper against Beckham's mouth.

He presses his hand against my spine and leads me out to my truck. I've mentioned a couple of times how I'm debating if I'm ready to find a different vehicle—something reliable to avoid putting miles on this one.

While it's sentimental to me, I don't want to get rid of it yet, but I know I can't drive her forever.

Plus, the gas adds up quickly.

Beckham grips the doorframe and leans in to kiss me as I slip the key into the ignition and melt into his kiss.

"I'll text you after the game." He steps back and waves.

"After you win." I wink, attempting to turn the key. It clicks, rumbling like it's trying to turn over but never does.

Beckham stands at the edge of the driveway, his brows furrowing as he studies me. I keep trying, but each attempt is futile.

"Shit," I mutter into the empty cab and grab my phone from my bag, hoping to catch Ava before she's too far.

I don't want Beckham to deal with giving me a ride, not when he has his game to worry about.

The door handle creaks, and Beckham is there by my side again.

"Why don't you take my truck, at least to your place, and then you can meet Ava and Mandy there to ride together?"

"What will you drive, though?"

"I'll catch a lift with one of the guys. It's not like I don't have other options," he reassures. "Plus, I'd feel better about you driving my truck. The last thing I want is for you to get down the road and this thing breaks down on you."

I squeeze my eyes shut and rest my forehead against my steering wheel. I swear, if it's not one thing, it's another. I try to calm my nerves and not get frustrated.

"C'mon, I'll go grab my keys quick."

He takes off jogging toward the house and returns a moment later with his keys. His hair is still damp from the shower he took this morning. He normally has product in it, enough to keep the long strands on top from being too unruly, but pieces fall onto his forehead.

My fingers itch to reach out and touch them before he runs his hands through it, moving the strands out of his face.

"Don't stress over it." He reads my expression. "I'll take some time tomorrow or Monday to look at it and see if I can figure out what's wrong. We'll get it sorted, okay?"

He tucks his fist under my chin, lifting my eyes to meet his, and I nod.

"Thank you." I smile, rising on my tiptoes to kiss him.

He unlocks the doors and opens the driver's side for me, and smiles when he sees me seated in his spot.

"I have to admit, I'm getting a bit turned on seeing you in my truck."

"One of these days, I want you to lift the armrest and fuck me on this seat," I say.

"Hallyn." His tone changes, and I grin.

"It was just an idea. You can think about it while you're on the road today to Keaton. Maybe use it as a little motivation?"

"Oh, I have my ideas too. Just you wait."

He steps back and slams the door shut, and I roll down the window to holler, "Good luck," to him. He doesn't take his eyes off me while I back down the driveway and pull away.

When I make it to our place, Ava is almost ready. I end up hopping in the shower and am still styling my hair when Ava pokes her head in my room.

"Mandy's here." She smiles.

I bite my lip and nod, focusing heavily on tying the ribbon in my hair. I'm too distracted to notice her standing in the doorway studying me.

"You seem different lately," she says when I finish, and I drop my hands to my side.

"Different how?"

She shrugs. "In a good way. You seem happier and more confident. It's just good to see my best friend again."

My eyes soften. "I certainly feel happier. Happier than I've been in a long time."

There have been a fair number of challenges in the past few weeks. From the assault and subsequent break-in at our apartment to finding my window open—the old Hallyn, the Hallyn I was when I was with Tanner, would've been ready to run for the hills.

By hills, I mean home or back to Tanner.

He was my first everything. I think, for a long time, I didn't want to let go of who he had been to me. At one time, I felt safe with him.

I try not to think about it. I've reasoned with the fact maybe it's the true crime nut in me that overthinks everything, but then I come back to his comments about having eyes on me at Braysen.

I get anxious when I try to decipher what he meant, realizing I trusted the wrong person.

"I'm grabbing my stuff, and I'll walk out with you." Ava nods toward the door.

I quickly toss all my stuff into my bag and shrug on my Braysen U jacket.

Ava talks about what happened at the party after we left on our way out the door. Mandy waits for us in the parking lot. We both drop our bags in the trunk, and Ava slams it shut. My fingers grip the door handle when I catch her eyeing Beckham's truck parked behind me.

"Umm... is that what I think it is?" She zeroes in on me.

I grit my teeth in a forced smile and burst out laughing. Climbing into the back seat, I avoid her question.

"Don't you dare ignore me, you little shit." Ava snickers, claiming the front passenger seat.

She reaches for the seat belt, turning her body to look at me, waiting for me to answer.

I play it off like I'm clueless as Mandy hits the gas and pulls out of the parking lot onto the main road leading out of Braysen.

"I'm waiting..." Ava adds. "We can sit in silence the whole way, but I'm not changing the subject."

"What are we talking about?" Mandy asks, confused. She flicks her gaze from Ava to me in the rearview mirror.

"Well, for starters, we stayed over at the guys' house last night. Hallyn, of course, slept in Beckham's room. We talked briefly before I left to come home, and her truck was parked outside. I figured she'd be right behind me since they were leaving to head to the stadium and board the bus."

I smirk, listening as she voices her thoughts out loud. I glance out the window as we hit the highway leading to Keaton. The drive is only about thirty minutes, so we should be there quickly.

However, Ava isn't going to let me out of this one easily.

"I noticed as we were getting in the car that Hallyn's pick-up is missing from the parking lot, and a certain Braysen quarterback's truck is parked in her usual spot."

"I have no idea what you're talking about." I smugly smile.

She bursts out laughing, and Mandy's eyes are bright with amusement.

"I have to admit, most guys aren't one to let anyone drive their truck," Mandy comments.

"Beckham won't even let his own brother drive his," Ava interjects.

I hadn't ever heard the topic brought up, but Ava's been around their place often, especially for those ten days during our apartment fiasco. I'm sure she heard a whole lot living with four guys for a week and a half.

"So, what's going on between the two of you? Are you dating? Is it getting serious? I mean, no one would be surprised if you were in love at this point." She snickers.

My eyes bug out, and I try to calm my racing heart and ignore the way my stomach flips at the mention of love.

"I don't think it's that serious." I play it off, shaking my head.

Ava presses her lips in a firm line and nods enthusiastically. "Right. What is it then, Halls?"

My heart seizes at the use of the nickname Beckham has taken to. I remember the first time he used it the night

Tanner came to Braysen, and we ran into Beckham with his friends at Whiskey Sinner's.

He cornered me outside the bathroom, away from our friends after Tanner took off.

"I know you think you hate me, Halls, but there's a thin line between love and hate. Sooner or later, that line will blur, and you'll find yourself falling for me, just like I knew you would."

I tried and failed at the whole "hating him" thing.

He didn't seem to care that I wanted him to hate me too.

This started out as a deal. I'd help him out by tutoring him, and in return, he'd fix my truck.

I had built up all these walls around me, around my heart. The only person besides Ava I ever let in was Tanner, but with him, it was for all the wrong reasons.

Beckham didn't give a shit what act I tried to play off, and he didn't stop when it came to seeing beneath the surface.

A part of me feared when I let him in that he'd turn out to be no different from Tanner. Or my dad, who walked out on me.

Except he hasn't. He's proven he'll be there for me time and time again. In ways no other man but my grandpa has.

Tears prick my eyes at the thought, and I look over at my best friend. Her smile softens, and she reaches into the back seat for my hand and squeezes it.

"What are you thinking, Halls? I can see it on your face, but maybe it'll help if you talk it out."

I wipe my fingers beneath my eyes. It dawns on me that I haven't even bothered with my makeup yet, which I guess is a good thing now.

Who cares, though? Beckham certainly never has. If anything, he seems to love the natural me more.

Wait. Love?

"I don't know what we are or where this is going between us…" I exhale a shuddered breath. "What I can say, though, is what we have is different from anything I've ever felt before."

"You love him…" Ava reassures me.

It's not a question but a statement. No one else on this earth knows me the way she does.

"You love him, and I think he loves you too."

I guess that's what happens when the lines between love and hate blur.

CHAPTER 30

BECKHAM

It's the game I've been looking forward to all season.

Not only is it a make-or-break game for the Bulldogs, but the win will be much sweeter when I can look across the field at the scoreboard and see we beat the Keaton Eagles.

"This is it," Coach hollers, slamming his hand against the side of the locker with a bang. "We're only up by three points, and we know they're gonna come out guns blazing ready to light our asses up. So what are you gonna do about it?"

"We're gonna fight!" Hayes shouts. "Every minute. Every play."

The guys all shout, "Yea!" in agreement, amping them up.

"This is always our biggest rivalry of the year. They won't give up without a fight. You have to be ready to put it all on the line," Coach adds.

Reed shoves his shoulder against mine, and I turn to face him, nodding my head. The adrenaline is already pumping.

Something about knowing Tanner is our opponent makes me want to go out and dig even deeper. Every time he's been out on the field, he looks along our sideline.

What no one else knows is how he wanted to be me, in my spot, on this team.

This win is even more personal for him now.

We have thirty minutes left on the field, and if we win, we've secured our spot in the conference championship no matter if we win or lose our next game.

I jog onto the field, football in hand, and soak in the crowd. The cheerleaders and dance team line the tunnel as players take the field.

The first thing that dawns on me is I don't see Hallyn among them.

"Where is she?" I shout to Ava as I pass by her.

"She had to run to the bathroom. I thought she would've been out here by now, though. She wanted to see you run out onto the field."

I nod and clench my jaw, taking off toward the end zone.

Our game today is in Keaton territory. Call me crazy, but something doesn't sit right with me when I look over at the sideline, and Hallyn's nowhere to be found.

I try to push away the thoughts spinning through my mind, focusing instead on getting my arm warmed up.

"Let's close out this half," Reed says, smacking his hands on my pads and knocking his helmet against mine.

I grip the football, spinning it around to line up the laces and throw it downfield to Hayes who's ready and waiting.

I'm distracted. My eyes keep searching for her, and it isn't until I see her rejoin Ava that I'm able to get my head back in the game.

It's safe to say both teams are thinking about what's on the line entering the second half. We each traded two touchdowns before we finally get them off the field in a three and out, forcing them to settle for a field goal.

We were tied coming down to the last three minutes. My nerves are shot to shit, knowing the only way we can win is to pull out a stop now or find a way to steal the ball and make a play down the field.

Our time-outs saved us, so when it's third and seven on their forty-two-yard line, our defense knows it all comes down to this play.

"I think I can feel my heart beating in my asshole," Reed groans next to me, and it's enough to break the tension.

Freeman lines up behind his center and calls out the play. We all watch with bated breath as he passes off the ball to their running back, and Knox barrels through their offensive line and punches the ball out of his hand, sending everyone scrambling onto the ground.

The whistle blows, and those few seconds waiting for the referee to make the call feel more like hours.

"The ball was stripped from Keaton, causing a fumble recovered by Braysen. It's Braysen's ball on the forty-three-yard line," the ref shouts through the microphone.

"You're a fuckin' menace," Hayes hollers at Knox as we take the field.

We run it for the next three plays, keeping the ball on the ground to take time off the clock. Reed turns it on when it's important, gaining us an extra sixteen yards.

When the clock runs out and we kick in the field goal, a grin stretches on my face, knowing the time has run out on Tanner's season too.

The whistle sounds when the time hits zero, and several of our offensive linemen stalk toward me, lifting me on their shoulders. Fans rush out onto the field, joining us in our celebration.

I'm too caught up in the moment to even notice what's going on along the sidelines until I glance over at Colter, and he motions with his head toward the girls.

I don't see Hallyn at first, until my eyes zero in on the Keaton jersey standing among a sea of blue and teal, and recognize the number sixteen with Freeman printed on the back.

I clench my jaw and stand there watching. Hallyn sidesteps him and holds her hand up. From here, it looks like she's attempting to evade his advances, trying to get him to leave her alone.

Freeman doesn't see me coming. He's too busy trying to convince her to talk to him in the midst of drawing a crowd from our student section. A few fans see me coming, judging by the "oh shits" and gasps as I barrel through the hordes of people toward them.

"Hey, buddy." I smack him on the shoulder, pulling him back by his pads.

His footsteps falter, swinging around to see who it is.

"I think you're on the wrong side of the field. Seems you forgot what team you're on."

I keep my tone light and joking, although the tension has my body wrung so tight, I'd love a few rounds with him to loosen me up.

"Get your fuckin' hands off me," he bellows, charging toward me and bumping his chest against mine.

I chuckle under my breath. "Or what?" I tilt my head to the side. "What are you gonna do about it?"

He takes his helmet off, lacing his fingers through the face mask. I glance around to see if anyone's onto us, thankful we haven't raised any eyebrows.

Yet.

I turn my attention back to Tanner and bump my chest against his once more. He drops his helmet on the ground and uses both hands to shove me. I stumble a few steps.

Colter hollers at Tanner to drag his sorry ass back where he belongs, but we ignore him.

"It has to grind on your fuckin' nerves to see me on your field wearing this jersey, with my girl on the sideline, when we both know you wish it were you." I grin, egging him on.

He flipped the switch now, and I'm ready to lay into him the only way I can.

"I bet it pisses you off to know everything you've ever wanted is mine."

His face falls, and I chuckle.

"I got your spot on the team and the record you can't compete with, and now I got your girl. Except she's not your girl anymore, Freeman. She's mine."

He clenches his jaw and turns to Hallyn. She wears a conflicting look on her face. I don't think she knows whether to feel bad for twisting the knife deeper or happy that I just declared her mine.

"I wouldn't count on it," Freeman says. "She always comes back to me."

His voice cracks, and a salacious smile spreads across my face. I pull off my helmet and jog over to Hallyn, tugging her into my arms and crashing my lips on hers.

She moans against my mouth, gripping the front of my jersey. I drop my helmet and lift her into my arms.

She yelps at first before wrapping her legs around my waist and slides her fingers into my sweaty hair. Her body relaxes, and her mouth opens, seeking entrance into mine, and I give in to her.

I don't have to turn around to know Tanner slunk back to join the rest of his team.

Hallyn breaks the kiss and slowly blinks her eyes open, sucking in a sharp breath, and I lower her to her feet.

I press a kiss against her temple and lean into her ear. "You better be ready to celebrate later."

She drags her lip between her teeth and nods.

I'm still amped up from the game and celebrating with my teammates when we board our bus back to Braysen.

My phone has been flooded with over fifty missed messages from my parents, Talon, and other friends from back home and Rixton. I scroll through them, my eyes landing on the one from Hallyn, more specifically the glimpse of the message appearing on the preview screen.

Hallyn: I've been thinking of ways to congratulate you on your win.

It's not the suggestive nature of the message that has my dick hardening in my pants. It's the kneeling emoji she follows it up with, hinting at exactly how she plans to celebrate with me.

I grunt under my breath, my eyes flashing around the bus. I have the row to myself near the back with Colter across the aisle from me, and Reed and Hayes in the seats in front of him.

Trying to keep it subtle, I adjust my dick through my sweatpants and lean against the window.

Beckham: You gonna get on your knees and take me in your mouth like a good girl?

Beckham: Or you gonna let me fuck you first so you can taste your pussy on me too?

Fuck.

She knew exactly what she was doing when she started this shit up. Now I'm sitting on a bus with a bunch of guys, hard as fuck.

I scroll through my music to A Rebels Havoc, needing something to drown out the sound around me. It's a distraction until I get home and can make good on my word.

It doesn't help I have to wait for her to get my truck and meet me at the school to pick me up.

All thoughts of distractions are out the window when she responds with a photo from the night of our date after I took her back to my house.

She's lying on my bed in nothing but my jersey, and the hand between her legs covers her pussy.

She's teasing me, tempting me in the delicious ways only Hallyn can.

Hallyn: Whatever you want, Carver.

My nostrils flare, and I clench my jaw. She agrees to let me have her however I want her, and the thought alone has me squeezing my eyes shut as my phone vibrates in my hand again.

Hallyn: Be safe, but also hurry your ass up. I need you...right now.

"Where the fuck are we?" I grunt, glancing out the window as we hit the bridge crossing the Savannah River into South Carolina.

We're still about ten minutes out, but not fuckin' soon enough.

I'm not waiting until we get home to have her.

I don't think she's ready for what I have in mind.

Beckham: *Meet me in the locker room.*

I pull into the parking spot outside of the school and shift into park. My heart starts pumping when I read the message.

He wants me to meet him *in* the locker room?

The rest of the parking lot is mostly empty now. We got caught up in traffic leaving the game, and Mandy dropped us off at our apartment so I could drive his truck to pick him up.

Which means he wants me to come into the locker room with him *alone.*

My skin pricks as I push the door open and hit the lock button on the key fob, stuffing it into my pocket.

With their win today, they have one game left before moving on to the conference championship. My adrenaline was finally coming down from the intensity of the game when I got here, but he ramped it back up with only one text message.

I glance around, checking for any players or coaches coming before I exhale heavily and reach for the door handle to slip into the locker room.

The walls are painted teal and blue, leading down a dimly lit hallway, with glass cases of trophies, team photos, game balls, and other memorabilia. It's so quiet, I can practically hear my heart beating in my ears.

"Beckham?" My voice echoes.

I walk around the corner and come to a stop when I see him sitting in a chair in front of his locker cubby. Each one is painted in Braysen colors with shelves next to it. His helmet is hanging from a hook behind him.

His head hangs between his shoulders, headphones on, dressed in nothing but a pair of athletic shorts and his white Air Forces.

"Beckham?" I say again. His head slowly rises, and his eyes lock on mine. "Everything okay?"

He takes off his headphones, setting them along with his phone in his bag beside him.

I don't know what to make of his demeanor. My first instinct is to worry that something bad happened until his face softens, and he pushes himself to stand.

My mind flashes back to my conversation with Ava and Mandy earlier in the car about my feelings for Beckham. Could I really be falling for him already?

His mouth curves into a small grin, and all thoughts and worries fall away as he captures my attention. Him and that fuckin' mouth that drive me crazy.

"Congratulations on your win," I say, my voice low.

He brushes his thumb along my jaw, using his fingers to push the hair out of my face. I lean into his palm and close my eyes, blindly reaching for him, skimming over his stomach.

His abs tighten, and when I open my eyes again, he studies me with a hooded gaze.

My fingers skate across the waistband of his shorts and continue lower, wrapping them around his hard length beneath the thin material.

He sucks in a sharp breath, and the sound is intoxicating. Something about it fuels me further.

Maybe it's the thought of us being in here alone and the temptation of getting caught. I drag my lip between my teeth and slowly lower myself to kneel on the locker room floor. The Bulldog logo printed beneath my knees.

"Hallyn," he mutters, his eyes widening.

"Yes?" I tilt my head to the side, slipping my fingers into the top of his shorts.

I pause, giving him the chance to stop me. When his nostrils flare and he widens his stance, I know he's gearing up for what's about to come.

Beckham runs his thumb along my lower lip, and I suck it into my mouth, biting on the tip, earning me another low gasp.

When I slide his shorts over his hips, his dick bounces free, and he reaches his hand out, gliding his tight fist over the head.

"You want me to fuck your mouth, Hallyn?" He leans forward so we're both at eye level.

My tongue quickly darts out of my mouth, and I nod. He kisses me hard, and when I open up to him, flicking my tongue along the seam of his lips, he pulls away and grins.

"Open," he orders, and the sound of his deep voice and the sight of him jerking off is a heady combination.

I obey, though, and flick my tongue over the tip. He grits his teeth and inhales before I wrap my lips around him, taking him as deep as I can until I gag.

"Mmm, fuck," he groans.

He slides his fingers into my hair, tugging on the strands. Something about his sounds and the raw desire on his face while he pumps his hips flips a switch in me.

I do it again, but I don't slowly back off this time. I wrap my hand around the base of his dick and increase my momentum, taking him as deep as I can and holding it until he pulls away and reaches for my arm to help me stand.

The move takes me off guard, and before I can even overthink it or let those niggling self-conscious thoughts enter my mind, he kisses me hard. His fingers reach for the button of my jeans.

I changed my clothes before we left the stadium. The temperatures were cold for early November, and I wasn't about to freeze during the drive home.

He slides my pants over my hips before he thinks better of it and grabs my hand, leading me over to his locker. Dropping his shorts on the floor, he claims the seat he was sitting in when I first walked in. His eyes run over my body, nodding toward me to lose my jeans too.

The fear anyone could be in the school and a whole roster of guys who could walk through the door and bust us at any second still runs through my mind.

"Get over here, feisty girl," he taunts me. I take a step between his legs and roughly drag my fingers through his hair.

His gaze darkens.

"You thinkin' about how at any moment, someone could walk in here and see you riding my dick?"

He leans forward and shoves my pants down my legs. Gripping my hips, he turns me so my back faces his front. He doesn't have to guide me any further, though.

We both have the same thought running through our minds. He positions himself at my entrance, and I catch us both off guard when I slam down onto his lap.

He growls in my ear, wrapping his arms around me. One slips under my top, gripping my breast through my bra while the other reaches between my legs.

"What if I told you I hope someone walks through the door right now," he moans. "Maybe I want everyone to know you're mine."

"Beckham," I exhale.

"Yeah, baby. Tell me who this pussy belongs to."

"It's yours," I mutter breathlessly. "I'm yours."

He releases my breast, his hand moving back to my hip, and we both start to move. The sound of our skin slapping together echoes around the empty locker room.

"Damn right, you're mine," he groans. "And I'm yours too. There's no one else I've wanted since the moment you stepped foot into my bedroom."

His fingers continue to rub my clit. This position and his fingers work together perfectly.

When he pulls me against his chest, resting my head against his shoulder, my hips buck, and he thrusts up into me. Stars dance in my eyes, but it's not until his teeth drag along the shell of my ear, and he mutters, "I'm gonna make you mine in every way," that we both go crashing over the edge together.

My body tenses, and he releases a low growl in my ear. It's like I'm floating on a high I don't ever want to come down from.

We sit there for a few minutes, his arms holding me tight, until we eventually come back to reality. He stops me when I move to pull my pants up, and I look to find his heated gaze on my pussy as he sucks his fingers in his mouth.

His eyes drop between my legs, and he grins. "I love the sight of our cum smeared on your thighs."

My face heats, and my mouth drops open at his words. He reaches down, pulling my pants up, making it clear he has no intention of letting me clean myself up either.

He hurries to get dressed, grabbing his gym bag from his locker, and reaches for my hand to lace our fingers together.

I guess he wasn't kidding when he said he wanted to make sure anyone who saw us together would know that I'm his. He lifts our linked hands to his mouth, pressing a soft kiss against the back of mine.

He surprises me with how he can be rough and dirty one minute and soft and sweet in the next. I don't think I'll ever get enough of all the sides of Beckham either.

On our way out to his truck, he makes a comment about a party his roommates are having to celebrate their win. He appears to question if I'd want to go to his place or if we want to head over to mine.

I still haven't felt comfortable staying at my place even though we've changed the locks and Ava's dad installed the security cameras. Even when I know he is there with me and would keep me safe.

It's fall, which means it's begun to get dark earlier. The sun has started to set in the distance. A chill runs through my body, and Beckham glances at me and smiles, tugging me into his arms as we round the front of his truck.

When he pulls away, his face turns serious, and I can tell something is on his mind.

"What's wrong?"

He shakes his head. "Nothing's wrong. In fact, everything is perfect."

My brows deepen, and I narrow my eyes. I'm not sure I want to believe him.

He pushes me against the side of his truck and buries his face in the crook of my neck. He inhales deeply, and I almost want to ask him again, out of fear of him keeping something from me.

"I was thinking about what I said back there," he says. He doesn't look at me, so I wait for a long pause for him to continue.

"You care to elaborate?"

He chuckles. "The part about wanting everyone to know you're mine."

I swallow hard.

"I've been thinking lately just about how different life has been since I moved to Braysen. In a good way. Football is goin' great, and school is goin' well now. Everything in my life is good, and a lot of it comes back to you."

I drag my lip between my teeth to fight off my grin, but it's no use.

"I'm falling in love with you, Halls, and I have to admit, it scares the shit out of me, but at the same time, it doesn't. I know what I want, and it's you."

I grip the front of his shirt, rolling onto my tiptoes, and wrap my arms around his neck. He lifts me into his arms and presses my body against his truck. I can't help but think about what he said, and I agree.

My life would be so different if I had followed Tanner to Keaton. There's no telling what our relationship would be today, but I know it would've never led me to Beckham.

"I love you," I whisper against his mouth.

The entire drive back to his house, his hand is in mine or holding my thigh, and every time I catch him looking over at me, I can't help but smile.

Cars are parked out front of their house, overflowing into the yard. Ava weaves through a group of people huddled up in the living room and hollers my name, bouncing on her feet as she flings her arms around me in a hug.

"Where the heck have you two been?" she asks. It's meant to be quiet, but there's no way everyone around didn't hear.

"So glad the two of you could keep your hands off each other long enough to join us," Hayes shouts from where he sits on a barstool in the dining room.

He grins, lifting a beer into the air, and cheers. I glance up at Beckham, and he smirks. He bends down, hoisting me over his shoulder, and climbs the stairs in the entryway.

Ava yells back at us, "Where are you two going?" while everyone else laughs and cheers him on.

He carries me down the hall to his room and tosses me on his bed, kicking the door shut behind him.

"What the hell are you doing?" I laugh, sitting up on my forearms.

He tosses his shirt over his head, and my eyes once again drop to the front of his shorts.

"I was making sure every fucker in this house knew you were mine."

He pushes his pants off, kicking them and his shoes to the side.

His hand wraps around my ankle, tugging me toward him.

"But now, I want to taste my girlfriend before I make love to her again."

CHAPTER 32

BECKHAM

"Things with you and Hallyn seem to be progressing well," Reed says, leaning against the front of Hallyn's truck.

Hayes stands on the other side, his hip resting on the front fender with his arms crossed.

"Or she just likes you helping her with her broken down truck," Hayes jokes.

I narrow my eyes on his, and his laughter stops, holding his hand up between us.

"Dude, I was kidding," he says, earning him an eye roll.

"Good, because I need you to give me a hand so I can get under here and see what the hell is goin' on."

He exhales, and we both walk into the garage to retrieve the steel ramps and position them in front of the truck. The truck won't start, so I shift it into neutral while Reed and Colter help push it until it's off the ground.

I kneel on the asphalt and position myself under the truck, searching for any rhyme or reason why it won't start now.

She didn't have any problem driving it over to my place, but randomly, when she needed to head home the following morning, it stopped running again.

"You don't think Freeman would fuck with her car, do you?" Colter asks, helping aim the flashlight from above.

"I wouldn't put nothin' past that fucker. From what Hallyn has shared, which isn't a lot because she doesn't like talking about him, he was pretty tore up over the fact she wouldn't follow his ass to Keaton," I grunt.

Reed lends me a hand and climbs into the driver's seat, attempting to start it again.

"Goddammit," I growl, pulling my phone out of my pocket to use it as a flashlight.

"What is it?" Reed asks.

"That stupid motherfucker," I grunt, pointing the light at her fuel line, and sure enough, it's cut.

My jaw clenches, and anger coils in my body as I slide out from under her truck.

"What'd you find?" Hayes asks Colter, standing next to him. His expression grim.

"Her fuel line has been cut. There's no way it happened here, not unless he figured out where I live."

"I mean, I guess he could find out if he really wanted to or if he's following her," Hayes adds.

My eyes flash over to him. He holds his hands up again and steps away. He didn't suggest it to piss me off more, but he has a point.

"Her truck could've caught on fire if he did it while she was still at her place. If that's the case, she got lucky she had enough gas in her line to make it over here."

Colter drops his arms he had crossed over his chest and rubs his hand over the back of his neck.

"Well, uh, there's something I think I should show you then," he says.

"What?" My voice drops low.

I glance at the house, checking to make sure Hallyn is nowhere in sight. I can't be certain it was him, and the last thing I need is to freak her out by telling her my suspicions.

"I found this next to her battery." He holds up a black circle puck the size of a small magnet.

"What the hell is it?" I ask, ripping it out of his hand.

"GPS tracker," Reed answers.

My eyes slowly rise to meet his, and he nods.

"Do me a favor, and don't ask how I know. Let's just say I've seen them before," he adds. My brows furrow.

"You can connect them to an app on your phone. It'll send the signal back with exact GPS coordinates. You don't put one of these on someone's truck unless you plan to track their every move."

Rocks crunching beneath tires has all four of us shifting our attention to see who it is. A black police car is the last person I expected to see turning into our driveway.

I toss the GPS back to Reed, and he shoves it into his pocket. We wait until the older man steps out of the car, his partner following him.

The older man looks like he's in his late forties or early fifties, judging by the salt-and-pepper color of his hair and the dark circles under his eyes.

He adjusts his belt and motions something to his partner. He couldn't be older than twenty-five and likely fresh out of the academy.

"Are any of you kids Beckham Carver?" the man asks.

"Yes, sir. That's me." I lift my hand.

I learned at a young age after getting myself in trouble a time or two that using words like "sir" goes a long way with cops. Never mind the fact I'd like to ask him what the hell he's doing here and how he knows my name?

At least half of Braysen knows who you are, Beckham. What do you expect?

I swallow hard, immediately my mind jumping to word getting out about a police officer showing up here and it getting back to Coach. He'd hang my ass out to dry real quick if I did anything to embarrass him or his program.

"I'm gonna have to ask you to come with me down to the police station. We need to speak with you about an altercation that took place outside of Whiskey Sinner's a few weeks ago with a man by the name of Ricky Meyer."

I clench my jaw and nod.

"All right. Come with you? Can I drive myself or does that mean I'm under arrest, sir?"

"Yes, son. We have to bring you in. You're being charged with second-degree assault and battery. I'm gonna ask you to turn around and put your hands behind your back."

"Are you fuckin' shitting me?" Hayes bellows. "He didn't do anything wrong. He was protecting his girlfriend, who was the true victim of the assault."

"Were any of you present when the altercation took place?" he asks the guys. They all look back at me, and I grit my teeth, shaking my head.

None of them can vouch for me because no one else witnessed the altercation. No one except Hallyn, but she was too drunk to even remember all the details.

They all mutter a low, "No," and he adjusts my hands behind my back, tightening the cuffs on my wrists.

"Where have I heard the name Carver before?" he asks me. "You play for Braysen U, right?" His grip on my forearm squeezes. I glance over my shoulder at him, and he studies my face.

I nod. "I do."

It's no secret that the football players get away with a lot in town. Mostly speeding tickets or parties, though. Nothing like assault.

"You're the one who had that dirty play against Osten last year, right?"

I grit my teeth at the sight of his smug expression. He mutters to his partner, "Go ahead and load him into the back seat."

The kid leads me by my arm to the car. He turns back to Hayes and says, "Son, I understand you're concerned, but I need you to let us handle this with him. We will need to get his statement, and he'll be booked at the Braysen County jail."

I glance at my brother to see if he heard the comment about Osten. Judging by the pissed-off look on his face, I'd say he did. He's close to seeing red.

Colter claps him on the back, and Hayes takes off toward the house. Colter nods to me. I know they'll make sure he's all right and won't get into trouble after that comment.

"All right, let's go." The younger officer pushes my head down and shoves me into the back seat.

The last thing we need is both of us winding up in cuffs, sitting next to each other in jail. I can only imagine what Coach would say when he got that phone call.

I guess it's best to rip off the Band-Aid now because after finding that GPS tracker on Hallyn's truck, I can't promise I won't find myself in this back seat again soon.

The screen door slams shut with a loud bang, jolting both Ava and me from where we're kicked back on the couch.

"Is everything okay?" I ask when Hayes races up the stairs. He paces in front of us, running his hand haphazardly through his hair, mumbling to himself.

Ava and I trade glances as I push the throw blanket off my lap and stand.

My eyes flick to the end of the driveway, where there is a police cruiser parked behind my pickup. I happen to catch the exact moment when the officer leads a handcuffed Beckham to the back of the car, and now Hayes's sense of panic sets in.

"What the hell is going on?" I yelp, racing around the coffee table toward the stairs.

Hayes reaches for my arm to stop me, but I yank it free, pushing out the door.

"Beckham!" I shout so loud my voice turns hoarse. I press my palm to my chest while I quickly shove my feet into my shoes.

The door shuts, and he leans against the window, a solemn look on his face.

Tears fill my eyes as I turn to his brother.

"What is happening? Why is he being arrested?"

Hayes's face is hard as stone. "The fight at Whiskey Sinner's. The fucker is pressing charges against him."

"What?" I shout. "H-h-how? How could he press charges when Beckham was just defending me?"

"I don't know," Hayes mumbles, reaching into his pocket for his phone.

My mind is a swirl of questions that I'm not able to answer. Each time I think I might have a way out of this, my mind forms two more.

"Did he say if we can bail him out?" I whisper as Hayes holds up his finger to me as he says, "Hey, Mom."

My stomach drops, realizing he has to make this call.

I haven't even had a chance to meet Beckham's parents, and this is how they'll be learning about me.

I'm the woman he was defending, the reason he could've just ruined his football career.

Hayes escapes into the kitchen, where he begins pacing again, his footsteps and his voice growing louder the further he gets into explaining the story. I don't want to interrupt him, so I hang out outside of the room, picking up bits and pieces of the conversation.

All I'm able to make out is that they were outside fixing my truck when the cops showed up. They explained they're aware of a fight outside of Whiskey Sinner's a couple of weeks ago and need to bring him down to the station for questioning.

The big question is, though, why did they have to cuff him and parade him into the police station like he's some sort of criminal?

Hayes exhales a heavy sigh when he reappears again, tucking his phone back in his pocket.

"We have to go to him. We have to bail him out," I mutter frantically.

"With what money? I'm waiting for my parents to transfer it to my account so we can go down there as soon as it hits."

I press my fingers to my lips, thinking about what Beckham's coach might say when he gets wind of this. He's already been in hot water.

They have one more game left of the season before the conference championship. There's no way his coach would sit him out, would he?

"I have an idea," I say, rushing down the hall to Beckham's room and grabbing my purse hanging on his desk chair. I throw on Beckham's sweatshirt and sling my purse across my body.

Hayes has his shoes and jacket on, and Ava is right behind us, doing the same.

"Will you take me to Whiskey Sinner's? There has to be something they can do, video footage or something from that night."

Reed and Colter sidestep us when we take off out the door. Reed says he'll lock up, and all of us pile into Colter's pickup since it's the only one that will fit everyone comfortably.

The parking lot of Whiskey Sinner's is deserted compared to what it was the night we were here. Most of the crowd stops by for lunch or dinner with a few beers before things pick up at night.

Reed, Colter, and Ava hang back while Hayes comes inside with me.

"I know this is your brother, and you're worried about him. I am too, but let me take the lead on this one. Okay?"

He studies me for a moment and nods.

A bartender sits at the front, smiling when she sees us. Reaching behind her to pull out the towel hanging from her pocket, she begins wiping down the counter.

"Hey there! What can I get you?"

"I'm not ordering anything right now. Do you have a manager or security, someone who might be able to help me with an altercation that happened outside a couple of weeks back?"

Her eyes flash in concern, glancing from me over to Hayes.

"You bet. Let me get him for you."

We stand there waiting. The song switches, and I tap my foot, trying to focus on the lyrics and not the worry coiling in my stomach as I think about Beckham sitting behind bars in a jail cell with Lord knows who.

"My name's Russell. Andrea says you want to speak with me about an altercation that happened here?"

He crosses his arm, resting one arm on the other while he grips his chin and studies me.

I nod. "That's right. I'm hoping you can tell me if you have video surveillance, and if there's any chance it may have caught it? My boyfriend got there shortly after it happened and found the man trying to force me into his car. He's now pressing charges against him, claiming my boyfriend assaulted him."

He grits his teeth. "We might have it still. I can see what I can do." He motions over his shoulder for us to follow him, weaving in and out of the tables leading down the hallway where Beckham cornered me the first night we were here.

We take a left, leading down another long corridor to where an office door is cracked open. There are two large computer screens and a TV mounted above them, equipped with video surveillance covering nearly every inch of the bar.

He asks me what day we're looking at, and I pull out my phone and flip through my calendar, trying to recall the exact night. I remember it specifically, though, because it was the night before the Bulldogs played the Lions.

I explain to him that the interaction started in the entry-way of the bar and finished with us out in the parking lot.

He pulls up the footage from that day, scrolling through until I spot myself leaning against the brick wall between the set of doors leading outside.

"Wait, stop. I think this is when the guy approached me."

He presses play and clicks on the sound button next to it, and then my voice echoes around the small space.

"I never did thank you for the, uhm, for the roses you sent me."

My face heats. "Go ahead and fast-forward it a little bit further."

He does. I don't notice it right away, but a man in a white shirt lingers near the doorway. I ask him to play it again.

"Beckham..." I say, clutching my phone tightly against my ear like I'm straining to hear him. "I pictured it was you. I wanted you to be there."

Well, shit.

I flick my eyes over to Hayes. The frustrated look on his face he had earlier has softened some, replaced with a glimmer of amusement.

If I had any hope that maybe he didn't know what our conversation was about, him pressing his lips together to contain his laughter gives it away.

"Hey, what are you doin' out here by yourself?" a raspy voice asks.

He takes a step forward, and I'm finally able to get a good enough look at him.

"That's him," I say, motioning to the screen. "Follow him."

He changes cameras, moving ahead to when we make our way out to the parking lot. The camera he mentioned earlier was positioned right above where his broken-down silver Honda was parked, but from this angle, we're not able to make out a good view of his license plate to confirm it's him.

"Is it possible you can export these clips to me and send them over to my email? I need to give them to the police so we can prove my boyfriend was just protecting me."

He appears to hesitate for a minute.

"My boyfriend is Beckham Carver. He's the..."

"Quarterback of the Bulldogs," he finishes, his eyes flicking to Hayes. "I thought you looked familiar."

Hayes flashes him a warm smile, turning on the charm I remember from the day we first met.

Before I realized he wasn't Beckham and was his twin brother.

Braysen U football players hold weight in this town. I've heard rumors about them getting into trouble and how members of the community would conveniently turn a blind eye.

Sometimes I think they care more about football than anything else, including the law.

"No problem, I can send it over to you."

It grates on my nerves, knowing he didn't mind helping me look at the footage just a minute ago, but he wasn't willing to give me a copy until I dropped Beckham's name.

Whatever, though. As long as it will help Beckham out, that's all I care about.

Before he exports the footage, we backtrack to earlier in the night, trying to get a glimpse of the plates on the Honda when he first arrived.

It takes us a while before we spot him. He came in through one of the side entrances.

"Who is that?" Hayes asks when Russell stops the Honda pulling into another space on the opposite side of the lot.

Another car pulls in next to him, and they both get out, circling to the back.

The video is in black and white, making it hard to recognize the vehicle they're driving at first glance. His hoodie is up, covering his face, until he turns toward the camera enough to get the side profile of his face.

"Is that who I think it is?" Hayes growls. "What the hell is that fucker doing talking to him?"

My heart feels like it plummets into my stomach and then turns.

Tanner?

"Do you know this person?" Russell asks as we all three lean in, staring intently at the screen.

We watch the two of them converse before Tanner pulls out his phone. The screen flashes before he turns it over to him to show him something.

"I think he's showing him a picture of you," Hayes says, reading my mind.

"But why?"

"Who is this?" Russell asks, interrupting.

Tears fill the brim of my eyes, and I shake my head, trying to blink them away. "The guy holding the phone is my ex-boyfriend. He's the quarterback at Keaton."

Recognition flashes on his face, and he nods.

My eyes stay trained on the screen, watching as Tanner reaches into his pocket for his wallet and retrieves cash tucked inside before he subtly shakes his hand, exchanging the cash in the process.

Now, there's no use trying to conceal my emotions.

"So what, he paid this man to try to corner me and get me into his vehicle? Beckham ended up showing up, which threw off his plan. The two of them get into a fight, and now he's trying to twist it to say Beckham assaulted him, but for what?"

"To fuck with him? To get between the two of you? Who the fuck knows." Hayes exhales harshly.

I shake my head, turning back to Russell, and thank him for his help. He writes down my email and promises to send it over in a zip file as soon as it finishes saving.

"C'mon, let's go," Hayes says, gripping my shoulder to usher me out of the room and down the hall.

"We have to go to the police station and tell them the truth." I wince, the tears spilling over now. "They're after the wrong guy. They should be arresting them, not Beckham."

CHAPTER 34

BECKHAM

My back strains from sitting on this uncomfortable-ass chair for Lord knows how long. They don't have a clock on the wall here. The room is cold, even despite the hoodie I'm wearing.

The door handle turns, and Detective Frazier reappears. After the first officer cuffed me and dragged me down here, I was brought into the office and escorted into the room.

I could tell by the detective's reaction he hadn't expected them to arrest me. He made a comment when he saw me in cuffs, telling the cop to release me.

Despite the seriousness of his concerns, he hasn't been a complete asshole while I've been here. Although he did keep me in this room for what feels like forever.

"All right, Beckham, I have some news for you. It turns out that girlfriend of yours pulled some strings and was able to turn over footage of the night of the assault. The videos we have validate your account from when you were present anyway. Our investigation has changed courses, so I might need you to come back down here eventually if we have any further questions, but for now, you're free to leave."

I exhale a sigh of relief, although the one question circling through my mind is the video footage and the mention of him getting it from my girlfriend.

What the hell was Hallyn able to turn over to him?

I don't question him on it, though. That can come later after I have a chance to talk to her.

I spot Hallyn and my brother sitting in a row of chairs on the wall outside the interview room. They both glance up at the same time. Hallyn's eyes glisten when she sees me, and she rushes toward me.

"We went to Whiskey Sinner's and talked to the owner. He was able to give us surveillance footage from that night. He took my statement and said you were free to go," she rattles off, reaching out to grip the front of my shirt.

I tangle my fingers into her hair, pulling her into my arms and pressing my lips to her temple. She melts into my side, looping her arms around my waist, and we stay that way as we walk down the flight of stairs and out the double doors.

I'm shocked and not surprised when I spot Colter's truck out front. He and Reed both hang their hands out the window with Ava sitting between them. Colter cranks up his stereo, blaring "Bad Boys," the *Cops* theme song, as they both smirk at us.

"Good to see you out of the clink, buddy." Reed snickers.

I have no idea how long I was in there or how long they sat outside waiting for me. I owe them big time, but they know I'd have their back if it came down to it.

Hallyn curls up under my arm and stays there during the drive back to the house, which isn't exactly short since the police department is in Lancaster, one town over.

We don't say a word to each other when we disappear to my bedroom. She seems to understand my intentions when I drag my hoodie off and nod toward the bathroom. I'm ready to wash the day away after spending most of this morning working on her truck, followed by sitting at the police station for the better part of the afternoon.

I expected her to join Ava in the living room while she waited for me, but instead, she slipped my sweatshirt over her head and reached for the waistband of her leggings.

"You don't mind if I join you, do you?" she whispers, and I shake my head.

"There's nowhere else I want you to be."

She drags her lip between her teeth before releasing it, her sweet smile stretching across her face.

I push my jeans down, kicking them with my socks in a pile near my hamper. She does the same, and I wrap my fist around my dick when she stands upright, her perky tits on full display for me.

Her nipples bead, and I resist the urge to reach out and brush my finger over them, taking one into my mouth while I lick and suck on her skin.

"Beckham," she whispers, but it comes out as a moan.

I bend down to grip her thighs, lifting her into my arms. She wraps her arms and legs around me while I carry her into the bathroom.

I set her down near the shower while turning on the water, waiting until it's warm enough for her to join, then I hold my hand out to her.

"What'd they say when you got there?" she whispers, leaning in close to me. Water droplets hang from the end of her lashes as she stares up at me from beneath the spray.

"They just wanted to ask me questions about what happened that night. I don't have any idea why they had to resort to the dog and pony show to do it, but it doesn't matter at this point."

I loop my arms around her, and she rests her cheek against my chest. She relaxes when I kiss her forehead and hold her. Her worry was still evident, despite the officer telling them they were releasing me.

"What videos did you give them?"

I listen intently as she recounts her and Hayes going to Whiskey Sinner's to talk with the manager and how he found footage of her standing outside the bar that night while we were on the phone.

She tells me about how they could see what happened clearly, how the guy lurked outside watching her before he approached, dragging her with him out to the car, and then when I showed up, how I fought him off to stop it.

There's more, though. Something she's not telling me. Judging by the way she's chewing on her lip, she's worried about how to say it.

"What's wrong?" I ask, trailing my hand over her hip, up her side, and along the edge of her breast.

Despite the water being hot enough to fill the room in a cloud of steam, she shivers. I love the way her body reacts to my touch. It's something I hope never changes.

"Before it all happened, when he first got there..." she states.

"Ricky," I correct. "Turns out, his name is Ricky. The detective says he used to play for Keaton."

Hallyn nods. "Well, that makes sense, considering how when we were trying to confirm who he was by his license plates, before he ever approached me, we saw him talking with Tanner in the parking lot."

Realization flashes in my mind. He had been tracking her movements with a GPS. It's possible he was staked outside that night and watched her and Ava leave to go to the bar.

I guess it also makes sense why the break-in happened too. Maybe he was pissed when he found out she went out that night.

Guess she wasn't too upset from their breakup if she was going out with her friends.

"I don't want you to worry about him anymore." I lean in and press a soft kiss to her lips. She circles her arm around my neck, pulling me into her.

Her tongue brushes along the seam of my lips, and I deepen the kiss, trailing my hands over her body. Her stomach trembles when one hand continues farther to brush over her clit.

I grin against her lips when her breath hitches, and she sidesteps, giving me better access before she pulls away, narrowing her eyes on me.

"What does that mean?" she asks.

I furrow my brows, playing it off like I don't know what she's talking about. I was hoping she wouldn't read into what I said. It's just better if she doesn't ask questions or know about my plans.

"I mean exactly what I said. I don't want him to be a thought in your mind anymore," I say, pressing a quick kiss against her lips.

When I trail my fingers lower, brushing the tip around her tight heat, she shudders.

"I want your eyes, these lips..." I kiss her again. "This sweet pussy," I growl, dipping my fingers inside her. "Your heart."

She quickly reaches her hands out, holding my shoulders to keep herself upright, but I have my other arm around her. I won't let her fall.

"I want every inch of you," I groan, pulling my fingers out and shoving them in farther. She thrusts her hips toward me, her eyes growing heavy. "In every fuckin' way I can have you."

"You can." She nods, crashing her lips against mine in a hard kiss. "Whatever you want, however you want." That earns her a low growl.

I fuck her like this with my fingers, thrusting in and out of her wet heat. When I adjust my position, moving to curl my fingers, I brush along the sensitive bundle of nerves.

Her movements grow erratic, and she quietly starts pleading with me, muttering, "Please," repeatedly. Her body shudders, and she collapses against my chest.

She reaches between us, wrapping her hand around my hard length. I'm desperate to feel her warm pussy tighten around me like a vise. After the shitty events of today, it's the only way to turn the night around.

I help her wash up, running soap over her body before we finish with our hair. When we step out of the shower, and

I use the towel to dry her off, she protests before I remind her I want to take care of her just like she would me.

Her face softens, and she nods, letting me finish, wrapping her towel around her. She steps into the bedroom while I do the same. I fully anticipate her getting dressed again, so when I find her reclined against my pillow, her legs spread while she stares at me intently, my mouth drops open.

"Hallyn," I order, and she grins.

"Do you remember what we talked about on the phone that night?" she asks.

It takes me a second before it connects to what night she's referring to, and a slow smile stretches across my face.

"I do." I nod, leaning against the doorframe.

My eyes trail down her body to where her pink pussy is on display for me. She moves her legs as if she's fighting the urge not to cover herself up but instead reaches her hand between her thighs.

I flick my gaze back to hers and quirk my brow.

"Don't get impatient now. You can watch, but I was trying to tell you a story first."

"I do remember our conversation that night, Hallyn. I remember how you thanked me for the roses I sent you." I grin. "I recall how you told me you used said rose to get yourself off and how you thought of me while you did."

I push off the doorframe and stalk toward her, crawling up the foot of the bed until I'm lying flat on my stomach, staring between her legs.

Her body trembles again when I brush my fingers along her inner thigh and over her hip bone.

She rubs her clit, her breath hitching, and my eyes zero in on the movement.

"Oh fuck," she groans. "That night, I was thinking about you at the bonfire. Do you know how often I got distracted watching you sit at the table in my dining room, bent over your textbook? How the veins in your hands pop when you grip your pencil, or the way your arms flex when you cross them? I could picture the serious look on your face when you were losing your patience with me, moments away from saying something smart to get under my skin."

I lean in, flicking my tongue over her fingers, and taste her sweet wetness. She spreads them apart, giving me access, adding my tongue as we work her clit.

She lifts her hips in the air, and I brush my finger over her opening and quickly thrust inside her. She moans my name, but I've had enough of her teasing me.

I pull out and kneel, leaning back on my haunches while I face her. Her chest heaves, watching as I tighten my grip around my dick. My fingers are wet from her pussy, and I use it to coat my hands as I fist my length.

"Tell me how bad you want this dick, Hallyn."

She reaches her fingers lower, dipping them inside her, and holds her hands up. "Look how wet I am for you."

I growl, grabbing her wrist and sucking the digits into my mouth. She moves toward me and climbs into my lap.

Her arms circle my neck. I expect her to take me slowly, to torture me in every way she can. She likes to take me by surprise, though, and she does when she bucks against me, fucking me hard. I throw my head back in pleasure.

Her tits bounce, and she rotates her hips, grinding down on me.

When I wrap my palm around her throat, a slow smile stretches across her face.

"Ride me, baby," I groan. "Damn, you fuck me so good."

She throws her head back, and I stare down between us, watching where our bodies meet.

"That's it, Halls. You take my dick so well." I shudder, feeling a wave of pleasure race through me.

Fuck, I'm not going to last long.

"Tell me who this pussy belongs to," she croons.

"This pussy is mine, Hallyn," I growl, earning me a smile.

"No one else," she says, and I repeat it.

"No. One. Else." I thrust my hips up, punctuating every word.

"Yesss," she sighs.

She fits so perfectly in my life the more she lets her walls down and opens her heart to me. She's it for me, and I don't want anyone else.

CHAPTER 35

BECKHAM

"I got eyes on the wounded eagle," Reed's deep voice echoes through the two-way radio.

I chuckle at the nickname. "Stay behind him. I'll see you there."

Reed, Colter, and Hayes are driving in Colter's pickup. I suggested my brother hang back. He's still agitated by the comments the police officer made referencing the game last season.

It's something he still struggles with, especially after how it's destroyed his reputation.

Being here with him these last few months, I've noticed how it's hardened him and his personality. He's still the carefree jokester he's always been, but it's different.

Knowing Tanner was behind what happened to Hallyn, and it led to them pressing charges, has him fired up like it has me. Same with Colter and Reed too.

I've only been here for a couple of months, but these guys have become more than teammates to me. They're like family.

And when family needs you, you don't give up or let them down.

I pull the hoodie over my head and adjust the skull bandanna wrapped around the lower half of my face, revealing only my eyes.

The brakes screech when I pull Hallyn's old pickup into the spot and shift it into park. I keep my head pressed against the headrest, my eyes trained on the rearview mirror, waiting for the headlights to appear behind me.

When I found the tracker under Hallyn's truck, I strategically chose to leave it there. It was the biggest clue we had, and if I was right as I suspected I was, it would be the nail in the coffin, solidifying Tanner was behind it all.

I sit there waiting for close to ten minutes before the headlights appear.

For a second, I wonder what Tanner thought he'd find when he pulled up to Greencastle and saw Hallyn's truck parked in the empty field near the cliffs overlooking Sugar Bottom.

He veers off the side of the road behind me and turns the key in the ignition, right as the guys follow him. He doesn't notice them at first until they're parked on his ass, leaving him only inches to work with if he tries to escape.

I leave the radio in the car. We don't need it now that we're here.

We thought this through—each of us left our phones back at our house, and they all drove together. The goal was to remove any clues pointing to us being here tonight if things fell through and Freeman tried to pull a bitch-ass move and take off crying to the police again.

Something tells me when he finds out what I have to say, he may think twice about going down that road, though.

Reed shoves the door open at the same moment I do. "I think you're on the wrong turf, don't you?" Reed asks.

Freeman glances behind him, his eyes flashing when he spots Colter and Hayes with him, each of them wearing hoodies and face masks of their own, as they pile out of the truck.

When I slam the door shut, his gaze flicks over to mine.

He can't see it, but a broad smile takes over my face.

Judging by the frozen look on his, he had been expecting Hallyn and not me even though the bandanna disguises my face.

I tilt my head to the side. "Not who you were expecting?"

He clenches his jaw, and I chuckle.

Colter pats him on the back before gripping his shoulder and yanks on his shirt.

"C'mon, buddy, you're gonna come with us."

Reed leads the way across the field into the trees. My memory flashes to the last time we were out here that night of Halloween.

We follow him down the dirty path a few feet into the distance. I wasn't familiar with this place until the guys told me about it.

The path leads to a walking trail that hasn't been used in years. There's an underground tunnel, and I guess, as rumor has it, it's supposed to be haunted.

I don't give a shit about all that, though. All I wanted was space away from everyone to talk to our little *friend* here.

"Where the hell are we going?" The fear is evident in Tanner's voice, but none of us say a word.

Once we get to the clearing near the tunnel, Colter shoves Freeman. He nearly trips over his feet.

"Why don't we ask the questions, and you be the one to talk?" I grunt, crossing my arms over my chest. "Starting with, why the fuck you've been following Hallyn?"

His mouth falls open, but he quickly snaps it shut. He flicks his eyes from mine, over to the guys, then back to me.

"C'mon, you didn't actually think you could follow me out here, pull up behind Hallyn's truck, and have me not piece it all together."

"I just saw her truck driving through town, so I followed her out here." He shakes his head, correcting himself. "I mean, you. I followed you out here."

"You just happened to see her truck in town?" I lift my chin, staring down my nose at him.

He fumbles over his words. He hasn't figured out that I'm onto him.

Did he think he would get away with fucking with her truck again, and I wouldn't have pieced it all together eventually?

"I'd think wisely about your words, Freeman. I don't particularly like a liar, and I sure as hell don't fuck with a snitch," I growl.

"I was just trying to talk to her." He holds his hands up and takes a step back. "She blocked my number and won't speak to me."

"So, you thought if you cut the fuel line to her truck, you could what? Trap her at home so you could show up again and harass her into speaking to you?"

His eyes go wide. I grit my teeth and close the distance between us, gripping the front of his shirt in my fists.

"You didn't think I would figure it out? Who'd you think would fix her truck, motherfucker? Me! Unlike you, I'm gonna take care of her every fuckin' day."

He winces, his throat bobbing when he forces a heavy swallow.

"Yeah, that's right. It's gonna be me."

I shove him roughly against the uneven rock wall, pushing my forearm to his throat. He coughs, arching his back away, begging me to get off him.

"Look at me," I snarl. "Look me in my fuckin' eyes, you little pussy. You can't handle being roughed up a little? If you don't get your shit together and stay away from my girl, I can promise you, you'll have far more to deal with."

"All right, man. All right." He holds his hands up.

"What else did you do? Tell me." My voice drops, the warning clear in my tone. "You break into her place too? Was it you who got into her room and left the window cracked?"

"You might as well tell him," Colter pipes up behind me. "We'll find out either way, and if we figure out you lied, you won't have just him on your ass. 'Cause I think what you failed to remember is that not only is it Hallyn's place, it's Ava's too. Don't act like you don't know we're together too. What's her brother think of you fuckin' with her?"

"H-h-he doesn't know, man."

"You told Hallyn you have eyes on her at Braysen. Who the fuck you payin' to keep tabs on her?"

His eyes gleam, and I tighten my hand into a fist. "Oh, that was easy. It's not like you don't have other girls vying for her spot."

Leslie. I honestly can't say I'm surprised.

Tanner grunts, the rock wall digging into his spine. It's the curl in his lip I'm focused on instead. The fucker thinks this shit is amusing.

I rear back, landing a hard fist into his gut. He hunches forward, grunting in pain. When I land another heavy blow, this time under his chin, it sends his head snapping back.

"We know what you've been up to, Freeman." I bend down, leaning in close to his face. "We figured out how you paid the fucker harassing her at Whiskey Sinner's that night, and you gave him money to press charges. We know about the text message you sent me. If you thought it was going to scare me off, you're sorely mistaken."

His brows deepen, and his eyes dart over to me, but he doesn't make the mistake of moving.

"Text message?" he mumbles. "I didn't send any fuckin' message. Everything I did was to Hallyn, okay? Not you, not Ava."

I pull back and glance over at my brother. His arms are folded against his chest, one hand gripping his chin. He still has no clue about the note left in my locker, and I never told him about the text.

Our eyes lock because he's the only person who knows what happened in Rixton.

Could it be that bullshit followed me all the way here?

Or am I missing something else?

"Don't fuckin' lie to me." He grunts when I follow it up with another punch, falling to his knees on the ground.

"Get the hell up," Colter scoffs.

His stomach heaves, and he coughs, spitting blood on the ground. Something about the sight of it smeared on the concrete is so fuckin' satisfying.

He was paying the price for his actions.

"Stand the fuck up," I mutter, gripping the back of his shirt, and he stumbles to his feet.

He wipes the edge of his hand along his lip, smearing blood on his chin and hand.

"This is how it's gonna go from here." I lean down to look him in the eyes. "You're gonna sit right here until we leave, and you're never gonna speak of our little chat. You hear me?"

He doesn't say a word, doesn't even make a move.

"You're gonna leave Hallyn alone. You won't reach out to her or even breathe her name again. Do you fuckin' understand? 'Cause not only would I use every piece of evidence we have to bury you, but I'll make sure you never throw a fuckin' football again."

I stare at him, his eyes locking on mine.

"Are we clear?"

"All right," he mumbles.

"I want to hear you fuckin' say it. Tell me you agree."

"I agree. Now, will you get the hell out of here?" He spits again, this time narrowly missing my shoe.

I stare down at him and curl my lip, only he can see it.

"C'mon, Beck," my brother says, reaching for my arm to jerk me away.

He has to know he got off easy.

We have video footage of him. The tape recorder in my pocket has him admitting to breaking into her apartment.

He claims he wasn't behind the text, but it doesn't matter. We have him for the shit that does.

All I have to do is pack it up and send a copy off to his coach, and his college football career is over.

I'm still dealing with the fallout of the charges being pressed and dropped, but thankfully, the video footage was enough to appease Coach. He may not have liked seeing his star quarterback getting into a fight in the bar parking lot, but when the door was shut and it was only the two of us together, he told me he would've done the same thing.

He didn't admit it, but I think it was his way of saying he was proud of me for it too.

"You good?" Colter asks as we take the path leading to our trucks. I hit the button on the recorder before shoving it into my pocket.

"Yeah," I exhale. "Let's just hope he sticks to his word and leaves her alone."

"He will," Hayes says.

I hope he's right.

As soon as I climb into Hallyn's truck, I pull my hood down and tug the bandanna off my head.

My hand aches a bit from the punch I landed against his jaw, but not like the fight the night at the bar. I stretch my fingers out, attempting to loosen it.

It might be a little sore, but at least we only have one game left of the season before fall break. I'm not worried about this one. As it stands, we already have the conference championship in the bag.

We head straight for our place. When I walk into my room, I drag my hoodie off and hit the power button on my phone before a flood of text messages roll through from Hallyn. Several asking where I am and for me to call her.

We made plans to meet up, only for me to stop responding and turn my phone off.

"You had me worried you were in an accident or something," she says, skipping her greeting when she answers.

"Sorry, my phone died. I just got home."

She goes silent for a moment.

"Hallyn?"

"Well, that's interesting... Ava was trying to get ahold of Colter, and he said the same thing."

I grit my teeth. I hate lying to her, but it's better if she doesn't know what we were up to.

"You still coming over tonight?" I change the subject, and she exhales heavily.

"Yeah, I'm with Ava. We'll head over soon."

"All right," I say, opening my dresser and pulling out shorts and a pair of underwear. "I'll see you when you get here."

"Okay." Her voice drops low.

"Halls..."

"Yeah?"

"I love you, baby."

This time when she exhales, it comes out as more of a sigh.

"I love you too."

I'm sitting outside the locker room after I wrap up dance. I'm not alone. A few other girlfriends are waiting too.

It's still relatively quiet, though, so when I hear heels clicking on the tile floor, my eyes flick over to where Leslie and her posse saunter down the hallway.

Thankfully, she's stayed away from us since the night of the Halloween party.

She stands across the hall from me. I curl my lip as she drags her eyes over me, pursing her cherry-red lips thinking she's once again gotten under my skin.

The door to the locker room clicks, and Beckham steps out, his bag hanging from his shoulder with a group of guys following him.

His hair is wet, and he shakes his head, letting the strands fall wherever, before he pulls his blue Braysen beanie on.

I grin at the sight of the dimple on his cheek. He holds his hand out and tugs me into his arms. I giggle, collapsing against his chest, and take a deep breath. Inhaling his familiar cologne, I sigh, pressing my cheek to his heart.

"How was practice?" I ask, pulling back to glance up at him.

"Good," he groans. "First day back after break, so they worked us hard. Gotta get ready for the game, though, right?"

I smile, pushing up on my tiptoes, and he kisses me softly.

Fall break came and went quickly, and I eagerly counted down the days until we had two weeks off for the holidays at the end of December. While the rest of the campus cleared out to go home to spend time with their family, the football players came back early to amp things up before their conference game on New Year's Eve.

If they win, there's a chance they landed their spot in the playoffs.

This is what Beckham and the team have been busting their asses for all season, and it's right at the tip of their fingers.

"You guys are gonna kill it, and I can't wait to stand on the sidelines and cheer you on the whole time."

He mumbles a low, "Thank you," and kisses me again as the door clicks behind us, followed by loud voices echoing in the hallway.

"Hey, Carver, why don't you pack it up and take that shit home," Zane jokes.

"On second thought, why don't you take that shit over to Hallyn's? Give us a break for one night," Hayes adds.

My cheeks heat, and I bury my face into Beckham's chest.

"Shut up, Hayes," he fires back. "Don't forget to pick up lotion on the way home. Lord knows your dry spell is like the fuckin' Sahara Desert, so you're gonna need it."

I clap my hand over my mouth and peer over Beckham's shoulder. Hayes raises his middle finger in the air, aiming it at him and then me.

He's joking, and we both know it even though I don't doubt the jab felt more like a sucker punch to the gut.

Hayes has tried and failed to get the attention of Lydia for weeks. She's holding his reputation against him, refusing to even give him a chance, and is convinced he's nothing but trouble.

He denies it to everyone, saying he doesn't give a shit, but it's no secret the comments about his character get under his skin. He claims to have given up on pursuing her. He plays it off like he doesn't care even though we all know damn good and well it's not the truth.

Those Carver boys are not ones to give up easily, that's for damn sure.

Beckham reaches for my hand, linking our fingers together, and lifts the back of mine to his mouth.

"Let's go," he whispers, and I nod, fighting off my grin.

We turn to head out the door and are met by Leslie. Her lip curls in a snarl. She quickly smooths it over though when she catches Beckham looking in her direction. He plays it off like she's not there, which gets under her skin more, until he takes everyone by surprise and stops when we pass her.

"Hey, Leslie," Beckham says. "How's Tanner doing?"

My head jerks over to him. His comment feels more like whiplash at the mention of Tanner. Beckham, on the other hand, seems unfazed and manages to keep his expression neutral.

"I'm sorry, who?" Leslie rolls her eyes.

Beckham chuckles. "I thought that's what you might say."

I pull on his hand, and he looks down at me and winks.

"I guess you could say I got eyes on you too."

My face drops, and I level Leslie with a murderous glare. He didn't have to explain himself any further. The statement alone said all he needed to say.

"Keep mine and Hallyn's name out of your mouth, and we won't have any trouble. We good?"

Her eyes are wide, and she nods. "It's not what you think, Beckham," she tries to reason.

He ignores her, moving my hand to grip his forearm.

"Let's go," he mumbles to me.

She's meddled with our relationship one too many times, but he's made his point clear now. Whatever he has on her, the warning ought to be enough for her to back off and leave us alone.

"What the hell was that about?" I exhale heavily as we push through the doors leading to the parking lot.

The temperatures have dropped below freezing. When the cold hits my face, I gasp to catch my breath, a puff of air billowing in front of me.

Beckham tugs on my arm and mutters, "Come on," as we jog across the parking lot toward his truck. There are a few patches of ice throughout. We make a point to jump over them.

He opens the door and helps me climb into his truck before he jogs around to join me.

"Are you gonna tell me what just happened?"

He shakes his head, reaching over to crank up the heat and sending a burst of cold air into the cab with us.

"I'm sure you put two and two together. Hopefully, she'll heed my warning and leave us alone."

He rests his hand on my thigh as he pulls out of the school. I'm so worked up at the thought of her filtering information about Beckham and me back to Tanner that I don't even realize where we're going or that he's driving in the opposite direction of his house.

I tug on the sleeves of my cardigan over my hand, attempting to keep me warm. One of these days, I'll learn my lesson and wear a coat, especially with my luck around cars breaking down, but I guess today isn't the day.

Eventually, I realize where he's heading. There's not much else out near Greencastle, especially after he passes the turn leading us to the beach below the cliffs.

He keeps driving past our normal spot along the trees. Instead, he pulls into the gravel area overlooking the pointe and puts his truck in park, lifts the center console, and wags his brows.

"C'mere." He nods, motioning for me to join him.

He stops me, though. Holding one finger up, he reaches into the back seat and pulls his jersey out of his gym bag.

"Before I forget, I wanted to give this to you. In case you wanted to wear it at our next game."

I take it from him and shrug out of my sweater and toss it in the seat behind us. This time, I'm the one wagging my brows suggestively.

The cool temperatures from the window feel good against my heated skin. All I'm wearing are my leggings and the tank top I had under my sweater.

His eyes drop to my chest, his face turns serious, and I smirk before pulling the jersey over my head.

"Get your ass over here," he groans, the number eighteen proudly displayed on my chest.

I grin at his reaction and crawl across the seat toward him. He reaches for the lever on the side and pushes back, giving me enough room to straddle his lap.

The fabric of my leggings and his sweatpants don't leave much to the imagination. He growls when I swivel my hips, pretending to make myself comfortable, and grips them to stop me from moving.

I bat my lashes at him, playing coy. "So, Carver, what brought us up here?"

I wrap my arm around his neck. He drags his hands down my thighs and under the hem of the shirt. His fingers brush along my skin, skating along the waistband of my leggings. My stomach trembles, and I suck in a sharp breath.

"I was thinking..." He looks between us to where his jersey bunches at my waist. "Remember what you said the day I let you drive my truck."

My brows furrow, trying to piece together the events of the day and remember what I said to him.

He wraps his arms around me and flips me onto my back, pinning me against the seat beneath him.

"Beckham," I gasp when he thrusts between my legs, then moan.

"Have I refreshed your memory?" He drags his nose along my jaw, peppering kisses in his wake.

He quickly pulls away, and I shudder from his absence. My eyelids lower, taking him in as he stares at my center and rubs his fingers over my pussy through the thin cotton of my leggings.

Instinctively, I raise my hips, desperate for him to give me more. A satisfied smile curls on the edge of his lips.

He glances around us, checking once more to make sure we're alone before he tugs my pants down over my hips along with my underwear.

The sound of his moan echoing in the small space hits like a shot of pleasure directly to my core. He slides his finger into his mouth, wetting the digit, before he brushes it over my clit.

"Oh fuckkk," I exhale, lifting my hips toward him again.

He gives in and jerks my leggings off, along with my shoes, dropping them on the floor next to us. My hand slips between my legs to touch myself before he pushes it away. His eyes flash with desire.

I smile when he wraps his hand around my legs, pushing them against my chest and burying his face between them.

Beckham has me right where he wants me. My legs pinned against my chest, spread open for him, with nowhere to go.

He devours me like I'm his last meal, and he's a starving man.

I drag my nails through his hair, pulling on the strands. He hums in appreciation against my clit. The moan creates a vibration as he sucks and licks my pussy, and I pull harder, forcing him not to let up.

His finger brushes over my center, teasing my entrance just enough before I start quietly begging him for more. He delivers, thrusting two deep inside me.

When he finally lets off, I release my hold, and he continues sliding his fingers in and out of my pussy.

I gasp, trying to keep up with him, while his gaze burns between my legs. The desire is written on his face.

"Do you know how much I love you?" he says, catching me off guard. The comment so sweet, so vulnerable, given the assault he's currently wreaking on my body.

"H-h-how much?" I question.

His mouth drops open, his nostrils flaring as he mutters, "So wet," under his breath followed by "fucking hot as hell."

I squeeze my eyes shut, my chest heaving as I grip the seat.

He fumbles for a minute before he pulls out of me. When I finally open my eyes again, he quickly shoves his pants down to his knees. I sit up, pushing him back against the seat, and he doesn't stop me.

We're halfway between the driver and middle seat, giving us enough room this time when I climb on top of him.

His eyes lower when I position the tip at my entrance and slowly take all of him.

"Tell me, Beckham," I whisper against his lips. "How much do you love me?"

He slips his palm along the side of my face, his thumb gripping my chin to look at him.

"Sometimes I wonder how I made it through life without you before," he grits out. "I hadn't realized how hollow I was inside until you came in and filled all the empty parts of me."

Tears prick my eyes, and I crash my mouth against him.

It's hard to believe the same man who was such an asshole when we first met can still take my breath away by saying the sweetest things.

I grind my hips, and his head falls back, rolling around until he finally looks at me again.

"One of these days, I'm gonna put a ring on your finger, and you'll wear more than my last name. It'll be yours too."

"You promise?" I ask him, lifting myself and slowly taking him again.

He growls, slipping his fingers into my hair, and kisses me.

"I'd make any deal or hold any promise you ask of me if it means I get to have you forever."

"Forever," I agree, trailing my lips along his jaw to his ear. "I've always been yours."

He presses his forehead to mine, and I wrap my arms around his neck. We both hold on to each other tight.

When he thrusts his hips up, matching my rhythm, a wave of pleasure washes over me. I'm close, and the look on his face says he's not far behind.

"I love you," I moan against his mouth.

I quickly dart my tongue out, brushing along my lips and the seam of his. He groans, his nostrils flaring.

"Show me."

EPILOGUE

BECKHAM

"Congratulations on your big win! Happy New Year, baby," Hallyn croons.

She holds the plastic cup in the air, swinging her hips while she sings along to the lyrics. When the cup passes by my face, I get a strong whiff of what she's drinking and glance down, smiling at my girl.

I'm not sure what number drink she's on, but she's letting loose and feelin' good.

Her eyes slowly blink as she stares up at me, a slow smile stretching across her face.

"Happy New Year to you." I chuckle, and she leans in, pressing her lips against my neck.

I inhale sharply between my teeth, digging my fingers into her hips as I press my mouth to her ear.

"Easy, or I'm gonna drag you down the hall to my room, and we won't be appearing again until the morning."

She snickers, turning around so her back is molded to my front, and continues her dancing. Every time her hips sway and she grinds her ass over my dick, I find myself growing closer and closer to following through on my word.

It's fine, though. We'll continue celebrating with our friends and my teammates for now, but at this rate, it won't be long before I haul her ass over my shoulder and make good on my word.

"Hallyn," Ava shouts as she steps back inside from the back patio, where she, Colter, and a few of our teammates were outside around the bonfire.

The song changes, and Ava weaves through the crowd. The two girls jump up and down like they haven't seen each other in years before they pick up dancing again.

Colter is two steps behind her. Our eyes meet, and we both shake our heads and smile as if to say, "How the hell did we get ourselves here?"

Reed is across the room with a girl seated on his lap, and they're huddled up, talking.

"Where the hell is your brother?" Colter hollers.

I shrug, pulling my phone out of my pocket again for the third time, checking to see if I have any missed calls or texts from him.

It's unlike him not to answer me, and it's even more unlike him not to be here.

"Any chance you have that girl's number he's been hangin' out with? What's her name, Everly?" Colter asks. "Maybe he's with her?"

My brows deepen, and I shake my head. I'm still not sure what to make of their relationship. He claims the two of them are dating, yet they act so awkward whenever I've been around them that I'd hardly even call them friends.

He swears it's not what I think and that they are serious, but I find that hard to believe.

"I don't have her number, and honestly, I don't know if I know anyone who would."

"Who?" Ava asks, picking up on pieces of our conversation.

Hallyn's in her own world, though, having the time of her life. All three of us stop and chuckle when she tilts her head back, belting out the lyrics to A Rebels Havoc at the top of her lungs.

"Everly… Shit, I can't think of her last name. The girl Hayes was with the other day in the cafeteria. We have no idea where he's at and think the two of them might be together."

"I think Mandy knows her. She might have her number. Let me see if I can find her, and I'll ask."

We nod, and Ava disappears into the crowd, heading back toward where she came in earlier.

"I don't know, man, but something doesn't sit right with me." I hold my beer in front of my mouth, leaning closer to Colter.

He presses his lips together in a firm line.

Call it twin intuition, or maybe I just know my brother. Whatever it is, something isn't right.

"I'll be right back. I'm gonna try to call him again," I grit out.

He nods and motions with his head to Hallyn who says, "I'll stay here."

The house is packed, with people spilling out onto the front lawn and into the back, where the bonfire is. Initially,

I was going to head out front before I pivot and head down the hall to my room.

I pull out my keys and unlock the door when I hear a loud scream before the music cuts out.

"Beckham," Colter shouts down the hallway, and I can't move fast enough to get to him.

In the back of my mind, I pick up the sound of the collective gasps and the concerned voices muttering things like, "holy shit", "what happened", and "is that Beckham" before I turn the corner.

None of it prepared me for what I saw when I glanced down the stairs to the entryway where my brother stands. He stumbles and nearly collapses before he hits the wall and slides down to the floor.

Blood stains the front of his jacket. I'm not sure if it's from the gash on his cheek, the massive goose egg on the side of his head, or his nose, which appears off-center.

"What the fuck happened to you?"

He shakes his head and stares up at me, slowly blinking.

The dazed look on his face shows all the signs of a concussion.

"Are you hurt anywhere else?" I mutter, reaching to help him stand.

He grits his teeth and pulls away, clutching his arm to his chest, and winces in agony. A part of me wonders what the hell we're going to do next week when we face the Hawks in the playoffs.

I can't let my mind go there, though. Not right now.

Not when my brother needs me.

"C'mon," I grunt, looping my arm around his waist. He wraps his around my neck and grits his teeth, his breaths coming out in heavy pants.

"My truck," Colter hollers. "We can take my truck."

I catch a glimpse of Hallyn with her arms around Ava. She waves her hand to me, urging me to go. I'll call her later when I get a second.

Getting my brother to the hospital is the only thing fueling me right now. I need to make sure he's okay.

We step out onto the porch, and I notice a lot of the crowd has dispersed, likely making their way into the backyard. It's cold as hell out here, and unless they want to freeze their toes off, I'm guessing they want to get around the fire.

Hayes stumbles down the stairs, but I have my arm firmly around his waist. There's no way in hell I'll let him fall.

"Beckham," he forces out, sending him into a coughing fit.

We stop, and he bends down, clutching his arm to his stomach while he spits blood on the freshly white snow.

"You all right, man?"

He forces himself upright again, and our eyes lock on one another.

His throat bobs when he swallows, and I know whatever he's about to say won't be good.

"It was him."

All the emotion drains from my face.

"Are you serious?"

He nods. "It was him."

There are two things I know for certain—you can't come for one Carver brother without thinking you won't have to get through the other too, and you better be prepared for the hell that will follow when you do.

Thank you so much for reading The Rivals We Hate!

I hope you could feel how much I enjoyed writing Beckham and Hallyn's story as you were reading it. Braysen U has been a blast for me to dive into and there's a whole lot more coming so stay tuned.

Want to find out what happens with Hayes? Get The Plays We Fake, a fake dating, opposites attract romance.

www.authorbrookeobrien.com/theplayswefake

Still want more Beckham and Hallyn? Keep reading for access to their bonus epilogue.

Don't miss a sneak peek at another one of my favorites, Brix, an enemies to lovers, stepbrother rock star romance. If you love rock star romances with lots of hate to want you vibes, then you'll definitely want to check it out the A Rebels Havoc series.

I hope you enjoy!

BONUS SCENE

Dear Reader,

I hope you enjoyed Beckham and Hallyn's story as much as I loved writing it.

I've loved living in the Braysen U world and I can't wait to share more about what's going on with the rest of the guys, as well as bring you along for Hayes' story. I decided to give you a glimpse into where things are at a year later in a bonus epilogue exclusively for you.

To read it, all you have to do is visit the link below or scan the QR code with your phone, sign up for my newsletter, and you'll get access.

www.authorbrookeobrien.com/bonus

If you want to stay up to date with my sales and new releases, you can follow me on Bookbub at: www.bookbu b.com/profile/brooke-o-brien

Brooke

BRIX

BOOK ONE

USA TODAY BESTSELLING AUTHOR

BROOKE O'BRIEN

CHAPTER ONE

IVY

"I'll take a whiskey. Neat."

"You got it!" the bartender shouts over the music.

My eyes scan over the crowd of people packed into Whiskey Barrel Saloon, searching for any sign of my friend. She promised to meet me here after she got off work.

I rolled into town less than an hour ago. The moment I saw the "Welcome to Carolina Beach" sign passing into the city limits, I contemplated pulling over on the side of the road and turning the car around, convincing myself there had to be another way out of this.

Returning home for the summer had been last on my list of options, but in the end, it was for the best. My scholarship covered the first two years and it had been rough balancing a job with a full class load last year.

My mom raised me as a single parent since I was five when my dad took off out of town. He never even bothered to look back. She's done her part in raising me, and I hated the thought of relying on her. All I needed was a place to stay for the summer. I'd work, save up the money, and get my ass back to Chapel Hill to finish my last year as a Tarheel.

When I saw the band A Rebels Havoc printed across the flyer on the door, the deal was sealed. I knew this was a huge mistake.

"Here ya go." Placing a napkin on the counter, the bartender set the glass down in front of me.

So, here I was, back home for the summer, waiting for Kyla to show up. Once I saw the flyer, I immediately knew why she asked to meet here tonight. I can't blame her for not telling me sooner. If I knew A Rebels Havoc was going to be playing, I would've come up with an excuse as to why I couldn't make it.

I spot Kyla's brother, Madden, duck through the door, causing a knot of unease to coil tighter in the pit of my stomach. Not at all because of Madden.

It had everything to do with the guy walking through the door behind him.

Some things never change.

If only there were an eject button, some way to get me the hell out of here undetected.

Brix was dressed in all black, from the baseball cap on his head to the t-shirt fitting him like it was tailor-made for him, to the black denim jeans molding to his body in all the right ways. Even from here, I can spot the thin, silver chain hanging around his neck. My eyes roam over the dark ink covering his left arm while he makes conversation with the bouncer, his dark eyes searching over the crowd.

"There you are!" Kyla yells, as I glance over my shoulder.

She's gorgeous, her lavender-colored hair styled in curls pulled away from her face with a black choker wrapped around her neck. Her lips are painted a fire-engine red, and

I'm starting to feel like I underdressed in my denim shorts, black tank top, and black espadrille sandals.

"Hey, girl." I smile at my friend, wrapping my arm around her for a hug.

"I'm so glad you're home." She bounces on her feet, clapping her hands. As much as I'm happy to see her, I wish I could say the same for myself.

"I didn't know your brother would be playing tonight."

Maybe it's the forced smile on my face or the sudden realization of the tidbit of information she forgot to share with me about tonight, her head turns away from me, eyes searching through the crowd. Mine follow along with hers until we both spot the guys near the front of the bar by the stage.

"If you don't want to stay to watch them, I understand."

"It's fine."

I'm not going to let him push me out of here. He's gotten away with embarrassing me and making me uncomfortable, to the point I'd take off running.

I'll be fuckin' damned if I let that shit slide again.

"Let's go find a table," she suggests while pointing her thumb over the wall wrapped around the side of the bar lined with booths. The name, Whiskey Barrel, fits the rustic feel. It's all weathered wood and iron beams.

Swiping my drink off the bar, I motion with the glass for her to lead the way. We find an empty booth near the front, which happens to also be close to the stage.

"Hey," Madden says, approaching us. "I had no idea you were going to be here tonight."

Madden's eyes bounce between his sister over to me. His narrow, trying to place me.

A lot has changed over the years. I'm not the same girl I was when I left Carolina Beach. Living on my own for the first time in my life forced me to learn a lot about myself. I found a voice, a confidence I didn't have when I was stuck in this hellhole of a town, and a style that suits me. I wasn't exactly the definition of pretty and popular back in high school. I've come a long way from my pimply face, oversized hoodies, and baggy jeans.

"Who's this?" Madden points to me.

"What the hell, Madd? It's Ivy."

Madden's eyes widen in recognition. They do a quick sweep of my body, as if seeing it for the first time, before finally meeting mine again. His mouth drops slightly, shaking himself from his thoughts, before he grins.

"Wow, Ivy. I didn't even recognize you."

He reaches his hands toward me, giving me a casual hug. When he steps back, I eye his black t-shirt with A Rebels Havoc printed across the front. His backward plaid hat paired with his well-kept beard gives off lumberjack vibes.

When I was in high school, I would often stay over at Kyla's house on the weekends. She was the closest thing I had to a sister, having grown up an only child. Madden took on the role of the pseudo big brother, looking after and protecting both of us.

Even when his band of dimwits came around, he would always keep an eye on us, threatening to knock some sense into anyone who didn't leave us alone. He'd never let anybody fuck with his sister, and I was thankful I was included in that, too.

"You look so... grown-up?" he mutters, bewildered. "Different... but in a good way."

"You ready to set up?" Brix interrupts. He may be the bane of my existence, but he's still one of Madden's best friends. He claps Madden on the shoulder before his eyes stop, falling on me.

I knew the moment Brix looked at me, the way his eyes did the same once-over Madden's just had, he didn't recognize me either. The only difference in how Brix looked at me was the not-so-subtle way he bit his lip before rubbing his hand over his chin, enjoying his blatant perusal of my body.

All the memories of him making fun of me growing up flash through my mind like a highlight reel of my high school years.

To say I hated Brix Ward would be a mild understatement. If he were to go up in flames standing in front of me, I wouldn't bother to offer him the glass of water in my hand.

"Yeah, man," Madden grunts, slapping him on the chest. "Give me a sec to grab a beer, and I'll be ready."

"I need a drink, too. I'll come with you," Kyla echos. She eyes me nervously, her eyes flash over to Brix, hesitant if she should leave us alone. I nod my head toward the bar, assuring her it's alright, I've got this.

"Be nice," Kyla jests, smacking Brix on the chest.

He has the nerve to act wounded, rubbing his hand where she had touched him, shouting over the music toward her asking, "What the hell was that for?"

I roll my eyes, taking another sip of whiskey.

"What's your name, sweetheart?"

The words roll off his tongue, and I don't hold back my cringe of disgust. Is this how he picks up women?

"Not interested."

"Oh, really." He laughs. He glances around us, checking to see if anyone may have overheard, before looking back to me. "Are you sure about that?"

"Oh, trust me," I chuckle, "I'm very sure."

"Is this some sort of hard-to-get move? 'Cause I happen to like a chase, but you should know, I always get what I want in the end."

My eyes widen, nodding my head at his audacity. I'm afraid if I roll my eyes any harder, they'll end up rolling out of my damn head. Does this garbage actually work on women?

Who am I kidding? Of course, it does.

I'm not blind to the heated stares blazing into him, eating him up like he's some sort of sugary piece of eye candy.

I'll admit it. He's not bad to look at if you're only looking at his appearance. If he hadn't been the sole reason for making my life miserable years ago, I might even be able to overlook the fact he's a player who's looking to score and give in to his advances for one night.

"I'm not playing hard-to-get. I don't think there's any-thing you could say or do that would ever make me want to sleep with you. Hell, I'm certain more than half of Carolina Beach already has."

His face falls for a second, but he recovers quickly. If I had to guess, he wasn't expecting this much resistance. Something tells me he's not used to being rejected.

"How the hell would you know?" he barks, the tension in his neck and shoulders growing stiff, his eyes narrowing into slits.

"This isn't the first time we've met." I smile, thoroughly enjoying this little taste of karma on my lips. I reach my hand out between us and say, "You may not recognize me, but my name is Ivy Thomas. I wish I could say it was nice to see you again, but we both know that's not true. Ain't that right, Brix?"

His eyes widen in recollection before a salacious grin spreads across his arrogant face.

"Ivy fuckin' Thomas. It's too fucking bad, even knowing that I'd still fuck you like it's the best you'll ever have."

"You're a real prick."

"So I've been told." Brix takes a swig of his beer, not taking his eyes off me.

"Yo, Brix!" a voice booms through the speaker. We both turn our attention toward the stage to find their other bandmate, Tysin, staring back at us with his hands up and an annoyed expression on his face.

"If you change your mind, come find me after the show."

He has the fucking nerve to wink at me before he turns, heading toward Tysin, Madden joining them as they start setting up the rest of their band equipment.

"What did he say to you?" Kyla asks, returning with a beer bottle in her hand.

"He didn't even recognize me," I snicker. "Tried hitting on me, probably assuming he could convince me to come home with him. I turned that shit down real quick."

"You're kidding," she snorts.

"Not in the least. You should've seen the look on his face when I introduced myself."

"Oh my God, I can't believe I missed it." She giggles, looking both amused and disappointed.

We slide into our booth, catching up. We spot a few people I remember from high school who stop by to chat with us before the show starts.

I've watched the guys play before, although it was years ago when they played on their makeshift stage in Madden's garage. Thankfully, their dad eventually said they had to find somewhere else to keep their equipment, which meant they started coming around less and less.

When they take the stage a little while later, I try to avoid showing any interest, but even I can't deny they're good. I'm thankful for the lights being turned down, so I'm able to hide in the darkness from the possibility of Brix spotting me.

The last thing I want is for him to see me watching him or give him the satisfaction of thinking I'm enjoying his performance. I've seen a lot of bands play while pursuing a career in music journalism. I'd never utter these words to anyone, but I'm surprised they haven't been scooped up by a major record label. They're talented.

Brix smiles flirtatiously at the crowd while he sings, leaning over the speaker, letting the women in the front touch him, thrusting toward their roaming hands.

Tysin plays the bass guitar next to Brix, nodding his head to the beat of the music. Madden's size alone makes him hard to miss sitting behind his drums.

I watch in awe for most of their set before I decide to cut out early and head to my new home. Exhaustion from packing up my car and making the drive back to CB weighed on me. A text from my mom came through around midnight as she was boarding her red-eye flight home. She left me with detailed instructions on where to find her hide-a-key and directions to the room I'd be staying in for the summer.

When she called me last week, I was in the heat of finals. My workload was piled high, and every available minute was spent with my head crammed in my books. When she broke the news she had gotten engaged, I couldn't believe my ears.

Honestly, I never thought I'd see the day she'd want to get remarried after her divorce from my father. I spent an hour on the phone listening to her gush over the man, Jasper, she recently met and how she'd been swept away in their whirlwind romance ever since.

I was shocked when she broke the news that not only had he asked her to marry him, but she had also recently decided to move in. It wasn't a big deal to me in the grand scheme of things. We had bounced around from place to place throughout my childhood, so it wasn't like I was coming home to a familiar house I had lived in all my life only to find out it was now gone.

It made the decision to come home for the summer all the more difficult, but in the end, I needed the help. I needed to find a job and save up money, so when I went back to school, I could put all focus on my degree.

I wanted to find a way to enjoy the next couple of months while I was here, but nothing could've prepared me for what happened next.

CHAPTER TWO

BRIX

I don't remember who brought me home, much less why I chose to crash on the couch, of all places. My back screams in agony from the pain and stiffness, moving to stretch, peeking one eye open.

The piercing ray of sunlight combined with the skull-splitting headache has me regretting the round of shots we had after wrapping up our show last night.

It wasn't the first time it happened, and it won't be the last.

I miscalculate the space between me and the edge of the couch when I roll on my side, sending me falling face-first onto the hardwood floor.

"God damn," I groan, bracing my hands beneath me, pushing myself up. Feeling weak, I reach for the edge of the oak coffee table to help me up.

Beer cans litter the surface, reminding me of the one too many drinks I put away when I got home.

"What the hell was I thinking?"

I wince hearing the sound of a throat clearing behind me. I expect it to be my father, which should have me regretting my choices from last night even more. Except that would mean I gave a shit, which I don't. I stopped worrying about what he thought of me a long time ago.

I rub the pads of my fingers over my eyes, delaying the inevitable moment when I glance up to find him staring bullets through me, adding yet another reason for being a disgrace of a son to the list.

"Are you waiting for me to answer that question?"

The soft voice from behind catches me off guard, sending my head jolting over my shoulder. The sharp movement causes a shooting pain to slice up the column of my neck. I roll my eyes shut, groaning in agony.

Her quiet chuckle follows. Whoever it is clearly relishes in my pain.

Pushing to sit on the edge of the couch, I fall back against the cushions, tilting my head in her direction. When I finally manage to open my eyes enough, I wonder for a second if I somehow misplaced where I was or what the hell happened last night.

What was I thinking?

Did Ivy end up coming home with me?

Hell no.

Thinking back to the scant denim shorts she wore showing off her sculpted legs nearly has me biting my lip at all the thoughts swirling through my mind. My eyes rake over her body once again, pausing as they land on her tan legs. She's active, judging by the clothes she's wearing combined with her tight body.

Recalling how she all too joyously turned me down, followed by the smirk lining those sexy-ass lips when she pointed out who she is, left the sting of embarrassment ringing clear in my memory.

Yeah... there's no way she would've come home with me. If that's the case, what the hell is she doing standing in my living room with the look of disdain painted like a neon sign on her face?

"What the hell are you doing here? Did you break into my fucking house? Or is this your way of twisting the knife deeper after last night?"

She laughs. The sound coming out both sexy and frustrating. Her head is thrown back and strands of her long, dark hair are falling over her shoulder.

"The fact you think I give a shit about you or would even consider wasting another second on your bullshit is hilarious."

Well, okay then. It still doesn't answer the question of why the hell she is in my house?

As if reading my mind, she continues, "I'm actually wondering the same thing." She clenches her jaw. She looks so fucking sexy, the way her cheeks turn rosy. If this is how she looks when she's mad, I can't wait to see her when she's turned on.

"Like I said, sweetheart"—I lean forward, bracing my hands on my knees to stand— "this is my house. I live here."

Facing her now, the subtle tick in her jaw at the term of endearment does not escape me. Anger blazes in her eyes when she crosses her arms in front of her chest. She widens her stance like she's gearing up for the argument that's about to ensue.

"Are you sure you still don't want to take me up on my offer from last night? I have no problem letting you take a little aggression out on me."

I reach my hand out, brushing my knuckle along the ink covering her forearm. Goose bumps rise over her skin, and despite her best effort to paste the look of hatred on her face, her body gives her away. She's trying to play it off, hoping like hell I won't notice, but I flash her a grin letting her know she's not fooling me.

"Something tells me the hate-sex will be some of the best fucking I've ever had," I moan, wrapping my hand around her wrist.

She grits her teeth, whipping her arm out of my hold. Seeing how riled up she is, I bite my lip to cover my be-mused smile. I have a feeling I'm going to enjoy letting her take her anger out on me.

Nails in my back, teeth marking my skin. *Fuck.*

"If you think I'd ever let your dick anywhere near me, you've gotta be fuckin' crazy. I bet you have shit growing on you from all the places that thing's been."

"You better watch your fuckin' mouth," I grunt, tension coiling in my body, taking a step closer to her. She smiles like the Cheshire cat, apparently liking how she's pissed me off.

Yeah, the hate-sex is gonna be real fuckin' good for the both of us.

A familiar sound of keys sliding into the lock followed by the click of the deadbolt has us both turning toward the door. Laughter filters through the room, and my eyes bounce back over to Ivy. The smell of her clean scent washes over me; the way her throat bobs when she swallows ignites a fire within me.

"Mother?" Ivy says, sounding both surprised and lighter. Like happiness was wrapped around one simple word. That is until I realize it's my father and his fiancée, Charlene, staring back at us.

For a second, I wonder if they heard us arguing from outside.

"Ivyana," she replies, smiling, and it all clicks into place.

My mind filters through the several conversations we've had about her daughter, Ivyana. The daughter who graduated high school with honors and has a nearly perfect GPA at the University of North Carolina.

Ivy is Ivyana. What the hell is wrong with me? Why didn't it click into place until now? I've never heard her called by her full name, not even when we were back in high school.

"Hi, Mother." She grins, crossing the distance between them to wrap her in a hug. The snarky tone she threw at me a moment ago is completely gone, replaced with something else entirely.

Reaching my hand up behind my neck, I massage my fingers into my skin in hopes of easing the tension.

"I'm so happy to see you, honey. I've missed you."

Already over this bullshit, I begin picking up the beer cans strewn over the coffee table along with the ones knocked over onto the floor.

"Brix, what the hell happened here?"

It wouldn't be a typical day if my father wasn't finding some reason to lay into me.

"What's it look like? I had a few drinks last night after my show. I'll fuckin' clean it up, alright? Chill out."

Holding the cans in my palm, I brush past my father, stalking into the kitchen. Like whiplash, the once happy moment between Ivy and her mom is gone.

"This can't happen anymore. You hear me? Just because I let you live here doesn't mean you can treat my place like a dumpster."

"Yeah, I got it."

"I'm serious, Brix," he demands, raising his voice even louder, "turn around and look at me."

Tossing the cans into the recycle bin, I turn the faucet on and wash my hands before grabbing the towel. Resting my hip on the edge of the counter, I stare at him with a look I hope says *get on with it already*.

"This cannot happen anymore."

"I heard you the first time. I said I got it."

Charlene whispers something to him about waiting until later to have this talk. He nods, apparently ready to let it go.

We only agreed I'd stay here because I promised to help look after the place. His job has him traveling a lot. Even when he's in town between trips, he usually stayed at the apartment near his office. It got to the point he was either going to sell the house or hire a groundskeeper.

"I'm glad to see you've met Ivyana. She's Charlene's daughter. You may remember us discussing her staying here for the summer. I didn't want the two of you to meet this way." He glances at Ivy, and she flashes him a warm smile as he says, "It's good to see you again."

Again? I thought.

"I didn't want you to meet this way," he repeats, "or for you two to find out under these circumstances." His eyes bounce back over to Charlene. She steps closer to him, grabbing his hand.

Ivy's eyes widen in bewilderment as if hanging on his every word waiting for what bomb he's about to drop. I know what's about to come before the words are even out of his mouth.

"Charlene and I… while we were away on vacation, we decided to get married."

"What the—?" I stammer.

At the same moment, Ivy says, "Oh my God!"

"Are you serious?" I scoff.

My father's eyes lock on mine, and I can see the daggers he's shooting my way the moment they do.

If he thinks I'm going to stay here and play house with them, he's out of his damn mind.

"Now you listen here, I won't tolerate any of your comments. If you have something to say, I suggest you swallow it. I don't have the time or patience to hear you anymore."

Tossing the towel in my hand to the counter, I cross my arms over my chest.

Ignoring my father's glare, I focus on Ivy. Her hand covers her mouth, and a dazed look shrouds her eyes when she peers over at me.

What the fuck?

If they are married, this makes Ivy, or should I say Ivyana, my sister. Judging by the wide-eyed look on her face, it's apparent the same thought just hit her, too.

I told my stepsister I wanted to fuck all my frustration out on her. Good fucking lord.

"I can't believe it, Mom," Ivy says, hugging her once again. Charlene holds her hand out between the two of them to show her the ring. Of course, like every one of my father's wives, they can't help but gush over their five-carat diamond ring.

"Wow, Mom," she says in awe, reaching for her hand, "it's beautiful."

"Well, let's hope you signed a prenup with this one. Huh, Dad?" I snicker, crossing through the kitchen toward the staircase leading to my bedroom.

"Brix Carter Ward, don't fucking move."

I stop momentarily, waiting for whatever insults he wants to hurl my way. Although, he's always been one to say them without other watchful eyes around us, so I know the real jabs will come later when it's just the two of us.

"I won't tolerate you talking bad about Charlene or our marriage. If you have a problem, I suggest you find a way to keep your mouth shut, or you can get the hell out of here."

"You got it," I mutter, deadpan.

"By that, I mean you aren't allowed at the beach house either. If you're out of here, you're on your own."

"Whatever. Congratulations, Charlene. You picked a real winner."

Not bothering to look her in the eyes as I say it, I stalk up the stairs toward my room.

Passing by the bathroom, I find the guest room door next to mine open. Pausing in the doorway, I notice the bed sitting directly across from me left unmade and two suitcases standing near the foot of the bed.

It looks like Ivy's made herself at home in her new house, in the bedroom next to mine. I can tell already it's gonna be a long fuckin' summer.

Do you want more Brix and Ivy?

Check out Brix today at:
www.authorbrookeobrien.com/brix

BOOKS BY BROOKE

Braysen U

The Rivals We Hate
The Plays We Fake
The Fouls We Make

A Rebels Havoc

Brix
Sins of a Rebel
Tysin
Trey
Madden

Men of Blaze

Personal Foul
Reckless Rebound (Cocky Hero Club)

Tattered Heart Duet

Torn
Tattered

A Heart's Compass Series

Where I Found You

Lost Before You
Until I Found You
Now That I Found You
Where You Belong

Standalones (In order of publication)

Wild Irish

Learn more and purchase your copy at:
www.authorbrookeobrien.com/booksbybrooke

ACKNOWLEDGMENTS

To my boys – I love you more than anything in this world.

To my AMAZING beta readers – Ana, Thorunn, Kristen, April, and Candyce. Thank you for reading Beckham and Hallyn's story before anyone else, for your honest feedback, and for helping me make their story better. I'm so grateful to you! <3

Jenny Sims and Rox LeBlanc – Thank you for your hard work on this project. You both have been so wonderful to work with and learn from. I wouldn't want to do this without you on my team!

To the fantastic bloggers and my Rebel Hype Team, thank you for being a part of this one. I'm excited to hear what you think of Beckham and Hallyn. I hope you know how grateful I am for every one of you.

My Rebels Readers – I love being able to connect with all of you in my Reader Group and across social media. Thank you for your love of this series. It's changed my life and I'm so thankful for you all!

ABOUT BROOKE

USA Today Bestselling author Brooke O'Brien writes steamy and swoon-worthy new adult romances. She's best known for her sports and rock star romances.

Brooke believes a love worth having is worth fighting for, and she brings this into her stories where her characters risk it all for love.

When she isn't writing or falling in love with a new book boyfriend, you can find her spending time with her family, cheering on her favorite sports teams, listening to ASMR, or binge-watching the latest true crime documentary. She loves rockin' a comfy hoodie with leggings and believes the best days include a good nap.

Brooke loves connecting with readers and hopes you'll join her on her social pages or reader group to stay in touch. To follow Brooke and join her newsletter, visit:

www.authorbrookeobrien.com/follow

COPYRIGHT

Edited by Jenny Sims with Editing for Indies
Proofread by Rox LeBlanc with Rox's Reads
Cover designed by Shannon with Shanoff Designs
Version: BMO10062023

eBook Edition – ISBN: 978-1-954061-46-0
Original Edition - ISBN: 978-1-954061-20-0
Alternate Special Edition - ISBN: 978-1-954061-49-1

www.ingramcontent.com/pod-product-compliance
Lightning Source LLC
Chambersburg PA
CBHW060852210726
48293CB00006B/1763